TURBULENT
WAVES

Praise for Ali Vali

One More Chance

"This was an amazing book by Vali…complex and multi-layered (both characters and plot)."—*Danielle Kimerer, Librarian (Nevins Memorial Library, Massachusetts)*

Face the Music

"This is a typical Ali Vali romance with strong characters, a beautiful setting (Nashville, Tennessee), and an enemies-to-lovers style tale. The two main characters are beautiful, strong-willed, and easy to fall in love with. The romance between them is steamy, and so are the sex scenes."—*Rainbow Reflections*

The Inheritance

"I love a good story that makes me laugh and cry, and this one did that a lot for me. I would step back into this world any time."—*Kat Adams, Bookseller (QBD Books, Australia)*

Double-Crossed

"[T]here aren't too many lesfic books like *Double-Crossed* and it is refreshing to see an author like Vali continue to churn out books like these. Excellent crime thriller."—*Colleen Corgel, Librarian, Queens Borough Public Library*

"For all of us die-hard Ali Vali/Cain Casey fans, this is the beginning of a great new series…There is violence in this book, and lots of killing, but there is also romance, love, and the beginning of a great new reading adventure. I can't wait to read more of this intriguing story." —*Rainbow Reflections*

Stormy Seas

Stormy Seas "is one book that adventure lovers must read."—*Rainbow Reflections*

Answering the Call

Answering the Call "is a brilliant cop-and-killer story…The crime story is tight and the love story is fantastic."—*Best Lesbian Erotica*

Lammy Finalist *Calling the Dead*

"So many writers set stories in New Orleans, but Ali Vali's mystery novels have the authenticity that only a real Big Easy resident could bring. Set six months after Hurricane Katrina has devastated the city, a lesbian detective is still battling demons when a body turns up behind one of the city's famous eateries. What follows makes for a classic lesbian murder yarn."—*Curve Magazine*

Beauty and the Boss

"The story gripped me from the first page…Vali's writing style is lovely—it's clean, sharp, no wasted words, and it flows beautifully as a result. Highly recommended!"—*Rainbow Book Reviews*

Balance of Forces: Toujours Ici

"A stunning addition to the vampire legend, *Balance of Forces: Toujour Ici* is one that stands apart from the rest."—*Bibliophilic Book Blog*

Beneath the Waves

"The premise…was brilliantly constructed…skillfully written and the imagination that went into it was fantastic…A wonderful passionate love story with a great mystery."—*Inked Rainbow Reads*

Second Season

"The issues are realistic and center around the universal factors of love, jealousy, betrayal, and doing the right thing and are constantly woven into the fabric of the story. We rated this well written social commentary through the use of fiction our max five hearts."—*Heartland Reviews*

Carly's Sound

"*Carly's Sound* is a great romance, with some wonderfully hot sex, but it is more than that. It is also the tale of a woman rising from the ashes of grief and finding new love and a new life. Vali has surrounded Julia and Poppy with a cast of great supporting characters, making this an extremely satisfying read."—*Just About Write*

Praise for the Cain Casey Saga

The Devil's Due

"A Night Owl Reviews Top Pick: Cain Casey is the kind of person you aspire to be even though some consider her a criminal. She's loyal, very protective of those she loves, honorable, big on preserving her family legacy and loves her family greatly. *The Devil's Due* is a book I highly recommend and well worth the wait we all suffered through. I cannot wait for the next book in the series to come out."
—*Night Owl Reviews*

The Devil Be Damned

"Ali Vali excels at creating strong, romantic characters along with her fast-paced, sophisticated plots. Her setting, New Orleans, provides just the right blend of immigrants from Mexico, South America, and Cuba, along with a city steeped in traditions."—*Just About Write*

Deal with the Devil

"Ali Vali has given her fans another thick, rich thriller...*Deal With the Devil* has wonderful love stories, great sex, and an ample supply of humor. It is an exciting, page-turning read that leaves her readers eagerly awaiting the next book in the series."—*Just About Write*

The Devil Unleashed

"Fast-paced action scenes, intriguing character revelations, and a refreshing approach to the romance thriller genre all make for an enjoyable reading experience in the Big Easy...*The Devil Unleashed* is an engrossing reading experience."—*Midwest Book Review*

The Devil Inside

"*The Devil Inside* is the first of what promises to be a very exciting series...While telling an exciting story that grips the reader, Vali has also fully fleshed out her heroes and villains. *The Devil Inside* is that rarity: a fascinating crime novel which includes a tender love story and leaves the reader with a cliffhanger ending."—*MegaScene*

By the Author

Carly's Sound

Second Season

Love Match

The Dragon Tree Legacy

The Romance Vote

Hell Fire Club in Girls with Guns

Beneath the Waves

Beauty and the Boss

Blue Skies

Stormy Seas

The Inheritance

Face the Music

On the Rocks in Still Not Over You

One More Chance

A Woman to Treasure

Calumet

Turbulent Waves

Call Series

Calling the Dead

Answering the Call

Forces Series

Balance of Forces: Toujours Ici

Battle of Forces: Sera Toujours

Force of Fire: Toujours a Vous

Vegas Nights

Double-Crossed

The Cain Casey Saga

The Devil Inside

The Devil Unleashed

Deal with the Devil

The Devil Be Damned

The Devil's Orchard

The Devil's Due

Heart of the Devil

The Devil Incarnate

Visit us at www.boldstrokesbooks.com

TURBULENT WAVES

by
Ali Vali

2021

This Trade Paperback Original Is Published By
Bold Strokes Books, Inc.
P.O. Box 249
Valley Falls, NY 12185

First Edition: October 2021

CREDITS
EDITORS: Victoria Villaseñor and Ruth Sternglantz
PRODUCTION DESIGN: Stacia Seaman
COVER DESIGN BY Sheri (HINDSIGHTGRAPHICS@GMAIL.COM)

Acknowledgments

There are certain characters that stay with me. They rattle around in my head, letting me know they have more to say, and Kai and Vivien had more to say. Thank you, Radclyffe, for the opportunity to keep telling my stories—your friendship means the world. Thank you, Sandy Lowe, for keeping me on track and for another excellent title suggestion. Thanks too to my BSB family. I appreciate every one of you.

Thank you to my awesome editors, Victoria Villaseñor and Ruth Sternglantz. Vic, thank you for all your lessons, and for making me laugh as you bend me to your will. You and Ruth have taught me so much and I appreciate both of you. I'd like to thank Sheri Halal for the awesome cover.

Thank you to my first readers Lenore Beniot, Cris Perez-Soria, and Kim Rieff. You guys are the best and I appreciate all the help.

A huge thank you to every reader who writes always wanting more. You guys send the best emails, so every word is written with you in mind.

Hopefully, we're one step closer to finally seeing each other at different events and catching up. There's plenty to do on my bucket list, and I'm ready for some new adventures with C. There's a whole world out there yet to be explored, and I can't wait to get to it. Verdad!

For C
and
To the adventurer in us all

CHAPTER ONE

Vivien Palmer woke in her childhood bedroom in her family's beach house in Key Largo, Florida. Growing up, she'd shared the space all summer with her younger brother, Franklin. As adults they made it a point to visit at least once a year to spend time together.

The last month had been like a waking dream that she had to convince herself was real. She'd gone from realizing she'd spend the rest of her life in misery, to staring at the woman who'd come back for her.

Kai Merlin first came into Vivien's life on the beach outside when they were children. She'd been playing with Frankie, and the tall girl with the blue wet suit had surfaced from the water and talked to them before diving under again and swimming toward two large sharks, disappearing from sight. Vivien and Frankie hadn't been believed, and it'd created friction between them and their parents that had carried on until recently.

Kai had reappeared years later as an employee of her family's business—Palmer Oil, based in New Orleans. Vivien had been instantly drawn to Kai because she'd understood her passion for exploring what was hidden beneath the waves. It was something Vivien had pursued all her life, and Kai knew it was more important than her duties with the company. They'd had a bumpy beginning the second time around, but it'd turned into a love that would bridge two worlds.

She'd spent the last weeks listening to Kai's explanation of exactly who she was and where she came from. It was still hard to believe. That Atlantis existed was difficult enough to wrap her head around, but that she'd fallen in love with the heir to its throne blew her mind. Kai was here, though, proving Vivien wasn't crazy.

She heard noise coming from downstairs, and she glanced behind her at the clock. It was a bit after six, and although Kai was usually up by now, she remained curled up beside her. They'd had a late night after Frankie returned from wherever Kai's people had taken him. The stories her brother had told her made her jealous that he'd seen some of the things she'd searched for under the water all her adult life, but Kai had preached patience. Her turn would come.

"Good morning, love," Kai said softly.

The length of Kai's body pressed against her made her sigh. "Good morning." She hummed when Kai kissed her and moved so Vivien was lying almost on top of her.

"Want to go down and help him out? Frankie's going to have an adjustment period, so he's going to need some pointers." She traced Kai's dark eyebrows with her fingertips and smiled. "I'll teach him to make coffee, and you can teach him how to talk to girls."

A birth defect had kept her brother in a wheelchair all his life, and the chair was simply a part of who Frankie was. She'd told him from the time they were children it wouldn't keep him from having a full life and family. Frankie understood that in his head, but in his heart the disability had stolen his confidence when it came to his personal life.

Professionally, Frankie was an accomplished attorney, helped run the family business, and was talented in procuring leases to expand their holdings. Dating, though, was something he'd shied away from. His explanation was he didn't want to be a burden to anyone.

Of course he was the only one who believed that, but convincing him otherwise was like emptying the Gulf with a spoon. That wouldn't be a problem any longer, thanks to Kai's return and the medical team she brought with her. They'd given him his biggest wish. Working legs and a healthy spinal cord had been pie in the sky fantasies, until they weren't.

"I'm sure he'll be fine. Once the shock wears off, it'll be like we never intervened."

"You're right, and I'm shocked he didn't spend the night running up and down the beach." She smiled when Kai rolled over and kissed her.

"He's got a lot to catch up on, and hopefully he'll figure out he was a wonderful man with the chair. The part that makes him the brother you love hasn't changed. The essence of any man isn't tied up in his legs, but in his heart."

"You say the nicest things, but you have to move before I throw up on you." Hopefully this would be over soon. Nausea and throwing up were a definite mood killer. "I'm sorry, honey."

Kai followed her into the bathroom like she always did. "Don't apologize." Kai held her head and placed a cool towel on the back of her neck.

"Man, I hate doing this." She rinsed her mouth out and rested her head on Kai's chest. "I appreciate that this isn't completely grossing you out."

"I've been reading, and this isn't great for you, but it's completely normal. Once we get to twelve weeks, it should disappear, unless you're an overachiever." Kai kissed her forehead and rubbed her back. "If there was a way for me to go through this for you, I would."

"You're sweet, and it's time to tell Frankie. I was getting ready to when you popped out of the water."

Once they were in the kitchen, Vivien had to stop when she saw Frankie standing and looking out the window. The picture was so strange, it made her cry, making her brother turn and smile. Frankie had never been an unhappy person, but now he seemed perpetually surprised at his newfound blessing. He walked over and kissed her forehead as he put his arms around her.

"Those better be happy tears," Frankie said, placing his hand on Kai's shoulder. "I can chase you down now if you make my sister cry."

"Believe me"—Kai put her hands on Vivien's middle and made a good backrest when Frankie let her go—"she's going to be my world for as long as she can stand me."

"Good." Frankie poured them all some coffee, and they took it outside to the deck. "I think you two have a story to tell me."

"Actually, I think Kai has a story to tell us both."

Kai looked between them. "You really want to start with that?"

"Yes," the siblings said together.

"It'll make our news seem normal in comparison," Vivien said.

❖

Queen Galen Merlin and Hadley, her consort, watched from the capital as Laud Mandina took a deep breath before she entered the cell where they'd imprisoned Tanice Themis. Galen was glad her old friend and chief protector had accepted the assignment of breaking this fool. Laud's family had been in service for generations, but she was only the second in her family to be elevated to head of the royal guard, and Galen knew she'd get the job done.

Tanice was a smallish woman with brilliant red hair and green eyes. It was interesting to see someone who'd come from their ancestorial home. Her ancestors had left it thousands of years before. Galen knew their long-ago home planet still existed because of communications from the ruling Oberon family, but they were in the last stages of annihilation caused by their own foolishness. Queen Nessa, their first queen, had the forethought to save the best of her people and had settled a new kingdom named after their home planet Atlantis, before the cavemen learned to walk upright on planet Earth.

That first settlement had been built on land, and they'd expanded there for generations, until their original city had been destroyed and they'd headed for the depths instead. Now the capital was deep in the Atlantic, and they had settlements all over the world, deep enough that man would never stumble upon them.

Nessa had led thousands of her people from their home planet, and after twenty generations or so they'd evolved to a completely female population sustained by the scientific breakthroughs they'd accomplished. Galen was the current queen and, along with her wife Hadley, worked tirelessly to expand the empire while keeping their people happy and away from human eyes. That someone had attacked and almost killed Kai, their only child, would not go unpunished.

She watched Laud glance around the cell and the tranquil scene the computers had generated, images of the planet Atlantis Queen Nessa had stored in their archives. There was a monitor on Tanice's head which prevented her from hiding her thoughts, but she'd done an admirable job so far of emptying her head of anything useful. She was only one of the seven who'd survived the battle where Pontos Oberon, the Prince of Atlantis, had tried to kill Kai.

You should kill me. Tanice's thought came through clearly.

Laud nodded and swam closer. With a flick of her fingers the view changed to the one outside the facility. They'd long ago frozen the polar caps to keep some of their bases secret, but as advanced as they were, even they couldn't produce sea life in a desolate place this far north. The temperatures kept the waters fairly barren, giving them an air of bleakness.

"I have the permission of our queen to leave you here until you're done with a very long life. You're a young woman, so do the math. Even the most trained soldier would go mad way before then," Laud said, touching Tanice's forehead and smiling. "Queen Galen is devoted to her family, and trying to kill her child won't make her sympathetic to your suffering no matter how long it lasts."

"Your queen has no stomach for that. She's a weakling who raised another weakling who was easily killed in battle." Tanice glared at Laud and pulled on her restraints for the first time with a sense of desperation. "Where is Pontos? I demand to see him. You have no right to keep him from me."

"Pontos, or Steve Hawksworth as he was called on land, has abandoned you." Laud brought up the other six prisoners on the wall monitor and showed Tanice they were in the same position as her. "Prince Pontos left all of you and ran like the coward he is."

"Liar, I'm his promised. He would've never left me." Tanice tried again to break the invisible restraints, but the only escape would be if she had the talent to stop her own heart.

"This is the only location we keep prisoners. Pontos certainly isn't here or in the palace, so try to guess where he is. If he was close, you could sense him," Laud said, wrapping her fingers around the talisman around Tanice's neck. "Do you feel him?" Laud smiled at Tanice's glare. She pressed the controls and emptied the room of the Arctic seawater. The only addition the space would get would be a cot. The walls would be a boring beige, all sense of the outside taken away. "Tell me the route he took to run back to Daddy, and I'll give you the oblivion you seek."

"I'll never tell you anything." Tanice coughed after screaming her response. She hadn't used her voice in weeks, since they'd kept the room flooded.

"You'll tell me everything. It's the only way to get out of this room. Prolonging the experience means you're a glutton for punishment."

"You'll have to kill me."

"That's a choice only you can make, but the goddess will be silent to your pleas. You and Pontos tried to kill Princess Kai. There aren't enough prayers to earn you forgiveness for that crime."

Tanice stared at Laud and shook her head. "No, the princess is dead. Pontos killed her."

"The princess is alive, and Pontos will have to live with the shame of his failure. That'll be easier to bear than the fact he's nothing but a coward."

Laud walked out of the cell, the heavy door slamming shut behind her, and appeared on another screen. The exchange made Galen wonder how long Tanice and her friends could hold out. She was ready for Laud to return to the capital and retake her post.

"What do you think?" Hadley asked Laud.

Laud smiled. "I give her another week. There are a few things we can do to quicken the outcome we're after, but I wanted to see where she was mentally. If we twist her brain like a pretzel, it's liable to snap."

"Good, you're missed, but I trust no one else for this," Hadley said, turning to Galen and waiting.

"Your wife wants you to hurry it along," Galen said, making Laud smile. "That and I'm sure my partner is tired of playing babysitter. You're the only person Hadley trusts besides Kai to protect me."

"Highness, I'll be here until I'm sure we have everything we want." Laud took a deep breath and tapped her fingers over her heart. "I have all the incentive I need to make sure that happens. Cari finished all her procedures and is anxious to start trying again," Laud said of her wife. "As much as I want that, my duty is to you, Consort Hadley, and Princess Kai. There's something not right, and the people we have in custody are the only ones who can tell us what that is. I don't want us to stand down until we know you two and Kai are safe."

"I agree with you, but my wife has already warned me about keeping you away too long," Hadley said.

"What about the people who assisted Pontos and his people?" Galen asked. "Especially Bella Riverstone and her mother, Wilma Yelter."

"I have a group dedicated to finding anyone who had knowledge of Pontos being here. No luck yet, but they can't hide forever."

"Then it's imperative you get Tanice to crack. Do you have everything you need to make that happen?"

"Don't worry. Patience isn't something I'm going to show these people."

Hadley smiled and raised her fist to her chest in salute. "Take care of yourself, and we'll take care of Cari until you return."

"Don't hesitate to contact us if you need to," Galen said, and Laud bowed her head. "It's imperative we not only remove the head of the snake but destroy the entire body."

❖

Kai sat on the chaise lounge next to Franklin and opened her arms to Vivien. She gazed out to the water, seeing her great white sharks, Ivan and Ram, swimming forty feet offshore. The two sharks were good about staying close but also out of sight.

"I'll try to tell our history as succinctly as possible." She held Vivien's coffee while she shifted so she could see her face. "It all started with Princess Nessa Poseidon."

"Poseidon? Really?" Vivien asked, laughing.

"Yes, really. You have to realize how the history of the world stems from our gentle involvement. The Greek gods were an extension of our beliefs and the lessons we tried to teach the humans we last shared our knowledge with. All the embellishments of the gods came from the human side after we disappeared into the depths." Kai linked her fingers with Vivien's and kissed her temple. "Our history, like I said, starts with Nessa's courageous journey sixty thousand years ago..."

Planet Atlantis, 57,980 BC

Kashim Poseidon stood before his throne with his hands on his hips. Nessa knew he was waiting for her to appear after his summons. He spent days telling her how displeased he was that she'd volunteered for the decree he'd given his people. After years of a Poseidon on the throne, their planet was beginning to decline, which had led to food shortages and extreme weather. For a civilization that depended on the oceans that covered ninety percent of the surface of their planet, their abuse had resulted in less fish and plant life.

"Where is she?" Kashim screamed at his sister. He was one of three siblings, and both his sisters had married men who lived to garner all they could from the throne. Nessa wanted to break that tradition.

From the shadows, Nessa watched her father grow angrier, but that wasn't an unfamiliar emotion to her. She was to blame for her mother committing the worst crime against her father. She'd died after giving birth to a *girl*. A girl who'd never be anything like him or follow his harsh rules. She was popular with their people and had tried her best to start changing the policies that were killing them like a slow choking disease.

"My apologies, Father." She moved into the room, bowed, and stayed at the bottom of the dais. Her team was hours from leaving, and she was anxious to go. "My team is waiting, so I ask your leave to go now."

"Make sure you make regular contact, and don't disappoint me." Kashim curled his hands into fists, and she could see him struggling to not say any more. There was no way he'd do that with so many people around. Whining would only make him seem weak.

Nessa bowed her head and felt nothing but relieved to be away from her father's contempt. He'd mentioned more than once what a mistake she was, and how weak her mother had been. No woman was worth the food they wasted on them, in his opinion.

When his advisors had come up with the idea of this expedition, she'd jumped at it. Her exploration trip was supposed to be the first step in finding them a new home. One she was sure her father would ravage like he had this one.

The lead scientists had narrowed the search to three galaxies, and once they were underway, she was going to the location her partner Jyri Merlin had pinpointed. It wasn't on her father's list, but he'd never know until they were gone. Jyri had also helped her put together the team. Each of the four ships in her fleet carried seventy thousand citizens, drawn from every profession, and were the best of their population, though unproven. There were a large number of career soldiers, and half, like Jyri and Nessa, were scientists of every discipline. Her father had agreed to let them go because he thought they were all expendable.

Despite her father's objection, Nessa had also included a group of priestesses and shamans from the temple of the goddess Oceanids. The goddess was important to Nessa, and the young women who'd recently taken their vows were happy to join her. The river that flowed through the middle of the largest land mass on Atlantis was thought to be the mother of all life, and she was worshipped as their creator. The temple and the high priestess had kept her sane, growing up with her father. Now, they were heading into an unknown future, and the guidance of the priestesses would provide comfort in the coming months.

"As you wish, Father. Until we return in glory," she said, bowing again. She never looked back, unwilling to carry any memory of this place or of him. Once they took off, the shackles he'd placed upon her would be severed, so this was the last time she'd ever see him. The thrill of freedom being so close made it hard to hide her smile as she walked away. It was impossible to dredge up any sadness, leaving a parent who'd treated her like a piece of trash all her life.

The lead ship was at the launchpad, and Jyri was waiting for her on the bridge. Nessa glanced out before giving the order to lift off, saluting the people who had come to see them leave. She'd wanted to take more of their population with her but feared her father would figure out the truth, that they weren't headed to any of the three possible locations the scientists had suggested. They were headed much farther away. She wasn't coming back.

They traveled a week following the plan her father's people had given them. Once they were sure they weren't being followed, they put their own plan in motion. Nessa put her faith in her lover, glad to be making her own future. She believed in Jyri's research of black holes and how they were the key to go where no one would follow.

"It's not too late," Jyri said as they lay in Nessa's quarters. The vastness of space stretched out into infinity, but finally the black hole had come into view. If Jyri was right, the vortex that appeared like a large gaping mouth would bend space and shorten their trip to the galaxy they identified as their new home. If she was wrong, it would be death by shredding destruction, but they would die together. It was a chance she was willing to take.

"We can't go back, my love." Nessa placed her hands on Jyri's face and pressed closer to her. "I want a future with you, and a new start where we can be together." That was something her father would never allow. Her fate at home was to be sold off to the highest bidder, so her father would finally be rid of her. "We need to give the others a choice, though."

The people who weren't willing to take a chance were given

shuttles to make their way back to Atlantis, but those numbered fewer than two hundred. That's when her father would learn the truth, but by then it'd be too late. Nessa held Jyri's hand as she gave the full-ahead order, and the gravity of the black hole began to pull them in.

Their four ships sailed into the unknown with the head priestess lighting the way with the water orb. The treasured relic had been brought on board by the head priestess, so Nessa would have protection wherever she was going. Once they'd settled, she'd build a temple befitting such a precious gift. The light of the orb and the ships were the only things visible once they made it through the mouth of the black hole, and a sliver of fear went through her until Jyri took her hand. So much had gone into planning this step, and if she killed so many on the sureness of their calculations…

It seemed like a blink of an eye when they entered a galaxy with a powerful sun and planets surrounding it. They orbited the blue planet, the one that seemed most promising and most full of water, before Nessa had them put down for the tests needed. After a day the surface was deemed free of radiation and perfect for their needs. She couldn't help the tears when she stepped out and felt the land under her feet for the first time. The whole planet was untouched, and the waters were pristine and full of life.

"Welcome home, my love," she said to Jyri. "Our children will be free."

CHAPTER TWO

T hat's beautiful," Vivien said, leaning up to kiss Kai.
"She wanted a realm completely different from where her father ruled, but the people with her insisted she take the crown and lead them as their queen. Still, she made sure her policies were totally different from where they'd come from. Her joining with Jyri produced three daughters, two of whom started the scientific research that shaped who we are even today. Their advances led to things like expanding what our shells can do."

"Why did they tell her father where they were?" Franklin asked. "They'd made a clean break by the sound of it. Why take the chance?"

"Nessa sent word back to tell the families of those with them they were safe, but she never provided a location. Giving her father that would have led to the same disaster Atlantis had experienced. From that moment on, the rulers of the planet Atlantis have had two objectives. Every new king claims our residents and lands as theirs, and they're intent on finding us." Kai took a deep breath and thought of what those early days must've been like. "The appearance of Steve Hawksworth proves they took the same route here and were planning something."

"He's from Atlantis? The planet, I mean," Franklin said.

"Steve's real name is Prince Pontos Oberon, heir to Sol Oberon's throne. Once Nessa left, her father was killed in a coup attempt, and the throne went to his sister after the rebels were executed. Her husband wasted no time in taking over, and the throne has been passed to his male heirs ever since. Pontos is another in a long line of bad kings who've brought them to the brink of extinction."

Vivien put her hand to her mouth and leaped toward the bathroom.

Kai followed and repeated her earlier ministrations. It also gave her time to collect her thoughts. She hadn't had to revisit so much of her history in a long time.

"You mentioned something about my niece," Franklin said when they came back. "Is that wishful thinking or reality?"

"Oh, it's reality all right, as you can tell from all my sick glory. I was freaked out at first, but Kai explained it so I didn't go insane. You're going to be an uncle." It still amazed Vivien that Kai had gotten her pregnant before she'd disappeared. The doctors had confirmed it, and Kai had been the only one in her life until she'd thought Kai had died. Thankfully, Kai'd made it back to help her through the toughest part of this so far.

They talked until the phone rang, and both Franklin and Vivien spoke to their parents, who were on their way to the airport to visit them for a few days. That would give Kai a chance to speak to them about her relationship with Vivien. This would be very different from what she'd expected to go through when she picked a consort, but she'd be no less respectful of Vivien's family simply because they weren't Atlanteans.

"After your parents visit, will you join me on a trip home?" She held Vivien in the shower as she brushed her teeth for the fifth time that morning.

"Really?" Vivien sounded thrilled. "I can't wait."

Vivien felt better but not up to a car ride, so she and Franklin stayed at the house to make lunch while Kai drove to the small airport. Palmer Oil's private plane taxied to a stop, and Vivien's parents seemed surprised but pleased to see her. She'd forgotten to ask Vivien what excuse she'd given them for her absence, so she kept quiet about that as she stepped forward to greet them.

"Kai." Cornelia put her arms around her and kissed her cheeks. "What a surprise. Maybe Vivien will stop moping," she said, laughing.

"Damn good to see you." Winston hugged her as well and slapped her back. "Hopefully your family is okay."

"Yes, sir, thank you for the time off." She helped with luggage and invited them for a drink at one of the resorts on the beach. It hit her then that in this world, she was just one of Winston's employees who was about to ask for his daughter's hand. She wasn't royalty, or some special kind of being. It was down to her as a regular person to ask for his blessing. Maybe that was considered old-fashioned, but she wanted to assure them she'd take good care of Vivien and love her like no one else could. That she was nervous was something new as well, but no matter where she was, she was still Princess Kai Merlin, heir to Queen Nessa's throne. That reminder helped, a little. "Thank you both for taking some time before we head back to the house."

"Vivien told us you were responsible for the voting block that put the family back in charge, so I'm glad you asked." Winston smiled and ordered drinks. "I can't thank you enough for that and so much more."

"You and your family are the best fit because no one will care for the company and the environment as much as you do. I'd like to talk to you about Vivien, though." The smile on Cornelia's face gave her the courage to go on. "Viv and I have become close, so I'd like to start by telling you how much I love your daughter."

"She's waited a long time for you." Cornelia covered her hand with hers. "You're the first person who's pulled Vivien out of her own head. If you're asking what I think you are, promise me you're serious. Vivien's a special woman who doesn't deserve to be taken for granted."

"I've never been more serious about anything in my life. And yes, I'd like your blessing to ask Vivien to marry me." Back home there would've been gifts and a court audience between her parents and the parents of the woman she'd marry. It didn't matter that this wasn't Atlantis—it was important to her that Vivien's parents understood her commitment. "If there's a perfect match for everyone, Vivien Palmer is mine, and I'll spend the rest of my life loving her."

"We say yes, and you'd better," Winston said. "I lost my mind with Steve, and I'm not making that mistake again. You ask her, and you better come through. I have enough boats at my disposal to cut you up and drop you in the middle of the Gulf where you'll end up as fish food."

"You have my word, sir, and *she* has my heart." Getting Vivien's parents to understand how she felt about their daughter was important to her, and it was nice that it hadn't taken much to convince them. Making Vivien a part of her world was going to take time, but having her sit on the throne with her was paramount to her happiness. There might be those who would object, but with their child on the way, they had to work together to pave the way for Vivien to take her place as her consort.

Above all else, she was going to keep her promise to ensure

Vivien's safety. The love they'd found would make whatever they faced bearable, and she couldn't wait for the life they'd share. She'd never been giddy in her life, and the new sensation fueled her dreams for what was to come.

❖

The warriors formed a circle and readied their weapons. Daria Oberon could sense their nervousness as well as their anticipation. She needed the distraction of the ring to take her mind off her father's rantings about her brother, Pontos. The fool had insisted on doing things his way, and now he'd lost touch with the realm.

She opened her eyes and advanced on her guards one at a time. There was no doubt in her mind she was the best of her father's forces, and she was tired of asking for permission to find Pontos and bring him back to embarrass him for his failures. She wanted to finish what Pontos started and also claim the woman who'd been promised to her. She cut and parried, kicked and blocked, and one by one, knocked each guard to the floor. Her breathing was heavy by the time they were done, and she was just as glad none of them got back up.

"Highness," Javal Ladner, the head of her guards said. "His Majesty would like to see you."

She wiped her face and put her sword away. Her father was getting on in age and now regretted he'd waited so long to have children. In his opinion they weren't ready to take the throne and keep it. If anything had happened to Pontos, she was next in line for the throne, and she was ready to prove she was worthy.

Her plans for her people would make her father's reign seem like paradise, but there was too much insurrection, and those who dared challenge the throne would be crushed. A tighter grip was required to bring the people in line. Her father's weakness had blinded him to the stupidity of her brother, and like all Oberon kings he'd placed much more value on his son than on his daughter. In this generation she was the better choice for heir, but her sex had disqualified her. She would change that.

"Still nothing?" she asked when she joined her father in his private rooms. The smaller dining room was a glass dome that overlooked the dying kelp fields. Like everywhere on Atlantis, the gloom seemed overwhelming and was closing in on what was left of their people.

"The way you speak to me isn't acceptable," her father said. The spread of food before him was excessive, but he was never one to deny himself. It never occurred to him that everyone else had to ration to the point of starvation. Not that she cared much about the peons, but there was no reason to provoke an insurrection against the throne by being blatant about it.

"The truth isn't disrespectful, Father—it's simply the truth." She waved at the server, and he prepared a plate. "The truth is that Pontos is either dead or captured. He would've reported in by now, but as it stands, the last transmission from him was when he was about to carry out some plan. Either scenario isn't good for us, and those bitches will continue to taunt you, especially if they either killed him or have him locked up somewhere."

"What's your plan? To go and fail as well?" Her father spilled the grease from the fish on his chest, and it disgusted her. The weight of the crown was starting to make him sloppy in more ways than one.

"Why not? You sent Pontos with only Tanice to keep him in line, and now it's laughable that you're surprised he failed." She pushed the plate aside, rising bile keeping her from eating, and stared at him. "I should say it *would* be laughable if it wasn't so sad."

"Get out of my sight." Sol squeezed a piece of bread in his fist and snarled at her. "When you remember who you're talking to, come back."

"Gladly. But remember what I said." She stood and leaned toward him, her fingertips white on the desk. "The more days that go by without word, the closer you come to mutiny. This planet is dying, and you put our future in Pontos's hands. His failure will be your downfall. Remember good King Poseidon. Will your head look just as good hanging from the gate?"

❖

"You're what?" Winston asked, louder than Vivien expected. After lunch she'd shared their baby news, and her father appeared stricken.

"You two have been after both Frankie and me for grandchildren, so don't be upset." Vivien gripped Kai's hand under the table. Her emotions were all over the place, and his outburst increased her breathing rate as her anxiety climbed. She was happy about their baby and expected everyone to share that joy, especially her family. The insecurity of being an inadequate partner for Kai was already on her mind, so adding objections from her family wasn't helping.

Once she knew the truth of who Kai was, *really* was, she doubted falling in love with a human woman was what Kai's parents, as well as their people, would find acceptable. The baby she was carrying was part of both of them, but as Kai's heir, would the people Kai ruled reject someone considered a half-breed? She hadn't voiced all those fears to Kai yet, but they were never far from her thoughts. What surprised her was that Kai hadn't picked up on that.

"Please tell me it doesn't belong to that bastard." Her father couldn't say Steve's name anymore, but she knew that's who he meant. "Did you know about this?" he asked Kai.

"Yes, sir, and this baby is as much mine as Viv's." Kai put an arm around her, and she rested her head on Kai's shoulder.

"I can't say I understand, but I trust you," her father said, his voice softer but still upset. "Do you not realize the order of this, Merlin? You marry a girl first, then you get her pregnant."

"I do, but I'm too excited about this news to care what order we go in." Kai placed her other hand on Vivien's middle and smiled. "And I'm planning on marrying her as soon as possible."

"Congratulations, you two, and I'll be happy to plan a wedding with you, sweetheart," her mother said.

"We want something simple," Vivien said. The chance of that was like getting bland boiled crawfish in a New Orleans restaurant, but she thought it was worth mentioning.

"Nonsense," her father said. "I figured I'd be too old to remember who you were when I walked down the aisle. I'm doing that even if I have to handcuff us together."

"We'd be honored," Kai said.

They spent the rest of the afternoon in the shade of the porch, laughing at the embarrassing stories her parents told about her and her brother when they were kids. When her parents went in for a nap, she followed Kai down to the water. It was strange to hear her parents' stories she'd heard all her life, but now the memories included Franklin walking. When Frankie had returned from wherever Kai's people had taken him, Kai had made him a new shell to wear at the base of his throat, next to the original one. The marking would block the memory of his chair from anyone outside their established circle of knowledge.

"You okay?" Kai asked as they entered the water.

She held on to Kai, draping herself along her back. As far as looks, they were polar opposites—Kai was tall with dark hair and eyes as green as a tropical sea. "I'm happy, and I'm in love." The ripple in the calm water made her stiffen, expecting Kai's pets. When a woman popped up instead, she startled her.

"Your Highness." The woman touched her fist to her chest, and she lowered her head. "Miss Palmer."

"Isla, you're being overly formal today." Kai sounded like she was teasing, but all Vivien could do was watch the gills behind the woman's ears close. It was both amazing and unbelievable. What would it be like to explore the depths with no impediments? "I don't know if it's allowed, but here we're just Kai and Vivien."

"Thank you, ma'am, but Edil's still here"—Edil Oliver was assigned to Kai's security team, along with Isla Sander and a few more—"and I'd rather not get toilet-scrubbing duty. Everyone's still on high alert until all the traitors are found, and Edil has stressed following protocol until it's deemed safe." Isla smiled and bowed her head again. "I wanted to let you know the queen consort called and would like you to get back to her at your convenience."

"Thank you, and if it's not an emergency, I'll use the comm unit tonight when everyone goes to bed."

"Will do, Highness, and enjoy your swim."

"Do you think I can get some of these?" Vivien asked, touching the spot on Kai's neck where her gills were located.

"If you like." Kai maneuvered her to the front and kissed her. "Hopefully our princess will be born with a pair, and the doctors can help you out. I don't want you to be left behind when we go swimming."

The kiss Kai started made her sex tingle, and she missed their afternoons alone. She murmured when Kai pushed her fingers inside her suit. There were plenty of royal guards around, but Kai assured her their privacy would be respected, so touching in the water was something she'd come to love.

"Let me see everyone's hands." The shout from the shore made them both laugh, and she expected nothing less from her best friend, Marsha Kessler.

"You think she could've waited another ten minutes." She gave Kai a quick kiss and lowered her legs from around her waist.

"I should've waited, huh?" Marsha laughed when they reached shore. "You've had enough sex in the last month to hold out a little while, and besides I've missed you, so I'm not sorry."

"It's a good thing we love you," she said, putting her arms around Marsha. "And is there such a thing as too much sex?"

"Listen to you." Marsha hugged Kai next and kissed her cheek a bunch of times. "And you, I should've pounced on you the second I saw you."

"I saw you try to trip Vivien once, but she's a wily one." Kai walked them up to the house where Frankie was preparing to grill steaks. "You two catch up, and I'll help Franklin."

Marsha gripped Vivien's arm and stared at Frankie as if something wasn't right. The new shell he wore would block Marsha's thoughts, that Vivien was sure of, but the hesitation meant there was something off. Frankie stopped what he was doing and smiled at Marsha like a guy in need of a prom date.

"I'm sorry." Marsha wiped her eyes and tried to laugh off her tears. "I'm not sure what's wrong with me, but it's good to see you, Frankie." She let Kai go, put her arms around Frankie, and didn't release him for a long moment. "Do you need any help?"

Vivien nodded in her brother's direction in an effort to get him to return the affection. "We'll be inside," she said, dragging Kai with her.

"How about a sail later?" Kai offered as she was practically dragged from the room.

"Sounds good," Marsha said, her attention fully on Frankie. From her expression it was like she'd never seen him before and found him fascinating.

"He knows how to talk to girls, right?" Kai whispered in her ear when they headed in.

"Not as smoothly as you, but he has his moments." The kitchen was empty, so she stopped to kiss Kai as if they were alone in the house. "If he can get her naked as quickly as you did when it came to me, she should be pregnant by the end of the weekend."

CHAPTER THREE

"Any news?" Hadley asked Laud. Laud was still at their northern facility, but Hadley was anxious for updates. This was one thing Galen didn't mind humoring her about.

"Tanice is still not talking, at least about what I want to know, so it's time to chum the water and threaten her with what she wants, but not how she wants it. Death is something none of us can avoid, and Tanice has said she'll die rather than talk, but how death comes and how painful we can make it won't be Tanice's first choice. I know your thoughts about tough tactics when it comes to prisoners, but it might shake something loose." Laud, as always, appeared confident. "She'll definitely tell us everything to make it stop."

"We need to know what else they have planned, and we need to find Bella Riverstone and her mother because of the position she had with Galen. Bella has way too much information on the inner workings of the Palace and my wife's schedule to not be brought in and questioned." Hadley had trained as a warrior all her life and had planned on a long career in their military, and then she'd married Galen. After they'd fallen in love there was no question she'd use all her skill not only to protect her, but to fight to the death to help Galen keep her throne.

Some people in the realm wanted someone outwardly stronger on the throne because Galen's first instinct wasn't war. Their queen believed everyone had a place, and the world thrived on peace. It wouldn't take much of a fight to force everyone on the planet to accept her as their queen, of that she had no doubt. Her answer to those who craved that, though, was: To what end? Enslaving a planet simply because you could was no great accomplishment.

The counterargument from those who wanted change was that by being in charge they could heal the planet of what the humans had done to it. But in reality they felt superior to humans, and they wanted to heal the planet by subjugating humans under their heel. Disrespecting the environment wasn't a sin the humans alone were guilty of. The planet Atlantis was in much worse shape than Earth was, and Galen had made reaching out to and educating human children a priority. It was starting to make a difference, but it'd never silence that fraction of their people who wanted total domination.

"There aren't many places for them to hide. Bella and Wilma both have very little experience with the world outside our realm," Laud said.

That was true, since Bella was the kind of person who'd be happy going from school to the job she'd be happy with forever. It was entirely possible she and her mother were still nearby. "If they're still in the realm, someone is hiding them. You find that out, and there'll be no forgiveness." Galen was tired of having the same conversation repeatedly and was as ready as Hadley for concrete answers.

"Highness, those who oppose you are small in number, but they're loud. That's a good description of Francesca Yelter. She read about the great Poseidon and the Oberons who ruled after them and wanted that same iron fist ruling our people today. Why anyone would want that I can't tell you." Laud shook her head and sighed in what seemed to be disgust. "The only lesson Francesca's people should heed is that she's dead. Treasonous actions deserve no less."

"Maybe it's time to give Tanice what she desires most," Galen said, making both Hadley's and Laud's eyes widen. "Like you said, Francesca is a dead subject."

"I think what Tanice wants would be her freedom, love. Or perhaps our heads on a plate." Hadley smiled and then laughed when Galen rolled her eyes at her.

"One of your team told me about Helena Greenwood's work. If Tanice thinks she's talking to someone she trusts, someone who isn't you, she might talk." Galen took Hadley's hand and smiled. "It's like gentle persuasion instead of beating her with a piece of coral or something. This situation needs a bit of finesse so we can get somewhere."

"Coral?" Hadley said, laughing. "You do have a vivid imagination."

They all knew of Greenwood's work with a program that created a mental image so accurate it fooled a person into thinking it was their reality. Implemented properly, Tanice would think she was at home talking to whoever she cared about.

"Do you have anything on Pontos we can use?" Galen remembered Kai had mentioned Pontos and Tanice had been more than friends.

"Have Helena look on Palmer's website. There should be something," Hadley said.

"We'd better hurry before they purge him from their history," Galen said. "If we can get his voice as well his mannerisms it'll work that much better."

"I'll take care of it myself," Laud said. "I'll be in touch."

The screen went black and Hadley nodded as she turned to Galen. "Are you done for the day?"

Galen smiled and tilted her head. "I have a few things left to do, but I thought I'd come and drag you out of your head." She tapped Hadley's temple and clucked her tongue. "I know when given time alone, your brain runs on a loop worrying about Kai and me."

"It's been a long month, and we haven't talked to Kai much." Hadley smiled as Galen tapped her nose next. "You miss her too, so don't give me any lectures, and you worry just as much."

"Would I do that? You're my big bear, but you're a cream puff when it comes to your kid. That's why I love you, though." Galen led her to a chair and sat on her lap. "I do miss Kai, and it's been a *very* long month."

"I know you're going to tell me not to give her a hard time."

"No, I'm going to tell you to remember what it was like when we first fell in love. I want her and Vivien to enjoy this time. They're getting to really know each other and build on the love they found. That'll cement the bond their shells have already made, by binding their hearts together. She's also used this time to heal, which I'm grateful for. That blast from Pontos's weapon almost killed her. With everything we have unanswered, Kai will need to be at full strength." She kissed Hadley again, taking her time. "If it helps, I remember when you and I were swimming around each other trying to build on what we felt for each other."

"I remember Mari giving me the evil eye every time I reached for your hand. I got a year of chaperones and our kid gets the girl pregnant inside a month. Times have changed."

Galen laughed. Her mother Mari was a lot like Hadley—she'd married a queen, was a warrior at heart, and tried her best to keep her family whole. Her mother Yara had retired and passed her crown to Galen because she felt it was time, and so she could enjoy her time in their archives. Both of her parents had been overprotective of her and her sister Clarice, and they'd kept Hadley on a short leash until they were sure of Hadley's love for their daughter.

"Vivien's condition will get tongues wagging, but you know how people feel about Kai. They'll be more excited than mad at the breach of protocol. What we need to be ready for is the fuel this will give those who want me off the throne. I'm excited for Kai, but what she's done might bring more people like Francesca out of the depths. If they find a leader who can sway the masses, that could start a civil war."

"There aren't that many people who think like Francesca, and before you say anything, I've already assigned enough troops to quell any uprising."

"You do love to plan, my love."

"Is what you have left important?" Hadley kissed her neck.

"Why?"

"I thought I'd talk *you* into breaking protocol with me."

Vivien's parents decided to join friends for dinner, so Kai took everyone to the *Salacia* by skiff. They'd sail and be back by sunset, so they could anchor again and have dinner on board. Franklin seemed more comfortable on the water, but she did see him scratching around the tops of his legs. He was still healing, but the new tissue had bonded well.

"What a great boat," Marsha said. "No wonder Viv fell in love with you."

"That had more to do with that gorgeous face and all her dive equipment," Vivien shot back. "And I didn't notice any of that until she took me sailing, but the boat was hard to miss."

"You need me to do anything?" Franklin asked.

"You and Marsha take the wheel, and we'll take care of the sails."

Kai raised the sails by hand even though she didn't have to, trying to hide the special features of the sailboat from Marsha. It also felt good to move and use muscles that had ached for weeks after Pontos's attack. Once they were underway, Vivien told Franklin to head to the bow so they could relax and enjoy the view. No one spoke much as they glided along the calm water. Kai tied off the wheel and put her arms around Vivien. They kissed as dolphins swam alongside them.

"I can't tell you how happy I am," Vivien said. She ran her fingers along Kai's collarbone to her shoulder. "You really won't mind if my parents plan a wedding?"

"Love, I want to do everything I can to bind our worlds. This baby..." She placed her hands on Vivien's abdomen and smiled. "This baby has been the subject of a prophecy and proves we have to care about everyone. We'll never really be open about our existence, but we have to be more involved so the planet we share doesn't end up like Atlantis. Besides, we'll have to officially be joined in Atlantis, so by the time we're done, we should be wedding experts."

"You turn me on when you talk like that." Vivien stood on her toes and kissed her. "I'm also impressed with your matchmaking skills."

"Franklin's a good man. He deserves the confidence to open his eyes to the woman who loves him." She turned them about so they could head back and have dinner. "Think we can talk them into skinny-dipping?"

"I'm not sure I'm ready to see Frankie naked, honey."

That made her laugh. "There would have to be ground rules. They can have the beach side of the boat, and we'll take the deep end. Think about how that moved us along. Once I saw you naked, you blinded me to the world."

"He could learn from your seduction techniques." Vivien slapped her butt and laughed.

Marsha and Franklin glanced back when the sails came down to bleed off speed. Franklin helped Marsha up and held her hand as they made their way back.

"He might not need our help, so I might ask him for pointers later." Kai tilted her head toward them.

"You get any better and we'll never leave the bedroom." Vivien grabbed her hand and bit her finger. "Hey, wasn't this great?" Vivien asked her brother and Marsha when they made it back.

"It's a great way to see all the houses along the stretch of beach you can't spot from the road," Marsha said, not letting go of Franklin's hand. "Thanks for inviting me. It's been a long time since we spent time here, and it seems like everything's new."

"Um, about that…" Vivien sounded hesitant and her blush was adorable.

"Viv and I have a ritual when we anchor, and you can either join us, or I'll put you on the skiff back to shore."

"Group sex," Marsha said. "That's kind of kinky."

"That's never going to happen, so stop teasing Viv," Kai said, smiling as Vivien buried her face in her chest. "We like to skinny-dip, and we'll stay on this side of the boat if you take the other side."

"Kai." Franklin sounded slightly panicked. "Can I talk to you?"

"Let's go below and get towels." She'd left a stack on the galley counter and already knew what his problem was.

"I can't swim."

Bull's-eye. "You can. All you need to do is have the courage to jump in."

"Ah, no, I can't. I've missed out on a lot of time with Viv because I'm terrified of water. I mean, I can learn now, but I don't think skinny-dipping in the sea is the way to learn. Marsha is going to think I'm some kind of loser."

"You also couldn't walk until recently, and when our medical team did what was impossible in your world, they also gave you more than those." She pointed to his legs then at his head. "The new parts instinctively know what to do in the water, but you also got some rewiring up here." She reached up and tapped his temple. "Jump in, and you won't drown, I promise. Concentrate on the pretty girl who's going to be naked."

"Are you sure?"

"That's what I'll be doing, so trust me. I wouldn't lie to you about this. You'll be able to float, hold Marsha, and convince her to date you. Running wasn't your only fantasy, was it?" She laughed when he quickly shook his head. "Then listen to me and strip."

"Is this how you hooked my sister?" The tightness seemed to go out of his shoulders.

"After she got over her full-body blush, she got the idea."

"Thanks, Kai." He hugged her and left quickly with no towels.

"I'm sure he's about to find out how long he can hold his breath when Marsha short-circuits his brain," she said to Viv once she was back on deck. She lowered the ladders at the front and back of the boat before stripping to join Viv in the water. "He'll be fine," she said when Viv wrapped her legs around her.

"He might not be when Marsha gets through with him, but the love is already there, for both. Marsha has always been interested in Frankie, but his insecurities kept him from acting on what she wanted. Now there's nothing holding either of them back."

Kai moved them deeper and nodded. "All I'm worried about right now is *our* love. I love you."

"I'm so lucky." Viv cocked her head back and stared into the violet sky. It was too early for stars, but the darkness descending on the waves was beautiful.

"Do you feel okay?" There was nothing more she wanted to do than to float here with Viv and enjoy their night, but there was plenty to get back to.

The primary thing was a joining and introducing Viv to her people. She didn't want it to appear rushed to Viv. Courting—as her parents called it—was supposed to be a drawn-out affair where you showed the girl how important she was to you. The baby was going to change that timeline, and she had to make sure Vivien was not only ready, but knew how much she loved her.

"You know," Viv said, not moving her head, "I'm naked with my wet sex pressed against you, and you're thinking about royal wedding protocol that will in no way change how I feel about you." Viv wrapped her hand around Kai's shell, resting over her collarbone, as if telling her she'd read her thoughts. "Not the most flattering thing to a hormonal pregnant woman, babe."

"Sorry, and it's not royal wedding protocol that's worrying me. I'm upset over not being able to give you all the steps that were required."

"Is sex involved at any step of this courting dance?"

"No." Her smile widened when Viv moved to bite her bottom lip. "That's definitely not one of the perks of dating royalty with the intention of marriage."

"Then we're walking down the aisle or wailing loudly at the moon naked—whatever the wedding ritual is, we're doing it. As quickly as possible, I might add." Viv pressed her hips into her and kissed her.

"One, I'd like to not be really pregnant when that happens, and two, I'm not giving up sex."

"Believe me, my mother Galen is pulling out the list of rules, to make it as fast as we can manage. I don't want to give this up either."

"How many steps are we talking?" Vivien asked. "I have a clue as to what my mother has in mind, but marriage to Atlantean royalty... not so much."

"She has to introduce you to the realm, get a blessing from the temple, and a few things you'll like but I'd like to surprise you with. Trust me, I'm going to keep you informed every step of the way, and if there's something you don't like and want changed, I'll do my best to do that." They were about to kiss again when they heard Marsha's voice carrying from the beach side.

"Nothing's going to literally bite me in the ass in the dark, right?"

"God, you have the worst timing," Vivien said just as loudly before turning back to Kai. "You have to talk to Frankie. If she's over there yelling about that, he's doing something wrong."

Kai laughed, loving how much Vivien made her do that. Vivien was a shift from what she'd thought her future would be, and she was a bit nervous that everything would go smoothly when she brought Vivien home. She had an obligation to the throne and to her mothers, but she wasn't giving Vivien up.

They'd discussed a visit to Atlantis, and the weekend would be the perfect time to go. The sooner they arrived and started the process of the joining, the better. There was also the reality Vivien had to face that Atlantis was going to be her new home. Although she wasn't going to cut Vivien off from her family, Kai couldn't rule from New Orleans.

It was a lot to process, and what gave her faith it would be fine was how much she knew Vivien loved her. The priority for them both was to be honest with one another and find a way to coexist in both worlds.

CHAPTER FOUR

W ill you be able to call?" Frankie asked Vivien when he joined her upstairs while their parents and Marsha packed. She was packing too, but her destination was rather different from theirs.

Vivien had to stop and close her eyes to try to keep the contents of her stomach in place. The news of her pregnancy had been a popular subject all weekend, but she was getting nervous. No matter what Kai said, she was sure a baby wasn't part of the rules Kai was supposed to follow. She couldn't lose Kai now.

"Stop it," Frankie said as he put his arms around her. "Her parents are going to love you, and nothing is going to happen that'll change Kai's mind."

"You're getting good at that," she said, holding his shells. It was like the new one added to the old had given Frankie the ability to see into her mind when she was upset.

"Is there any way you can talk her into making one of these for Marsha? It'll be a plus if I can see if she's thinking sexy thoughts about me."

"I don't think you need a shell for that, buddy. All you need to do is study her face. I've known her all my life, and it's safe to say she's thinking all kinds of things about you." She mentally went through the list Kai had given her and packed a few more items. The zipper on the bag got stuck, and she turned to the door and smiled when Kai came forward and took care of it for her. "My knight in a wet suit."

"I'm more of a soldier than a knight," Kai said, kissing her.

"You have your fantasies, and I have mine, lover." She let Kai go and pointed to Frankie. "Frankie wants to know if I can call him once we get there."

"Your cell will work perfectly, so call whenever you like." Kai glanced at Frankie then at her and cocked her head.

She couldn't seem to hide her nervousness from Kai, and she tried smiling, but her lips wouldn't cooperate.

Kai put her arms around her and rocked her gently in place. "My love."

The compassion in Kai's voice brought on a bout of tears, and Kai held her tighter. "Sorry, I'm a mess today." She noticed Frankie tried not to be intrusive as he sat back down on the bed.

"Never apologize for showing me your feelings. I know you're nervous. You don't have to be." Kai placed her hands on her cheeks and looked not only into her eyes but what seemed like her soul. "I'll give up my title before I give you up."

"You can't do that, but I can't let you go." The thought of having to walk away from Kai made her cry harder.

"Hey, you won't have to." Kai sat next to Frankie and put her arms around her when she sat on her knee. "I have no intention of letting you go, and I can prove it. How about the next chapter of Nessa's history?"

"I'd love to hear it too, and make sure you don't get ahead of me while you're in Atlantis," Frankie said. "Hopefully I won't have to wait long for the next chapter."

"You're too important to both of us for me to keep Viv away too long. I'll keep Nessa's story for our visits," Kai said.

"Do we have time?" She placed her hand under Kai's T-shirt, needing to feel her.

"Marsha and your parents ran to grab lunch for everyone, so yes, we do." Kai settled more comfortably with Viv still on her lap. "It wasn't long after they got there…"

Two years after arriving on Earth

The birds outside Nessa's window held her attention after she'd tried her best to concentrate on the mound of paper scattered on her desk. It was hard to work today, and she held the talisman around her neck and thought of Jyri. They'd only had a few minutes together that morning before Jyri had left for the mission she was in charge of. The sound of construction scattered the birds outside, and she sighed.

Their four large ships had been retrofitted to serve as quarters for everyone until the engineers and architects finished with the dwellings they were constructing. They were replicating the prototypes that had survived for the last year, using both materials found on the surface and what they'd brought with them. The site they'd chosen was a large island where the weather, according to Jyri's findings, stayed mild and warm most of the time. It was close to water and had a good supply of the natural resources they needed to complete their construction. She and Jyri were still in the rooms they'd been assigned for the trip here, and she was comfortable.

Adjusting to their new home had been both easy and challenging, but they'd worked together to deal with the problems as they arose. They had enough food for another five years, but they had to plan ahead to start producing a steady supply to feed everyone. Jyri's team were almost done compiling the list of what was both edible and harmful to them. Their diet had changed for the better, in her opinion. Tasting all the wonderful new plants was almost as exciting as exploring their new home.

Their new home was different from Atlantis—there was much more land with a bigger array of animals and birds. They had a few species of birds, but Nessa was enjoying studying not only the varieties but the varying sizes. Some of the animals they'd found were very dangerous, and that was a new experience as well. The water was their natural habitat, and while Earth had a great variety of sea life, it was nothing like Atlantis. Jyri and the others had started introducing some of their home planet's fish and mammals, and from their reports, it was going well.

There were other beings living close to their camp who seemed to study them from a distance, appearing afraid of coming too close. Her guards observed them as well and had reported they were living primitive lives. Some of the scientists with Jyri had ideas about those inhabitants that sounded interesting, but she hadn't made up her mind about interfering with anything on this planet.

"What are you daydreaming about?" Jyri surprised her.

"You—always you," she said, looking at her consort. Their joining had been the year before, so of course now their people wanted an heir. "What are you doing back so soon? I thought you were on the shuttle headed east to explore the area for an outpost."

Jyri knelt next to her and kissed her. "Did you think I'd forget our anniversary? I'm here to kidnap you for the afternoon. I told your staff I didn't care what you had going on and to clear your schedule."

"I love you. A day off with you sounds lovely. Lately, all the people around me talk about is my womb and how I need to use it." She tried to laugh it off, but having a child that wouldn't be a part of Jyri made her want to skip the whole thing. "I know what you said, before you repeat yourself." She put her hand over Jyri's mouth, not needing to be assured again how she'd love *their* child no matter who they used as a donor.

"Plenty of the women have used the bank we brought with us." The scientist who worked with Jyri had thought of future problems and packed thousands of sperm donations to bring with them. It would guarantee gene variation, and they wouldn't have to depend only on the men with them. "I know how you feel about it, but I promise if that's how you want to do it, I'll support you."

"It might be stupid, but I feel like doing that means my father wins. I can hear him in my head, how my choice of partner is lacking, and how you can't do everything a man can do. To him it proves we can't exist without men." She rested her head on Jyri's shoulder and sighed. "Sorry, it's not the day for my depressing ramblings."

"I do know that's how you feel, and I also know how you feel about children." Jyri kissed her again and started unbuttoning Nessa's top. "Right now, I need you to only think about us and how much I love you."

"That's something I love thinking about." She put her arms around Jyri's neck once she was topless, and Jyri paused as if enjoying the sight of her. Their room was flooded with sunlight, but they were high enough that no one could see in.

They kissed as Jyri laid her down and took off her clothes. The only thing left was the talisman around her neck. The stone was precious on Atlantis, and so far they hadn't found it on Earth. Jyri's stone was the other half of the one Nessa wore around her neck. The stones amplified thoughts and feelings. Once you learned to harness the power of reading others' thoughts, you could read anyone's thoughts, but when you loved someone, like she did Jyri, it was easy to mesh your thoughts together. The etchings along the surfaces had been made when she shared her power with Jyri and her mate had done the same with her.

"Touch me," she whispered before pulling Jyri down.

"Tell me something first." Jyri placed her hand between her legs and hummed at the wetness she found. "Do you want us to have a child?"

"I only want your child, so if you can get me pregnant, I'll be thrilled." She smiled up at Jyri and lifted her hips. "Right now, all I want is you."

"You can have me, but first…" Jyri uncovered the tray on the side of the bed and showed her the clear orb about the size of a soft bean. "I've been working on this because I want us to have a child. I know what's been holding you back, but your children will be the best choice to lead into us into the future."

"Don't you mean *our* children? And what is that?" Nessa stroked Jyri's face with her fingertips. The first time she'd noticed Jyri wasn't in a laboratory but on her father's training grounds. Jyri had believed in enlisting to serve her people as well as to pursue her love of science. If their people deserved someone to carry on their lineage, it was Jyri's child who should do that.

"The prototype of what I hope will help people who have the same mindset you do." Jyri kissed her and opened her mind to her. The talisman at her throat warmed, and all of who Jyri was opened to her. "This," Jyri said, as she pressed her finger to the orb and it stuck to the tip, "is the essence of who I am."

She suddenly understood what Jyri was trying to tell her. She'd managed to encapsulate her biology in such a way that it would combine with Nessa's. "Make love to me."

Jyri touched her, and she felt the connection as they both climaxed. What Jyri had done would make what she'd dreamed for the future possible. They spent the rest of the afternoon in bed, and she daydreamed of carrying Jyri's baby.

"Do you think it'll really work?" she asked when Jyri held her tighter.

"We'll keep trying until I give you everything you want. I wanted to make it so all it takes is the love that powers the talismans that are unique to us." Jyri rolled over and kissed her. "This baby will belong to both of us, my love, and I can't wait to share that with you."

They left for the temple as the sun started to set to receive the priestesses' blessing and the congratulations of the court and their people. The head priestess asked to meet with her in the queen's chapel once they were done, and Nessa took the opportunity to pledge her faith again. With the responsibilities of making sure everyone was thriving in their new home, she'd neglected the spiritual side that was important to her.

"You look happy, Highness," Xendra, the head priestess, said as she poured them a glass of juice.

"I've been happy since we arrived here. It's such a wild but free place, and I see such a future for us."

"As you know, it's taken the orb time to bond with this world, so I haven't been much help to you, and for that I apologize." Xendra bowed her head and knelt before her.

"Please, come and sit with me." She waved Xendra into the seat across from her. "You have nothing to apologize for, and I promise I'll come more often than I have. Perhaps it's been my negligence that has made the process take longer." She glanced around the room at the murals the artisans had completed, dedicated to the goddess. They were beautiful and so different than the stuffiness of the temple back home. The artists seemed to capture not only the beauty but the wildness of their new home.

"Today I entered this chapel and prayed for your and Consort Jyri's happiness, and the orb finally spoke to me. I want to tell you about my vision before you leave to enjoy the rest of your evening. Your consort has unlocked the secret to life, and soon you both will hold the proof of that. Your reign will last for a thousand years, and those who come after you will continue your vision of peace."

Nessa pressed her hands to her abdomen and prayed that was true. Their numbers were growing with the births they'd had since their arrival, but she didn't want to waste one life on the civil war that would break out if she perished without an heir. "You've seen this?"

"Yes, Highness. Your daughter will start a long line of queens who will grow in wisdom through the ages. Our people will prosper until the one who comes that will—"

Xendra stopped talking so abruptly that it made her curious. "Please, speak freely."

"It is of no consequence tonight, Highness. We'll speak of it another time because it'll not come to fruition in your lifetime. You have my word on that."

"I'll be back soon. I don't need the orb to tell me we'll be good friends. I also have so many more questions." She hugged Xendra and took Jyri's arm when she entered. There'd be so many more anniversaries.

"I know we will, Highness, and congratulations."

Nessa nodded as she held Jyri's hand. The way Jyri smiled at her and winked made her father, all they'd fled, everyone who'd underestimated her, and the people she was responsible for fly from her mind. She had a life to live with a partner who loved her more than anything. Whatever else the orb shared with Xendra could wait. Tonight was for enjoyment and relishing the love she had for her mate.

❖

"Do you carry those orbs around with you?" Vivien asked Kai. The story had helped curb her nervousness, and she had to laugh at the expression of shock on Kai's face.

"I would never do that to you. It took a few more years and a slight change in our makeup to produce the same results with only the shells." Kai held Vivien's shell and closed her eyes when they briefly connected, their energies merging as only soul mates could.

"I was kidding, honey." She closed her eyes as well when warmth started in her chest and radiated out to the rest of her body. It was as if she was standing in warm rain that also kept her safe.

"What Jyri found was that the secret to joining with another person lay in the conduits of our beings. The stones their talismans were made from on Atlantis don't exist here, but we found the shells work just as well." Kai pointed to the shell around her neck that could be found on any Florida beach. On its own, the crown cone shell was a good find, but with the added etchings it was something much more special. "They carry the memory of the seas that make up a large part of who we are." Kai closed her eyes and started to speak in a language she didn't understand. "We are born to be part of a community and to find the one person who makes our mind and heart grow." The warmth from before intensified, and Frankie's gasp signaled he felt it too.

"Why doesn't everyone feel it?" she asked, wanting to understand. "Why have Frankie and I been able to read each other's thoughts at times? Why can he feel you touching my shell right now?"

"You and Frankie were close and your love for each other made it possible. To make the shells work, you needed the etchings on them, and the longer you wore them, the more your connection grew." Kai stretched her fingers after letting Viv's shell go. "The talismans Nessa and Jyri wore are in the historical archives, but the etchings are done now the same way they were done then. I do want to ask my mother and the head priestess why you two found the secrets to the shells without any guidance. The reason I made them for you two in the first place was to read your thoughts, so I could learn to be more human when I needed to be. But when I did that previously, whoever wore the shells discarded them eventually. You two didn't do that."

"So the process that achieved conception is what happened when we"—she waved her hands between her and Kai—talking about this in front of Frankie was not her plan—"you know. That's not the norm between two women."

"When my ancestors arrived here, humans were pretty…basic, and a lot hairier," Kai said and smiled. "We are responsible for the jump in human evolution by giving you a genetic head start. Granted, it was done to help humankind and not as some kind of weird genetic experiment."

"That's a strange change of subject," Frankie said.

"Our wiring needed a boost to help us procreate. If we hadn't, the only option would've been early humans once the men who made the journey with Nessa and Jyri eventually died out. They brought a sperm bank with them, but eventually you need to introduce variation in your genetic code, and in some cases couples wanted the option of having their own child." Kai leaned back, and Vivien followed her and pressed against her chest. "Nessa's dream was a nation of only women, able to share what every couple should. With the work Jyri started, we were eventually able to pass on the essence needed to create life. Not like men, but still as effective."

"Why all women, though?" Vivien asked.

"We have some women in Atlantis who are as aggressive or more so than any man, but Nessa's vision was a home where women ruled, and no man was tempted to take over. That stemmed from her father's influence in her life, and she eliminated the possibility of another man like her father being responsible for our people." She smiled and placed her hand on Vivien's middle. "Like I said, it's a different way of going about it, but it's just as effective."

"I see a lot of kids in your future then, sis," Frankie teased.

"You guys ready for lunch?" Marsha asked. She'd been in the kitchen helping and seemed to miss Frankie when she sat next to him and held his hand. "Are you sure you don't want Frankie and me to come with you to meet the in-laws?"

"I'm sure they'd love you, but I want this one all to myself a little while longer. We'll only be gone a couple weeks tops, and we'll get together when we get back."

They headed down and Vivien smiled when she saw her father staring at her throughout the meal. She caught his gaze, and he nodded when she pointed to the door. She held his hand when he headed for the beach. Her father wasn't prone to emotional outbursts, but he hugged her when they were at the water's edge.

"Are you sure about all this?" He kept one arm around her and started walking again.

"I know you weren't expecting a daughter-in-law, but I love her. She makes me happy." She could feel the tension in him and couldn't guess what all this was about. He'd never given her any indication he had a problem with her relationship with Kai. "You can tell me if something's bothering you."

"I…" He stopped and pressed the heel of his hand to his forehead.

"Daddy, I promise whatever you say isn't going to change anything between us." The same warmth from before happened again, and she saw Kai standing outside as if giving her strength.

"What really happened to Steve?" Her father gazed down at her, and she couldn't decipher his expression.

"He and his family left."

"Maybe your old dad is finally cracking up. I have these images in my head, but it's just glimpses of things that don't make sense. When I saw Kai again, I wanted to cry from relief, but I don't know why." His voice trailed off, as if admitting his memories would damn him.

Vivien wasn't sure what to say, and her silence seemed to embarrass him. "Daddy, you're not crazy." Whatever Kai's people had done that day hadn't worked, and she couldn't understand why. Seeing the fight between Pontos and Kai wasn't something easily explained, so Edil and the others had effectively reset her parents' memories. She placed her hand to the shell at her throat and asked Kai to join them.

"I don't think you understand." He sounded as if he was pleading for her to believe him. It was quite a twist of fate since he'd never believed her and Frankie when they'd told her about the girl and the sharks when they were children. "Kai shouldn't be alive. I remember her dead in the yard, and I can't stop thinking about it. Then I saw you right after all that, and you were so sad. It made me think I was right."

"Sir." Kai was there, and Vivien exhaled in relief. "Mind if I join you?"

"Give us a minute, Daddy, and we'll catch up." He nodded, but his pained expression was tugging at her need to make it better. "He's starting to remember," she told Kai. "How is it possible?"

"What happened was too big to wipe from someone's thoughts without doing damage unless the person was open to it." Kai held her and spoke softly. "It's like when someone goes through a trauma and their mind blocks it out. When Steve came to your house that day, your parents and Franklin had no point of reference for what they were witnessing. Edil did some gentle manipulation but left the choice to forget up to them."

"So why is he remembering now?" Her father had stopped and was staring at the water as if he was lost.

"My best guess is you and Franklin are the answer to that. His love for you both supersedes his need to find comfort in forgetting." Kai kissed her and took her hand. "Sir?"

"Kai, we're going to be family—call me Winston." Her father walked on the other side of her and took her free hand. "I'm sure that intense short conversation just now was about how to talk the old man off the crazy ledge."

"Not exactly," Kai said and laughed. "There's no simple answer, but can I ask you a simple question? It might make all this easier."

"What?" Her father stopped moving, and Kai seemed to be working something out in her head.

"Do you want to know?" Kai's question was both simple and loaded. The truth meant giving up all her secrets.

To add to the eeriness of the moment, her mother walked up and put her arm around her father's waist. Like she'd needed Kai, her mother seemed to know when her dad was in need of support. "Sorry, I couldn't help but overhear," her mother said.

"You don't have to answer yet," Kai said. "I'm taking Viv home to meet my parents, so in a week I'll answer all your questions if you decide that's what you want."

"You already know our answer will be yes—we want to know," her father said.

"Viv inherited her curiosity from someone. I'm not surprised that's your answer."

"Do you promise she'll be okay with you?" her mother asked Kai.

"Vivien will always be my priority, ma'am. You have my word on that."

The way her father stared at Kai made her think he was trying to crawl into her thoughts. His very apparent overprotectiveness was new and in a way humorous. He'd waited until someone else wanted the job before he showed interest…No, that wasn't exactly true. Her parents had always been involved, only they'd wanted to make all the decisions both important and minor. It was their children's job to follow the plan they'd laid out. Having your life mapped out for you was something she'd rebelled against.

"I believe you," her mother said.

Vivien smiled when her mom hugged her, and her father joined in. "We'll be fine, and we'll be back soon." They walked back together, and her parents appeared more at ease. "Thank you both for everything. It's good that you've welcomed Kai."

"Of course, and thank you for finally making us grandparents." Her mother hugged Kai again after saying that. "And thank you for loving our child. She's always been special, and I'm happy she's finally found her match."

The feeling of finally making her parents proud brought more tears. It was neither depressing nor elating, but somewhere in between.

Making her parents proud had never happened before, or it seemed like it hadn't. How strange that all it took was Kai and the life they'd created.

"You're a lucky bastard," her father said to Kai, making her mom smile and nod. "Viv's the most brilliant person I've ever known. I don't say that enough, but that's the truth." She smiled when her dad wiped her face. "I'm sorry for doing such a lousy job as your father. I promise to do better."

"I love you, both of you, and thank you. I'm glad you're my dad, and we'll both do better."

She stood with Kai and gave Marsha and Frankie one more hug before waving them all good-bye. She was having trouble figuring out if her emotional overload was coming from the conversation with their parents or the pregnancy. The weekend had been eye-opening as to what her family dynamic *could* be, and she hoped it was a glimpse of their future.

"It'll be exactly what you hope it'll be," Kai said, holding her against her chest. "The love was always there, and I messed up how they showed it. If you're going to blame someone, blame me."

"The one thought that's run on a loop in my head is that my mother's right. We were so young the first day we met, but I couldn't help the feeling that I'd found my match. You were there, and then you were gone. I figured I'd be alone for the rest of my life when I realized you weren't coming back, and it dimmed that part of me that wanted to love someone. That we found each other again makes us lucky." That was the truth, and it gave her the boost to make it through the next week. Nothing could make her walk away from Kai—nothing.

CHAPTER FIVE

"A re you ready?" Kai stood on the deck of the *Salacia* as she considered what Viv had said about them finding each other again.

"What are you thinking about?" Vivien stood on her toes and kissed her. The people coming with them on the *Salacia* ignored them, and she walked Viv to the seat that stretched across the stern.

"I know you're a little nervous, but I can't wait to introduce you to my parents. They were the ones who assigned me to work for your father, and I'm sure they're waiting to gloat a little." She kissed Viv again as she placed her hand on her back. "Now do you need more time, or are you ready to go?"

"I've been ready from the moment I met you when we were children. This shell"—Vivien held her shell and Kai's warmed—"it led you back to me, and I can't wait to see what I've searched for all my life. This is so exciting."

"From the time I learned to swim, my mothers drummed into me the importance of never showing our true selves to the world. Everything they taught me didn't matter the day I saw you and Franklin playing on that beach." She held Viv as she pressed against her.

"What made you come up to us? You've never told me, and I'm sure you'd passed plenty of people when you were out exploring." Viv gazed up at her and ran her fingertips along her forearm.

"You did. I wasn't old enough to know what to do with a girl, but I knew enough to realize you were pretty. That was part of it, but it was your story of how if you threw the shell back into the sea, the water would gift you something more precious." The picture in her mind of Viv standing on that beach, trying to make her little brother feel better, had touched her to the point of stopping. "It sounded like you really wanted to keep it, but you made Franklin happy. You're such a caring soul."

"Then stop thinking about the downside to what happened, and think about how it turned out."

"My mistake started the schism in your family." Kai had stayed close by and listened to what a hard time the Palmers had given their children.

"Honey, please." Vivien moved closer and whispered in her ear. "You are everything I want, and I want to move on. Neither of us can change the past, but we can agree that it turned out okay." She kissed her neck under her ear, then bit her earlobe gently. "Let's get going, so I can meet your parents."

"Take this." Kai handed over a blue pill with a bottle of water. "The doctor sent them to make sure you do okay with the pressure."

There were a few things to do before she lifted anchor, so she put out a call to Ivan and Ram. The two massive great whites had been with her for years, and their connection allowed them to survive wherever she was. Vivien stood next to her as they watched the sharks swim for the boat, their fins above the water.

"No wonder I had nightmares for years," Vivien said and shivered. The story she'd told her parents was that the girl they'd seen had talked to her and Franklin and then swum off into the jaws of two sharks. "You couldn't raise some friendlier pets?"

"My boys are friendly. You just need to get to know them." She secured the hatches that held Ivan and Ram, her guards, as Edil Oliver, Talia, and Isla took care of everything else. "Are we set?"

"We can get underway, Your Highness." Edil held her head slightly bowed, then stood aside to allow them to go down into the *Salacia*'s galley ahead of her.

"The boat really dives?" Vivien asked.

"It's not your average cruiser." Kai stepped to the controls and checked their radar. They'd sailed out to a spot in the Gulf that was completely desolate. It would be hard to explain a boat that sank and powered off. "I designed the *Salacia* myself for my quest. It wasn't just a good way to get here but served as my quarters as well."

"Not to mention attracted girls," Vivien said and laughed.

"I was interested in only one girl." She kissed Vivien and put her arms around her when Edil took over for her at the controls. "Let's go home."

❖

"We're on track for fourteen hours, Highness," Talia said to Kai. They were cruising along the outer shelf of the Gulf with nothing on their radar.

"Let me know if there's any problems," Kai said.

Vivien accepted a cup of tea from Edil and was content to stay at the table watching the small group navigate. Kai had mentioned there were another two ships, one in front of them and another tailing as a precaution. That her brain hadn't exploded from everything was unbelievable, but seeing all this on top of what had happened in her father's yard with Pontos meant it was real. Everything she'd searched for all her life, Kai had shown her since coming back.

"Let's relax," Kai said, offering her a hand.

Vivien followed Kai to her cabin and smiled when the door clicked closed. From the way landmarks outside were flying by, their speed was extraordinary. Whatever kind of motors this silent-running vessel had, there was nothing like them in the human world. As curious as she was about that, being alone with Kai had a way of short-circuiting her thoughts. The last month of her life had awoken feelings she'd only read about in books.

"Fourteen hours, huh?" She tugged Kai's T-shirt with the sailfish emblem over Kai's head.

"We need to get it out of our system," Kai said, dropping her shorts. "Once we get home, my mothers are going to deliver a long lecture about waiting for marriage. That you're pregnant means no long, drawn-out engagement."

"What? I'm sorry," she said, staring at Kai's perfect body. "Did you ask me to marry you?" The way Kai smiled at her made her wet— well, wetter. "You picked a Southern girl, and I might have more old-fashioned notions than I thought."

"What notions?" Kai stepped closer and pressed against her back. "I need to drop to a knee?" she asked as she cupped her breasts.

"Yes," she said in a low throaty voice. Her nipples were so hard she was going to have to beg for Kai's mouth on them. She wanted Kai on her knees but not to propose, at least not right now. Her shirt was lifted off her, and her bra went just as fast. "Jesus," she said when Kai pressed against her again, and her naked skin intensified the feeling.

"A ring should come next, right?" Kai unbuttoned her pants. "You're soaking wet, my love. Now, answer my question."

"Honey, it's not the time for long conversations." She moved her hips forward and wrapped her fingers around Kai's wrist. The need to have Kai between her legs was overwhelming. "I need to lie down."

Kai picked her up and gently placed her on the bed. "There's never been a woman who's made me this desperate."

"Also not the time to talk about any other women." She pulled Kai on top of her and kissed her when she lowered her head. "You're mine, and I have no intention of sharing you."

"I am yours, and I have to have you." Kai sucked in her nipple, making her feel like it was connected to her clit.

"God, baby, you have to make me come. You know what I want." She ran her fingers through Kai's hair and tugged before moving her hands down.

"Fuck," Kai said when Vivien squeezed her ass.

The shell at the base of her throat warmed, and she opened her mind like Kai had taught her. It magnified their connection, and the strength of it was proof that this was her true mate. She didn't need a ceremony or any other trappings of marriage to know who she was in Kai's life. Having insight into her thoughts showed her the intense love Kai had for her.

She'd spent her life with only Frankie seeing who she truly was, and he'd loved her nonetheless. Kai had unlocked the secrets of the shell, and it had demolished the walls she'd erected to protect herself from the world. The depth of Kai's love gave her a sense not only of belonging, but of fierceness as well. She'd battle anyone to keep Kai safe and to stay at her side.

It was that overwhelming feeling that'd intertwined the essence of who they were as individuals, so they became one. She still didn't fully understand how that had created life, but a trip to the doctor had proved the impossible. The baby she carried was Kai's, and her reservations about motherhood had vanished when she knew the baby would belong to both of them.

She reached down and opened her sex since any shyness over

intimacy had also disappeared under Kai's hands and interest. "Give me what I want. I'm already pregnant."

Kai laughed and brought her hips down. When Kai's hard clit came down on hers, she moaned and wrapped her legs around Kai's hips. It was so good it electrified every cell in her body, and she had to smile when she heard *fuck* very loudly in her head. The shells were connected, and Kai was an open book.

Kai held herself up with one arm, placing her other hand on Vivien's ass to pull her closer. She rocked her hips, and Kai started their intimate dance. Her gasp made Kai open her eyes, and she shook her head.

"Don't stop." She raked her nails down Kai's back to her ass and pushed her back down.

"I want you," Kai said.

"I belong to you so…yes…oh yes." She moved with Kai, and the pressure started in her sex. "Like that, baby, like that."

Kai reached up and squeezed her breast, making both of them moan. The dim light in the cabin made her notice the thin line of golden light between the shells. It appeared both fragile and strong, and it thickened as her orgasm started.

"Let go for me, love," Kai said as she pumped her hips faster. The loss of control made Kai's movements jerky, and it sent Vivien off the cliff. "I can't…fuck…I can't—"

"Come with me." She spread her legs as far as she could and pulled Kai's head down to kiss her. "Yes, yes, yes," she gasped as the orgasm washed over her like a warm wave. It took her a moment for her breathing to go back to normal. "Good Lord."

"We say good goddess where we're going, but I totally agree." Kai rolled off her and put her arms around her. "I love you."

"I love you and it's wonderful when I sense it. These," she said, holding Kai's shell, "make it possible to see it. And that's just…damn. I love it." The shell warmed in her hand, and she smiled at the peace it brought her. "We might have to leave these in another room once the baby's born."

Kai laughed and tightened her hold. "You'll be happy with only one?"

"No." She lifted up to see Kai's face. "Honey"—she placed Kai's hand on her stomach—"I want this with you. You also know how important Frankie is to me. I want our baby to have someone to depend on and befriend. A sibling is that one person always in your corner."

"The way it works, my love, is we both have to be happy and want it. If you're ovulating, though, we'll have to be careful, or we'll end up with a dozen."

"There's no way I'm going through that much morning sickness," she said, feeling the blood drain from her face at the thought.

"Don't worry." Kai ran her hand up and down her back. "I'll take my shell off until we're ready to try again."

"Good, because giving this up isn't in my plans either."

The calmness that overtook her was new. She'd never been so comfortable in her own skin and not worried about what came next. Her job had come with some satisfaction, as had the treasure dives she'd done, but not having anyone special to share that with had left her lacking. Falling in love with Kai wouldn't make life perfect because she didn't think perfection existed, but it would make it fuller. No matter what they faced, she was looking forward to building on their love.

❖

"Is everything prepared?" Galen asked Oba.

They were in Galen's office, and Galen realized this would be the first time her high priestess and friend would see Kai in love, but not with her. Oba had always told Kai what they shared could never go any further than a casual thing, but facing the reality of someone you cared for being with someone else would be difficult. That and there had been no natural conclusion to their relationship either. Kai had left on her mission with the thought of returning to Oba and what they'd shared. Until Vivien happened.

"The court and the magistrates will gather in the throne room tonight to receive them. Your first order of business is to declare Miss Palmer a citizen of the realm and introduce her. I'm sure Kai will appreciate a few days to complete what's required."

"How quickly can we have a joining?" She knew their people well enough to guess what the rumors would be. Kai getting Vivien pregnant would be both smiled and frowned upon. It was up to her and Hadley to set the example. "As much as I'm looking forward to being a grandmother, I'd like this not to turn into an episode of that dreadful TV show. The one that always turns into a brawl."

"Jerry Springer? I didn't realize you watched that," Oba said, laughing.

"Hadley flips to it to aggravate me at times, and every time I see it, it makes me think something's going horribly wrong in human evolution." She stood and poured them each a glass of wine. "Are you okay?"

There was no pretense about not understanding what she was referring to. "You know how special Kai is to me, but I'm truly happy for her."

"Oba, you don't have to pretend with me." She handed over one of the glasses. "Kai should've talked to you."

"It was me who tried to talk to her, Highness. She never heard me when I spoke of my devotion and the vows I've taken to the goddess and what it meant for anyone in my life. I don't have to be celibate, but I can't bond myself to anyone." Oba took a large gulp, as if to stop her rambling, and coughed. "All I want is for Kai to be happy."

"I never really put much credence in prophecies, but listening to both you and Kai speak about fate from different perspectives makes me believe this one. If anything, it's proving to me that love can make anything possible." She looked up to the glass ceiling. The water above was dark, but the stars still shone brightly in the depths.

On nights when she could, she loved swimming out there. The silence was overwhelming, and she enjoyed letting go of everything and simply being alone in her head at times. She was born to carry the responsibilities of a nation, and she wouldn't change her fate. Only now, the one person she brought into the world would no longer need her. Kai had met her mate, and she and Hadley would take a lesser role in their daughter's life.

She took a moment to let that sink in and didn't give in to the sadness of the truth of it. There was no doubt in her mind that she and Hadley had given Kai the foundation to swim off on her own and find a woman to love. Their lessons had also been about finding the person who fit with you and loved you that way in return. The truth was Kai would always be her child. Her age, her experiences, even building a family of her own wouldn't change that. It was just going to take time to adjust to the truth that she and Hadley wouldn't be the first ones Kai would turn to any longer.

"We all need to realize Kai has done the impossible. What she found with Vivien Palmer should've only been a brief affair. The bonding shouldn't have worked."

The conviction in Oba's voice made Galen smile. "Kai is someone I'd believe in even if I wasn't her mother. She gives you the sense of confidence to follow her anywhere, be it battle or for a walk. If anyone could create a bonding where none should be, it would be her."

"You raised a wonderful daughter." Oba smiled and stared up as well when she placed her empty glass on the small table between them. "If I'm honest with you, it's why I couldn't resist her."

"Hadley is very like our daughter, so I'll never blame you for what you shared with her. They're hard to resist. Am I right?" she asked, and Oba nodded. "Kai isn't perfect, but I truly believe she'll be a good queen." She remembered being at the point in her life where Kai was now, and it filled her with warmth.

Beginning a life with Hadley had been exciting, but when they'd finally been ready to have a family, she'd fallen in love with Hadley all over again when she watched her with Kai, and they'd loved their daughter from her first breath. They'd planned for a bigger family, but once Kai had been born, not even their doctors had been able to reverse the damage. Kai would be their only heir.

"When's she due back?" Princess Clarice Merlin asked when she came in and sat next to her. "And you're wrong, she's totally perfect."

Clarice had a habit of walking in and immediately dropping herself into the conversation. It was one of the things she loved about her sister. "Tonight, and you need to be there early so we can meet Vivien before we throw her in front of the nation."

Oba stood and bowed. "I'll be waiting in the temple, ma'am."

Clarice stared at her until they were alone, wiggling her eyebrows when the doors closed. "Is she okay? I don't think she expected Kai to come back with a ready-made family. That kid is efficient, if nothing else."

"Oba is one of the most insightful priestesses we've ever had, and the orb seldom hides anything from her. I'm pretty sure she had an idea what was coming." The chime from her comm unit signaled they had an hour. "Oba loved Kai in her own way and taught her what love should be."

"The goddess bless her then. You lucked out with Hadley, and you made one that looks and acts just like her."

"That's true, and I'm sure Dete will be thrilled to know you think Hadley's good-looking," she said of Clarice's wife.

"Hadley is good-looking, and Dete knows that. I also realize Kai's rock-star status." She hesitated slightly. "A human woman being the one to have won her heart won't play well in certain circles." Clarice glanced at the time and then to her.

"I realize that too, which is why I need you there tonight. We need to present a united front, and you need to celebrate that you'll be a great-aunt." She was pleased about the pregnancy. Holding Kai's child seemed surreal in a way, but the goddess had truly blessed them.

"Don't worry, you know how I feel about Kai. My girls are also wild about her and can't wait to meet Vivien. All I know is that you need to find and punish all these people who helped Pontos, so your family and heir are safe."

She shook her head and smiled. "You sound like Hadley, and neither of you need to worry. Some of our citizens planned and participated in the attempted murder of my child—my *only* child. There'll never be forgiveness for that." One of the servants stopped at the door and bowed her head. "Is everything all right?"

"Kai's close, Highness. We have everything ready on the veranda."

Clarice took her hand, and they walked to the space in the palace that overlooked the capital. The throne room would come soon enough, but from what Kai had told her, she thought Vivien would like to see what she'd been searching for all her life. Her experience had been that only certain humans were born with the imagination and drive to find the secrets of the depths. Vivien had spent a lot of her young life trying to find the origin of the markings on her shell, instinctively knowing it would be found in the depths. No one could've guessed what Vivien was really searching for was the love missing in her life.

She saw the *Salacia* headed for the docking station at the side of the palace. The sight of Ivan and Ram made her happy—Kai was home again and safe. Hadley joined her with both their parents, and they also appeared happy to see their grandchild again.

"Now you'll see the best part of being a parent, my love," her mother Sibyl said.

"When your child finds love?" She kissed Hadley's parents, Brook and Yara, hello and took Hadley's hand.

"No, when they find love *and* give you grandchildren. They, more than anything, will cement your legacy," Mari, her other mother, said. "Being a grandmother has been the best part of my life."

"Good to know Clarice and I are expendable, but you're right. The addition of a daughter-in-law won't be bad either."

She took a deep breath and wanted to speed up time. A montage of memories from Kai's birth and childhood went through her mind. When they'd placed Kai in her arms, the joy of the moment had given way to a bit of guilt. Children were always gifts, but in her case Kai was their future. Her life would be one of service and heavy responsibility, and she'd had no say in the matter. Fate had cast her die, and there was no changing it.

Her only fear was Vivien. Not that Kai had chosen incorrectly, but Vivien hadn't been raised being trained in service to a nation she didn't know even existed until recently. If their people didn't truly accept her, Kai's years on the throne would be much more difficult. Vivien would have to open herself up to what was required of her, and that meant giving up a huge part of who she was.

Love was easy, but would so much sacrifice break that bond between them? She doubted it, but there was no way to be sure. She knew Kai had explained it, and Vivien probably thought she understood, yet until she stood on the dais and looked out into the crowd, knowing some were happy to have her there and some weren't, there was no way to know for sure.

CHAPTER SIX

Kai had changed into her uniform, and Vivien had put on a dress Kai assured her would be fine for everything planned in their honor. The nerves over meeting her future in-laws had given way to the excitement of what she was seeing out the window. How a city as large as this could exist without anyone ever noticing it was unbelievable, but here it was, and it stretched as far as she could see.

"This is incredible," Vivien said with her hands flat on her stomach.

There were lit streets lined with glass-top structures that reminded her of Bubble Wrap. There were other sections with larger structures, all under glass-like domes. A variety of vessels glided over the city, and it was still amazing to her that none of the people riding them had to wear any type of breathing apparatus. In the last month she'd met most of Kai's security team and had watched them come and go, swimming from the ship they were staying on offshore. They popped up and spoke to Kai about different things while Vivien studied their process of transitioning from breathing underwater to air.

The gill system completely closed when they were on land, so no one who didn't know would ever guess they weren't human. Kai and the others also had better eyesight and hearing, and were stronger than the average human. It was like having her own version of Supergirl, but the Atlanteans also seemed more empathetic than anyone she'd ever met. She attributed that to their ability to hear the thoughts of humans. You never knew what struggles someone had until you saw what was in their head. Kai's people could do that, and they seemed to act accordingly by providing support.

She looked to where Kai pointed—the large structure on the

highest point was the palace. It appeared to be built into the side of a canyon, and she could see women swimming on the perimeter with tridents like Kai's.

"Put into airlock three," Kai told Edil.

Vivien smiled at Kai when she stood next to her and took her hand. "Don't lose me, okay?" This statement was meant as a joke, but not entirely.

"If you think I'm letting you out of my sight, you're crazy. Trust that we're doing all this together, and you'll be fine because everyone's going to love you." Kai kissed her as they came to a stop and straightened up when the hatch opened.

"Welcome home, Highness." The tall blonde who'd greeted Kai bowed and stood aside.

"Vivien, I'd like to introduce you to Belm Gaff. She's second-in-command of the royal guards."

They stepped into a large room with the most beautiful mosaic tile floor Vivien had ever seen. It appeared to be a goddess of some kind with constellations surrounding her.

"Ms. Palmer, welcome to Atlantis." Belm sounded nice but looked imposing in the navy uniform.

"Thank you." She tightened her hold on Kai and was on overload as she tried to take everything in. This place was extraordinary, and she couldn't wait to see what was under the domes. "Bow, right?" she murmured softly. She didn't want to get anything wrong when she met Kai's parents.

"I have to follow the same protocol, so follow my lead." Kai greeted others who moved aside as they walked forward.

The space was a glass dome with a great view of the city and the ocean floor. "How is it we can see the stars?" The space above them was ablaze with stars and a full moon.

"There're reflectors on the surface that mirror whatever is topside," Edil said. "They're completely invisible and have sensors to move out of the way of any passing ships. You've probably sailed by some if you've ever come this far out."

Her attention landed on a group by the railing and the woman with her arms out. She was beautiful, and the proud-looking woman at her side gave her an idea of what Kai would look like when she was older. Kai let her hand go and hugged the first one.

"Welcome home, love," the woman said after putting her arms around Kai.

Vivien enjoyed her laugh when Kai lifted her off the ground and swung her around.

"Mama, it's good to be back," Kai said, putting her mother down. "Let me introduce you."

Vivien stepped forward and took Kai's hand. The only royalty she was familiar with were the British family. Kai's family so far seemed much more relaxed, and crazy about their kid.

"Your Highness," Kai said. "I'd like to introduce my fiancée, Miss Vivien Palmer of New Orleans."

"Kai, the formality will come later." Her mother stepped forward. "Welcome to our home, Vivien. I'm Galen and this is my mate, Hadley. We've waited for you a long time, and we're glad Kai found you."

Vivien relaxed and smiled when Galen hugged her. "Thank you, Highness, and I've been waiting for her since the first time I saw her."

"Our little rule breaker does have a tendency to follow her own mind, but this time I'm glad she did," Hadley said. "Let me finish the introductions."

They moved among the crowd, with Galen and Hadley introducing her to people while Kai lagged behind just a little, allowing Vivien to be the focus of attention. It was overwhelming, and she'd never remember all the names, but she felt welcomed. It had been less than an hour before Galen whispered something in Kai's ear. Whatever it was made Kai smile and nod before she took her hand again. "Let me give you a tour, love."

It was good that Kai seemed to understand her need to explore and see, so they walked slowly until they reached another space that overlooked a much more desolate area. There were a few lights but not as many as the rest of the city. She hoped once the sun was up again she could see the bottom. There was no way of knowing where they were, but Kai had said they were in one of the deepest parts of the Atlantic Ocean.

"See, I told you they'd love you," Kai said as she put her arms around her. With a flip of a switch the area outside came into view. There were ruins spread before them. "Eight thousand years ago, we started searching for a new home, safe from the exploits of humans. This was the first palace built."

"You left the ruins up?" It seemed strange to leave this and only expand in one direction. There seemed to be nothing but darkness on the other side of the ruins.

"This palace was built on the ruins of part of the old one. We left a section of the old as it was because we never want to forget the pioneers who led us forward." Kai pointed to an area where a group of guards swam, their hair, though short, floating upward in the current. "The section that was lit before I turned on the floodlights is where the temple was located in that palace. It was the original resting place of Queen Nessa and her consort, Jyri. By vote, they were moved to the new temple, but that area out there is one of our most sacred."

"It's amazing you know where they are, considering how long ago they arrived." This whole thing was like a movie, but this time, the fantasy wouldn't end after a few hours. "I'm so glad you love me enough to share this."

"I do love you, and when I was little, this was one of my favorite places to come and daydream. The old palace was my playground, and my friends and I would pretend to wage great battles." Kai moved behind her and kissed her neck. "When I was older, I came here to think about my future and the peace that was my responsibility to carry on. I didn't have a lot of choices about that, but I did want a woman who'd share my life."

"I have a lot of learning to catch up on, but I'll always be here." She took Kai's hand and kissed her palm. "You're every dream I never thought to have."

"And what do good Southern girls dream about?" Kai whispered in her ear as she held her tighter against her.

She laughed at that. "I doubt my parents ever considered me a good Southern girl, but I wanted someone to love me and share my life."

Kai let her go, stepped in front of her, and knelt. "I want that and so much more. Vivien," Kai said taking her hand. "I love you, and you're also everything I never thought to wish for because I never thought someone like you existed. That proves to me I don't have imagination enough. You have my promise, though, that I'll always be at your side loving you." Kai took a small pouch from her pocket and emptied it in her hand. "Will you marry me?"

She wanted to cry. She was in the deepest part of the Atlantic Ocean with a woman who'd been brought up there. A royal woman, who looked at her as though she was the only thing worth looking at. It was every dream and fantasy she'd ever had. "I thought you'd never ask."

"Is that a yes?"

She laughed, giddy at how Kai made her feel. "It is a yes. I just meant—"

Kai cut her off with a kiss and slid the ring on her finger. "You are my match, love. Never think you aren't enough."

The stone in the ring was a blue that reminded her of the waters on a pristine beach, and it was beautiful. "Thank you, and I love this."

"It's a blue diamond. I thought you'd like something a little different, and it's not that I didn't want to ask." Kai walked her to a bench that was close to the edge of the drop-off outside.

"Honey, I was kidding, but I'd be lying if seeing you on your knees wasn't nice." She hoped the guards weren't spying on them as she kissed Kai.

"I plan to give you everything you want and more, but I waited until we were here with so much history for a reason. We'll eventually be part of that history, as will our children, and I also wanted to talk to your parents first. I want your family to be a part of all this."

"You asked my parents? Really?" The expression on her father's face must've been priceless.

"Does that bother you?" Kai leaned back to see her face.

She considered the question as she stared into the depths. "No. Granted, had this happened a few months ago, it might've, but I'm glad you did. I want them to love you too, and you talking to them probably got you points." Her relationship with her parents was so much stronger than it had been over the years, and she wanted to keep going in the right direction. "Are your parents okay with this? They didn't have some other woman in mind, did they?"

"Tonight, we have the reception, but tomorrow my moms invited us to an early lunch. It'll give you a chance to talk to them, and to get their blessing for our joining. If you don't mind a bit of a rush, we could have our service before we go back." Kai seemed as nervous as she was, and it didn't make sense.

"You want that, right? You haven't changed your mind?"

"Of course I haven't. The audience with my mothers is the first step before we're free to meet with the high priestess for a blessing from the goddess." Kai's voice seemed to fade away, but she didn't look away from her.

"What? Are you not religious or something?" She loved making Kai laugh. "Or"—she tapped Kai's head—"you and the priestess spent a lot of time *praying*?"

"I did love her…I still love her, but as a friend. The only woman I want to share my life with is you."

"She knows that too, right?" Jealousy was a new experience, but she couldn't help it. "You didn't wait until now to tell me you can have a harem of wives, did you?"

Kai laughed that deep belly laugh Vivien loved and shook her head. "I only get one like everyone else, so it's good I picked so well. As for Oba and me, we spent time together while I was healing, and she was the one who voted our stock." After Pontos tried to overtake their business as an initial move to take over the oil industry as a whole, Kai's family had voted with her father, giving them the majority. "We both understand we have a good friendship and nothing more." Kai seemed to be bracing for a bad reaction, but Viv kissed her instead.

"Good, and I love you. I'll be happy to join with you whenever you can arrange it."

She stood when Isla told them it was time. As excited as she was to explore, she figured the night would mean a separation from Kai. They were flanked by guards, which didn't feel normal, but Kai didn't seem upset, so she simply took in her surroundings as they went. They stopped in front of a set of grand doors carved with different sea life, and she could hear what sounded like a crowd on the other side.

"I'm right here." Kai's voice comforted her as they were announced. The throne room was majestic in every sense of the word. Galen stood with Hadley on the dais at the end of the center aisle, and the applause for Kai was thunderous. Mixed into all that was the drumming of the soldiers beating their tridents on the floor. She placed her hand in the bend of Kai's arm and tried to keep her features relaxed.

"Sisters," Galen said, and Vivien noticed the event was projected on various screens around the room. "Today we welcome a new citizen to our home." More applause followed, and Kai covered her hand with hers. "Come forward, Lady Vivien Palmer."

She did as Galen asked, climbing the steps with Kai, and bowed her head. "Thank you, Highness."

"I bestow upon you all the rights and privileges of a sister of Atlantis, and we welcome you to our family." Galen touched her head and smiled. "Let us all welcome Lady Palmer." There was more applause, so she turned and faced the court made up of women from all over the realm. From what Kai had explained, the capital was just one of many cities they had around the world.

"Thank you all." She glanced up at Kai and laughed at her wink.

"The throne would also like to announce the engagement of Lady Palmer and Princess Kai Merlin," Hadley said as the applause rose in volume.

She gazed at Kai and back out to the audience, noting only a few who didn't seem thrilled with the news. They'd have to talk about that later, but after what'd happened when Kai almost died, it seemed important. The ceremony didn't last much longer, and she was ready for some quiet once Galen called it to a close.

Kai walked her to the guestroom and stopped at the door. "Tomorrow we'll go to lunch with my parents, but Mama said she's already cleared us to go to the temple to prepare. Oba has to say prayers, and after three days we'll stand before the goddess and join. Are you okay with that?"

"So I'm stuck here alone until then?" She stepped into Kai's arms and pressed her lips to Kai's chest. "I'm going to miss you."

"It seems ridiculous to me, considering you're already pregnant, but this is to make everyone happy that we're following some protocol. If you need anything, I won't be too far away." Kai kissed her forehead before moving to her lips. "And I love you for doing all this."

"I love you too, and it's fine. I'd like to meet Oba." She smiled when Kai lifted an eyebrow. "You're a trained warrior, so you should know sizing up the competition is a good move." She had to laugh at Kai's look. "Honey, close your mouth, and don't worry—I'll do whatever I need to as long as I get you. I'm looking forward to meeting you at the end of two aisles. Remember, once all this pomp and circumstance is done, you'll be subjected to Cornelia Palmer's version of it."

"I can't wait." Kai held her hand and kissed the top of her head. "I love you, and Edil will look over you until the morning. If you need anything, use the comm unit next to the bed, and have them call me."

"I'll miss you." She wasn't in the mood to be alone, but three days wouldn't kill them.

"Eventually you'll want to get rid of me." Kai kissed her softly, with a world of promise held in her lips. The guards thankfully had turned around. It appeared privacy was going to be at a premium in the future if they were constantly in the middle of a pack. Kai gave her a final quick smile before she slipped out to go about whatever royal duties she had to attend to.

The way Kai held her and loved her made her willing to put up with whatever was coming. She leaned back against the door and stared out the windows at the schools of fish that swam by. That there was this much life where none should exist was still hard to believe, and that she'd become such an important part of it all was still a work in progress. She'd tackle it like everything else in her life and work until she'd won over the skeptics. Being a woman in a male-dominated field hadn't been easy even if her father owned the company, and this would be more of the same, only it'd be those who wanted one of their own with Kai.

Her phone rang, and she sighed when she saw Frankie's happy face. "It's like you have ESP. Thanks for keeping me from spiraling into my head."

"How'd it go?"

"I have dual citizenship now, but I'll wait to get back to tell you the rest." She moved to the large windows and pressed her hand against the glass. One of the patrols went by on what appeared to be Sea-Doos.

"Is it everything you imagined?" Frankie's voice brought her a sense of normalcy and eased some of the pressure the day had built up. "I've been thinking about you since you left."

"It's so much more, and I've never been happier." She enjoyed his laughter. "And I'm getting married in a few days." She laughed as she fell on the bed. Not having Frankie with her felt wrong. They'd gone through everything in life together, and she didn't want to leave him behind. "I wish you could see this place."

"I saw a little from a distance, and I wish I was there too, but don't tell Mom that. The planning is in full swing, so don't take too long. I'd hate to see you end up in ruffles because you're not here to rein her in."

She laughed and wondered if their mother was disappointed in having to deviate from the wedding she'd probably had in mind all her life. "I trust you won't let it get that far."

"She's actually having fun putting things together and is looking forward to meeting Kai's family."

"Are you sure?" She bit the tip of her finger to stem her nerves. "Are they really happy about Kai?"

"Are you kidding? I think Mom and Dad like her more than they do us. Stop stressing. I had a long talk with Mom to make sure we're all on the same page. She loves Kai—it's not an act. She said Kai loves you the way she's always wanted for you."

"How about you? How's it going with Marsha?" That the couple she'd always wanted to get together finally had was thrilling. Marsha had always been her best friend, but she'd love to have her as a sister.

"I have to say that Marsha is everything I ever imagined her to be. You can go ahead and tell me I told you so."

"Would I do that?" She made him laugh and she joined in. "I'm sorry it took you two so long, but if it makes you feel better, she waited out of respect for what you wanted. It was never from a lack of interest."

"I know and thank you. Now make sure you don't start some international incident, and I'll see you soon."

"Take care, and make sure you take Marsha somewhere nice."

"You do the same, and have fun. Hopefully you're allowed to take a few pictures, so I can see it."

She held the phone against her chin and stared back at the bed. After a month of wrapping herself around Kai to go to sleep, tonight was going to be tough. "Three more days and you get everything you want." She shivered, suddenly cool, but she was too tired to think about anything else. These were her last nights of being alone. That would be something to be thankful for when they went to the temple.

Her family had never been terribly religious, but she remembered a verse from her catechism classes. She was sure this wasn't what her priest meant, but it was appropriate. The quote from the book of Ruth was how she felt for Kai, and what she was taking on by marrying her: *I will go where you go, and I will stay wherever you stay. Your people will be my people, and your God my God. I will die where you die, and be buried there. May the Lord bring a curse upon me, if anything but death separate you and me.*

She'd never in her life had the connection she had to Kai with anyone else, so perhaps some goddess really had prophesized it years before. That it'd been her who'd been chosen to be loved by Kai was something she'd treasure more than anything she'd ever found beneath the waves. This was her destiny, and she prayed their first blessing was years to share, to build on what they'd started.

It might take time for her to completely fit in to a world that was as foreign to her as flapping her arms and taking flight. What seemed true was that no matter where people came from, they were all susceptible to drama, and Kai's realm was no different. No matter how hard you worked for what you had, someone was trying their best to take it away from you. People had schemed to kill Kai, and she doubted it'd be any different when it came to their child.

If someone tried to harm an innocent baby or Kai, she'd be happy to be the one to spear them through the heart. The next few years would be filled with a baby and a new marriage, but she'd also dedicate herself to learning what she needed to be a good wife to Kai. All she had to remember through all of it was that Kai loved her and only her.

❖

Daria lay on the massage table naked waiting for the woman who usually took care of her. She'd spent the day on the training grounds again, but the thrill of taking the competition down was losing its appeal because of the ease. Tomorrow she was headed to the armory to check the realm's one remaining ship capable of making the journey she'd planned. Her idiot brother had taken the others, and she knew those were lost forever.

"Highness." The woman bowed and didn't move until Daria gave her permission to rise. The idiot would've stayed in that position until she keeled over.

That kind of power over people had been the biggest turn-on from the moment she could reason. "Get to it." The ability to wield it belonged to her because she'd been strong enough to take it.

The muscles in her back were tight, and she moaned when the

woman started a deep-tissue massage. She'd reached her lower back when Daria noticed the boots standing in front of the table. Whoever they belonged to had guts for entering unannounced, and for staring at her naked. She was no prude, but there had to be rules and stiff consequences for breaking them.

"What?" She didn't lift her head as she decided whether to kill for the intrusion.

"His Highness demands to see you." Joel. She recognized his voice. He was the head of her father's forces, and this intrusion was a sign he'd let the power he'd been given go to his head. "Right now." He didn't avert his eyes when she pushed up and sat on the side of the table.

She stood and stared at him, waiting for him to lower his eyes, but he didn't. The defiance was blatant, and his smile made her move swiftly. There was never a time she was unarmed, and she laughed before driving her dagger into his kidney. He dropped to his knees and tried to reach for his weapon.

"Did you enjoy the view?" She stabbed through the other side and laughed again at his cry of pain. "Your disrespect is rewarded. How dare you order me to do anything? And what gives you that right or the right to look upon me?"

"Your father promised me," he said, breathing hard and sweating.

"My father promised you what?" She placed her fingers on her forehead and waited. "Tell me, or you'll have problems talking with your balls in your mouth."

"You," Joel said with a hand on either side of his body. "You need someone like me to keep you in line."

"My father said that?" She didn't need convincing to know that was true.

"You need me."

"So you felt free to do this because I belong to you?" She moved quickly and plucked his eye out. When he stopped screaming she showed it to him before taking his other eye. She finished by placing his testicles in his mouth after she'd cut through his uniform. "Set him adrift, and save on fish food today." The men with Joel saluted and bowed their heads. "Wait for me in my room," she told the woman.

This would be her last day on this dead rock, and her father could deal with the consequences of his actions. She was done wanting to rule the people left on Atlantis. Her destiny was to rule the world Galen and all the bitches who bowed down to her inhabited. All she had to do was get there and find the network she'd pieced together and use them to finish the job. Pontos had taken advantage of her work and taken credit for it, but without her they would've never reached this point. The women in Galen's realm had kept up communications over the thousands of years with a few select families, if only so they could keep tabs on what was going on, on planet Atlantis. She'd used that information to track them down, and now she'd take what she deserved.

"I've been waiting," her father said when she walked in.

She threw Joel's eyes at his feet and enjoyed the shock it caused. "Joel said he'd see you around."

"You killed him? Have you completely lost your mind?" Sol stood from the throne, stepping on the eyes and making them pop as he came closer. "Joel will be missed by the troops. You're risking them turning against us."

"You, Father. Turning on you." She accepted a towel for her hands from one of Joel's men. "Your stupidity and blindness are going to be our doom. Enjoy your crown while you still have a head to set it on. I'm going to finish what I started. Pontos is dead because he listened to you, and I'm not making that mistake."

"I forbid it." The way her father was acting meant he'd not heard one thing she said. "Your place is here with me."

"Shut up, old man. You spend so much time talking, you never see or hear anything around you." She grabbed his hand when he moved to slap her. "Be careful, or I'll free our people from you before I go. What do you think they'll do to you? All that mounting frustration from the state of things won't be pretty."

"How dare you speak to me like this." His face showed pain when she squeezed his hand. "Take her," he said to the soldier closest to them, who didn't move, staring at them wide-eyed. "Now!" But her father's guard stayed still.

"Who is Joel's second?" she asked the guard.

"I am." A tall woman stepped forward, and Daria was surprised Joel had a woman in that position. "Bronti Carper."

"I name you the new royal commander in charge while I'm gone," she said, and Bronti as well as the others saluted. "You're to detain my father until I send for you all. Release the stores of food, and tell

everyone my father is dying. Anyone who says otherwise, kill them."
She looked at her father. "Freedom for the people it is."

"Your commands will be followed," Bronti said.

And just like that, Atlantis had a new ruler. She'd deposed him
more easily than she'd eaten breakfast. She let her father go as she
pushed him back. "Like you always say, Your Highness, death comes
to everyone. You've done everything you can to invite it in way before
your time."

"You'll pay for this," her father said, spit flying from his mouth
when he screamed. His guards stepped away from him, their attention
on Daria.

"The future belongs to the strong." She walked out and headed for
the launch pad. The route to Earth was programmed in, and all she had
to do was survive the trip. "The throne awaits." She'd bring strength
to Galen's realm by taking it for herself before she conquered the rest
of the planet. From what little she knew of Earth, it had millions of
slaves who'd either fall in line or litter the waters when she had them
eliminated. This was going to be sweet. And Atlantis could disintegrate
into cosmic dust for all she cared. She had no intention of coming back.

CHAPTER SEVEN

K ai glanced at the pools in the temple's garden, then at the clear sky visible through the dome. That was the direction Vivien was squinting in. She was leaning against her and seemed lost in thought. The best part of coming home with Vivien was seeing it through fresh eyes.

"We can swim in any water on the planet, but it's a pain to be wet all the time, so we dome places like this. The sensors on the surface correspond to the ones down here, so it mirrors the surface. It's how we can farm and enjoy the sun on our beaches." Her explanation made Vivien turn in a circle, glancing around them from ground to sky.

"When the etchings on my shell grabbed my imagination, this isn't what I expected." Vivien was in awe, but she also appeared a bit green. They'd made it through breakfast okay, but morning sickness had a mind of its own.

"Are you okay?" She put her arms around Vivien and rubbed her back.

"Eh, you know what mornings are like." Vivien scratched the side of Kai's neck and took a deep breath. "That's part of it. The other part is I missed you last night."

"Good morning, Your Highness and Lady Palmer," Oba said. She was wearing her priestess robes, and they were blindingly white.

"We've been friends too long for such formality, Oba." Kai didn't let Vivien go, but she wanted to put both women at ease.

"Today is all about formality, Highness. If you both will follow me, we'll begin." Oba smiled at Vivien and pointed to the building surrounded in columns close by. The temple resembled the Parthenon in its original form. Inside, the open feel set off the large statue of the goddess and the water orb at her feet. The perfectly round clear crystal sat in a wooden cradle, but today it seemed to come to life.

The orb glowed at times, but Kai had only witnessed it on certain occasions. As they neared, though, it started to glow like a small flame at first, but it was like a laser by the time they stood feet from it. Kai blinked, but her eyes were starting to water from the brightness. Vivien gripped her hand, and she could sense her fear.

"Princess Kai Merlin, you were written about in a prophecy that everyone believed foretold a curse, but in reality you were our salvation." Oba lifted the staff that held the orb and stood before them. "You and Lady Palmer will form a bridge between the depths and the land that will lead to everlasting peace." The orb seemed to be pulsing, and the light was starting to heat Kai's shell. "State your intentions before the goddess."

"We will live our lives in service to the goddess and our people," Kai said, bowing before the statue.

"We will bond together to raise children to lead our people for a thousand years." Vivien said the words Kai had taught her.

"Join hands," Oba said.

She faced Vivien and took her hands. It looked like Vivien had a halo around her, and Kai noticed her shell glowing as bright as the orb. The heat emanating from hers was becoming uncomfortable. "Viv," she said when Vivien's eyes fluttered closed.

She had no choice but to close her eyes as well when the light became blinding, and her hands felt like they were melding with Vivien's. Something bizarre was happening, and she could barely hear Oba and her priestesses chanting as the searing heat burst from the center of her chest. Her mind stayed calm, and it linked to Vivien's, and her excitement had nothing to do with fear.

As suddenly as it started, it ended, and she had no concept of how much time had passed. She opened her eyes, blinking, and studied Vivien's face. It was the same, but not. Something was different, and the smile Vivien gave her held no hint as to what it was. She lowered her head when Vivien moved to kiss her, and when their lips met, the chanting stopped.

"The goddess has blessed you and your choice." Oba placed the orb back at the goddess's feet and faced them. "Vivien, you're a true daughter of Atlantis, and you will give birth to its heir. Those who oppose you will perish in the turbulent waves of their own making." Oba spoke in the ancient language only used for religious ceremonies, and Kai was about to translate when Vivien answered.

"Thank you, I dedicate myself to her and thank her for her gifts." Vivien bowed to the river goddess without releasing Kai's hand. "And for her." She bowed to Kai next. It was as if Vivien had grown up speaking a dead language no one on Earth knew existed.

"You are bonded in the eyes of the goddess but must return in two days for your joining before the nation." Oba smiled and stepped closer. "May I?" She pointed to their shells.

It was then that Kai noticed the shell she'd made for Vivien was now a clear material with different etchings. They resembled the stones Nessa and Jyri wore, only they'd retained the shell shape. What else was to change?

"Kai, take Vivien to the pool for a cleansing bath," Oba said with a smile. "We'll leave you and close the gardens."

"Okay," she said, lengthening the word. Apparently no explanations would be forthcoming.

The priestesses all bowed and left them on the altar staring at each other. "You want to tell me what just happened?" Vivien asked and laughed. "Do you have any idea how I understood what she just said? Or how I replied in the same language? It feels like someone's rewired my head."

"Did you just get really hot?" Kai was trying to understand, but there was no logical explanation. Religious teachings had been part of her education, but there was nothing like this experience in the tomes.

"It was more my head than my chest. Did that have anything to do with it?" Vivien pointed to the orb. "Or was it the bond we share?"

She shook her head. "I'm not sure, but I think something plucked all that information out of my head and shared it with you."

"Seriously? You have the technology for that?" Vivien followed her outside, and she headed for one of the small pools that wasn't one she'd shared with Oba.

"No, which is why I'm confused. Right now, I believe we've been given permission to get naked, so let's talk about this later." She dropped her shirt, and Vivien pulled the drawstring on her pants, leaving her in her underwear.

"Goddess, you look good in nothing but skin," Vivien said, lifting her sundress over her head. "Is it going to be freezing and kill the mood?" She blushed. "I doubt water sex has a part in the cleansing bath. Sorry."

"I guess two days won't kill us, but no one said we couldn't hold each other. And the pools are heated by the sun, even at these depths. I promise I'll keep you warm." She held Vivien's hand and helped her in. She looked at Viv when she sucked in a breath. "Too cold for you?"

"No, I feel like the water's different for some reason." Vivien cupped a handful of water and let it flow through her fingers.

"Different, how?" She placed her hands on Vivien's hips and took them deeper.

"I've always felt at home in the water, but now it feels like a part of me." Vivien kissed her and mentally asked to go under. "It's hard to explain." The water was cool in a way that made it perfect, and they both kept their eyes open. *Shit!*

The word exploded loudly in Kai's head, and she kicked to keep them from sinking to the bottom. She looked around, thinking something was coming close to harm them, but there was nothing but the usual tropical fish they cultivated to repopulate the oceans.

I have gills. Vivien's thoughts came into her head and she smiled. *How?*

Whatever happened in the temple gave you more than an understanding of an old language. Total freedom in the water was something she thought she'd never be able to completely share with Vivien, but this changed everything. *When Oba said you were a true daughter of Atlantis, she was right.*

They swam and played so Vivien could enjoy her new gifts. Vivien had no trouble adjusting to the changes in her body, and she appeared to be an excited child with a new toy. The small sand shark swimming around them came and bumped against Vivien's chest. So understanding the original language and gills weren't the only things the goddess had given her. Vivien was perfect before, but now she was the only match that fit perfectly with her heart.

Vivien put her hands to the sides of her throat when she surfaced, and the gills closed. "This is beyond amazing," Vivien said as Kai reached for the towels that'd been left out for them. "Is the orb technological or magical?"

"It's…it's hard to explain." Galen had told her true devotion would come with age. When she truly had something to pray for, the orb would speak to her as a future queen. "The orb bonds with the head priestess and gives her sight of the future. The only two people who touch it are Oba and my mother. Let's head to lunch and maybe we can ask her about what happened. In all the classes I took in my training, I've never read of something like this."

Vivien put her dress back on and handed her the T-shirt. "Do you think it will upset her?"

"I don't think that'll be it at all. She's going to find it fascinating, if anything."

They rode a small shuttle back to the palace and walked to her mother's private dining room, which was used mostly for family dinners, and she pulled a chair out for Vivien. The paintings on the wall were done during the Renaissance in Florence, and she could sit and look at them for hours.

"Is that a Leonardo da Vinci?" Vivien asked. She stepped close to the large painting of an angel hovering over a turbulent sea.

"It is." She pointed to the one across the room. It was actually first in the series. The second painting was of a beautiful day that was either dusk or dawn. It included the same angel, but this time his head was bowed.

"Is this the morning or sunset?" Vivien asked.

"The series is done at four different times of day. This is the beginning of the day and the Lord's warrior is giving thanks. It's my favorite." The painting was masterful and had been rescued from one of the many senseless wars started by humans throughout history. "Da Vinci was truly touched by the angels he included in much of his work."

"You're a true romantic, my love." Vivien smiled up at her and kissed her hand.

"She gets that from Hadley," Galen said. "They both have a core of steel, but they show their soft side to the women they love." Her mother kissed both their cheeks and sat at the head of the table. "How did this morning go?"

"It wasn't what we expected," Kai said. She looked at Vivien and winked. "Go ahead, honey."

Vivien explained in detail, and Kai had to chuckle at her mother's expression. The gods didn't manifest themselves in their lives in such blatant ways, but it was the only way to explain what happened. She was still trying to process it, and even with her experience, she couldn't come up with a plausible explanation.

"May I?" Her mom's question snapped her attention back to the conversation. Vivien nodded and her mom stood and reached for the shell. "The etchings match yours, Kai?"

"They do now, and even the lines on mine are changed."

Vivien raised her hand. "What does it mean?"

"We exist in the world as individuals, but we're all born and belong to the realm as a whole. The shells link our thoughts, so we know we have a place here. But when I made yours, that's not why I did it." She stood and knelt next to Vivien. "I wanted to hear your thoughts, but you and Franklin formed a bond that allowed that and shut everyone else out."

"What does that mean?" Vivien repeated her question.

"I didn't need the shell to hear your thoughts or to feel your emotions. Your despair is what made me visit your room that night." She held Vivien's hand and felt the love Vivien had for her like a physical, tangible thing. "The markings on your shell were missing the history of my family but did include what Franklin is to you."

"And now ours match? Does that mean something now? Will our relationship change?" Vivien reached for her hand, then let her go when she glanced at her mother.

"It's okay," she said smiling. "I'd like to think it means the goddess approves of our match."

"If you don't mind, I'm going to speak to Oba about all this." Her mom tapped her fingers together and just stared outside. "Your sudden transformation should quiet any critics you have, because you're right. The goddess gave you this gift, even if we could've done it the way we did for Franklin."

"Some people won't change their minds even if the goddess asked them out for a beer and begged them to." She enjoyed making them both laugh. "In two days I'm going to marry this incredible woman and share my title with her."

"And then my parents would like to give us a wedding," Vivien said, her attention on Hadley.

"Kai told me, and we're looking forward to it. It's been years since we've been to New Orleans, so I'm ready for some fun. We don't visit the surface as often as we used to anymore, but we do make regular trips."

Her mom called for lunch, and they had a great hour. She knew there'd be more to this, but she'd wait until they had time. What happened today had been miraculous, and those kinds of things never came free.

"We're going to explore the ruins before we're due at dinner tonight." Now that Vivien was physically transformed, there was no reason not to have fun. That, and she wanted to test the limits of Vivien's capabilities. In her gut she knew they'd be important going forward.

❖

Daria stared out at Atlantis as the planet became smaller and smaller. The force she'd brought with her was small, but it was enough to take over Galen's primitive realm. Once that was complete, she'd have access to their ships, giving her the resources she'd need to take over the rest of the planet. The one thing Pontos had said about the human population as a whole was that they were weak and petty. All their wars were based on greed and power. That she understood, but they didn't understand what was coming. Atlantis's advanced civilization would crush them if they didn't surrender. She wanted a new, undying planet with plenty of resources to exploit. She'd have no issue with taking it.

"Highness," the navigator said, standing next to her chair. "From the logs Prince Pontos followed, we're a week from the jumping point."

"Are you set at top speed?" Atlantis finally disappeared from view, and the only thing she regretted leaving behind was her mother, whom she hadn't bothered to say good-bye to. Rhea had fallen in love with her father and condoned how he'd treated Daria, so Rhea's future was tied to her father's.

"We are at limit, ma'am. This came through for you." The man handed her a slip of paper and bowed.

The message was from her father. It was a plea for her to return and proved how weak he was. It was freeing to leave him and all that behind. There would never be a time when she bowed before anyone and begged for their mercy. This conquest was her beginning, and she would never show the cowardice of her father and brother. Her destiny was greatness. Atlantis could rot.

"Good, call me if anything goes wrong. I'll be in my quarters."
She wanted to read the history of Nessa again. The traitorous bitch was
the seed from which the new Atlantis had grown. It was time to kill
what she built and show this new world real power.

"How long do you think Bronti will keep things from devolving
into chaos?" Frem Nye, her second, asked. Frem was naked on her
bed and bent a leg when she stared at her. In a life full of competition
for her parents' attention, Frem was the only person she thought cared
about her.

"Sol Oberon will curse the day he pushed me aside. His reign will
not last a thousand years. I'll be shocked if he lives out the week, and
I doubt Bronti will keep the people from overrunning the palace, but
that's not our problem any longer. I have no intention of going back."

"Forget that now and come." Frem lifted her hand and smiled.
"Victory awaits us tomorrow, so let's enjoy the moment."

"When we win, you'll stand by my side through all of it."

CHAPTER EIGHT

The underwater Atlantis was a different world in so many aspects. It was modern, advanced, yet ancient and strange. The sun shone through the domes in the morning, it even rained in some sections, and people went about mundane things like shopping and bringing their daughters to school. While they were inside the domes, their clothes resembled what Vivien would see on a daily basis in New Orleans, yet when they were outside, the suits they wore were not of this world.

Tonight, the navy blue uniforms were similar to a marine's uniform without as many embellishments. The gowns were made of a shimmery material she wasn't familiar with, but it felt good against her skin. The style reminded her of a Roman toga like the priestesses wore in the temple. They were a bit more form-fitting, though, with a slight dip in the back. She'd picked a deep blue that varied slightly from Kai's uniform and liked that they looked good standing together. Not that she'd seen much of Kai tonight.

Vivien was getting a crash course in Atlantean politics and ceremonies. After her visit to the temple, she and Kai had given an interview to the capital's news, and then they sat for their first state dinner. In the oil business, politics played a big role in how successful you'd be, but it wasn't anything like this. A matriarchal monarchy seemed to have a different feel to it, but the politics were there right under the surface.

The difference here was that Galen's rule was respected by most, and those who opposed her were mostly on the fringes of society. Except for Bella Riverstone, who she'd been told was close to Galen, whose family was planning the downfall of the royal family. At dinner there were a few people who'd brought that matter up and hinted that Vivien's presence in the capacity Kai had elevated her to wouldn't sit well with some people. Vivien's gut told her it wasn't sitting well with the gossiping hinters, but only time would tell. But the fact that those people were sitting at the royal table, close to the throne, was worrisome.

"Are you having fun yet?" Kai asked when she was able to make it across the room to her.

"Only three more days to go and you're stuck with me, which means all these people will be stuck with me too. Some of them give the impression that they'd rather drink scum water than have that become reality." She squeezed Kai's fingers and kept a smile on her face. Surprisingly, it was her father's voice in her head telling her never to show fear that was helping her through this.

"My life is set in so many ways, but I'm not compromising on who I love. The pond scum people will have to come to terms with that." Kai kissed the back of her hand and opened her mind to her. The words *I love you* did make her feel invincible. "But you know better than most that in every group there are a few nutters."

"Your world is so beautiful and amazing, and I guess I was hoping everyone was equally beautiful and amazing. Wishful thinking, huh?" The place really was much more than anyone could imagine. When she'd first started diving, trying to find the secrets her shell told, this wasn't what she thought she'd find. It was actually mind-boggling that an entire society lived in the ocean, with technological means far beyond that of the people living on the land above them. They were so far advanced, and they made humankind look so primitive in contrast.

"We may not be human, but we've been here long enough that we can probably claim aspects of humanity. And human nature is what it is. People act like people, especially when it's in their best interest. Some people think their best interest will be served by someone else's family taking the weight of the crown off my mother's head."

"Is that even a possibility?" Finding a civilization no one knew existed was strange enough, but finding one that could have a civil war right under the Atlantic Ocean was downright bizarre.

"Anything in life is a possibility, but they'll have to get through me and everyone loyal to my mother. Even if that happens, you still hold our future."

"*We* hold our future, so make sure nothing happens to you. There's so much more for me to learn, and I happen to love your lessons." There was applause when she kissed Kai, and their embrace ended too soon for her liking.

"Anything else bothering you?" Kai asked.

"It's not that anything in particular is bothering me, honey."

"Don't hold back, Viv. I can't help you if you don't tell me."

"It's been a long few days learning all the political stuff, as well as the stuff I need to know about the temple and goddess. I don't want to disappoint you or your family." Insecurity really sucked at times.

"I can say you're never a disappointment until I'm hoarse, but you have to choose to believe it. In three days I'm going to marry you because I love you." She smiled at the people milling around them. "And you pick the most interesting places to have talks," Kai said and laughed.

"I'm sorry. This is the last place I needed to do this."

"I'm glad you did. I'm over here talking to you instead of talking to some of the windbags over there." Kai kissed her hand again and placed it on the bend of her elbow. "How about I walk you home, so I can kiss you where no one feels the need to clap?"

"That sounds wonderful."

That's what Kai did, and Vivien had learned what it was to be the center of someone's world. Kai might've been the future ruler of Atlantis, but she was excellent in getting across how she felt about her to the exclusion of everything else in their lives. Three days passed much quicker than she'd expected, and Kai's family had truly embraced her. She was ready to join her life to Kai's and take on the responsibilities she'd have as future consort.

Galen had talked extensively in a way that was different than her own mother, but she'd appreciated Galen's openness and curiosity about her life. It wasn't that she didn't love her own mother, but the relationship they'd had for so long was distant and adversarial. That had changed recently, and her mom finally saw her as an individual capable of making her own decisions and choices. But Galen had seen her, understood her, and recognized how much she loved her child from almost their first encounter.

Her future mother-in-law was someone she was happy to have as a friend. She'd made her laugh with stories about Kai, and about her life with Hadley. She'd accepted Galen's help with her wardrobe for the big day, since aside from Kai and her family, she had very little support here. It was a reminder, however small, that she was an outsider. Would it always feel that way?

The dress she was getting married in had belonged to Galen, and she hoped it brought her the kind of luck Galen had been gifted with Hadley. After dinner the night before, Kai had dropped her off at her room and promised her a lifetime of happiness after kissing her until her knees were weak.

She was sitting thinking about that as a way of trying to calm her stomach. A mixture of nerves and morning sickness made her crave Kai's presence. It never stopped her from throwing up, but she felt better with Kai close by. A few more hours and she'd get her wish.

The comm unit chimed, and she smiled when she saw it was Kai. "I have to get dressed, and then I expect you in the throne room. You'd better show up." She put her hands on her stomach and tried to breathe through the nausea. "Your daughter's making my morning interesting."

"If you throw up on me while we're up there, it'll be memorable," Kai said, and she could imagine the smile on Kai's face.

"Don't worry. I'll try to hold it until the honeymoon. My father probably thinks that'd be apropos since I'm pregnant and single." Damn, though, if she didn't miss her father today. Hanging on to him as she walked the aisle would've been nice.

"You won't be single for long, and you can throw up on me anytime."

"Neither will you," she said, teasing. "All those pretty women trying to get your attention last night will be sad when you say *I do*."

"If I owned bells, I'd be putting them on. See you soon, love."

Kai had explained where some of the wedding rituals had come from, and she wasn't surprised the traditional human wedding ceremony was born here. It had evolved on Earth since then, but it made her wonder what other customs humankind had clung to from those early lessons of the people of Atlantis.

For the ceremony today she was going to have to walk alone, which made her melancholy in a way. Except for Frankie, she'd been alone for most of her life, but her parents had tried their best to make amends. This was the first of the two weddings they'd have, and she was looking forward to the one her mother was planning. Starting her own family made her see how important her parents and brother were to her life, even if it hadn't always been perfect, and she wanted to share this incredibly pivotal moment with them too.

She smiled at Edil's and Isla's partners, who'd come to help get her ready. "I never thought I'd get married," she said, looking at herself in the mirror. She'd been told a silver gown was the traditional wedding attire, but she was marrying royalty. Her gown was mostly gold with bits of blue beading that matched Kai's uniform. The A-line with a bateau neckline and court train was beautiful. It was backless, and Galen had teased her about how quickly that little design would get her to the honeymoon once Kai saw it. "Now I can't wait."

"Hopefully some of that excitement has to do with the girl who's waiting for you," Galen said as she entered quietly.

They all bowed, and she smiled at Galen. "It has everything to do with that, Highness. She was infuriating at first, but she woke me to everything I'd missed before her."

Galen nodded and laughed. "Yes, the tadpole is a carbon copy of the one who wakes all sorts of things in me." They all laughed when Galen winked. "I wanted to come to congratulate you as well as be the first to welcome you into our family. The life you're about to embark on will not always be easy, but I know my child will love you through all of it."

"I love her just as much."

"That we know from the way you look at her." Hadley joined Galen and handed her wife a box.

"We also know the customs of your world," Galen said, taking her hand. "I believe it's something old, new, borrowed, and blue." Vivien nodded. "The dress will count as borrowed and blue."

"It's beautiful," she said. "Thank you for letting me use it." She hadn't gone wedding-dress shopping and she knew her mom was probably looking forward to it. With only a week before they'd decided to come to Atlantis, she hadn't had a chance to think about what she'd wear for the ceremony, but Kai had assured her they'd find something in the city. Right now she had a connection to Kai's past by using her mom's dress, and it felt special in a way nothing store-bought ever could.

The dress had been altered quickly, as it'd been Galen's from her wedding day. "I'm honored you accepted my offer. I also wanted to deliver this for Kai. It will count for something old since she found it in an old shipwreck." The box contained a necklace that was strung with diamonds and sapphires. "It was a seventeenth-century ship that went down in a storm close to here on its way back to Spain. Kai researched it and this was meant for the queen. She said it was fitting for the woman who'd be her queen."

"It's beautiful." She turned so Galen could put it on her. "Thank you both for your welcome and for getting all this done so quickly."

"You're welcome, and I promise to always do my best to guide you through all this."

"I promise to always do my best," she said with her hand to her throat. The moment felt beautifully surreal.

"You'll be fine. Let me go take my place." Galen took Hadley's hand and smiled at her.

"I'll see you out there."

"And we have a surprise for you, to honor another one of your traditions." Galen nodded, and the door opened to reveal Frankie. His suit was much different than anything she'd ever seen him wear, and he appeared unsure what to do as he smiled at her and gave a little shrug. It was like Kai's uniform in the cut but without her adornments. The navy pants and jacket set off Frankie's blond hair that matched her own in color, and the white of the shirt underneath made his tan stand out. "This one time I've given permission to allow a topsider to visit because he has an important job to do. It's good to be queen sometimes."

Frankie bowed as the royal couple left and then hugged her. "You look beautiful, and this place is off the chain. I only caught a glimpse of it when I was down here before, and this is so much better." He let her go and stared out the windows. "I'm having trouble believing all this, and I'm sorry Marsha's missing it."

"Just remember that Kai will probably rip your tongue out if you ever tell anyone."

"I know. She already threatened me," he said and laughed. "You really do look like royalty, sis."

"We're ready to begin, ma'am." One of the attendants motioned toward the door.

"Let's go," Frankie said as if he suddenly knew what he was doing. "Don't worry—Kai told me what I have to do. Once we're done, there's plenty we need to talk about."

"Is everything and everyone okay?" She took his arm and followed the attendants out, her stomach flipping.

"Everything's fine, and it's nothing bad. Right now, smile and concentrate. From what I understand, everyone in the realm is watching this thing, and you don't want to screw up."

"Thanks so much for putting me at ease." She put her hand on her stomach and told her daughter to behave.

They stopped outside the throne room and waited for the music to begin. She'd always known in the back of her mind that this was going to be broadcast throughout the realm, but right now it was front and center. She took a deep breath and gripped Frankie's arm. The aisle ahead seemed endless, and the place was packed.

"Don't let me fall on my face," she whispered. Frankie laughed, and they started walking.

The people present stood and bowed as she and Frankie walked by. From what both Kai and Galen had said, some of the women in attendance went back and forth between the cities of Atlantis and the outside world. A very few who considered themselves purists had never set foot on land, so Frankie was the first man they'd ever seen in person. Those were the women who appeared the most upset that Kai was marrying her, as if the taint of having a male relative would somehow rub off on the crown. But at the moment, she couldn't bring herself to care.

At the dais, Kai waited halfway down the stairs. That wasn't where she'd said she'd be standing, and her smile widened when she felt her shell warm. Kai's thoughts came to her gently, and it was enough to make her let her nerves go and enjoy the moment.

"Beautiful." Kai's compliment made her ears warm. Her attention flicked to Oba momentarily as she stood to the left of the throne. Her robes were gleaming white, and she was holding a water orb that was crystal clear.

"Today we gather for our future." Oba's voice echoed in the now silent room. "Lady Palmer will join with Princess Kai. Who brings her forward?"

"I, Franklin Winston Palmer, would like to present my sister, Vivien." Frankie bowed over her hand. He walked her to the dais but didn't place a foot on it.

Kai walked down the rest of the steps and shook Frankie's hand.

"Thanks, I'll take it from here," Kai said softly. She took Vivien's hand and escorted her up.

Oba went through the ceremony, and she tried to pay attention to every word, but Kai in that uniform was distracting. Leave it to her to wait until her late twenties to start noticing things like that. She stopped daydreaming when it came time for the vows and all the things she had to say to Kai. Once that was done, the last thing they had to do was kneel before Galen and Hadley.

"You have made your vows and have chosen each other," Galen said and raised her head to the people. "The goddess has blessed Kai's choice by making Vivien a true sister. Today we crown a new princess and future consort." The crown in Galen's hand was a smaller version of the one she wore as queen, but it matched Kai's. "I give you Princess Kai and Princess Vivien."

The cheers went up, and Kai lowered her head and kissed her. "Forever, my love," Kai said.

"Forever," she said and smiled out at the people. This time no one appeared reluctant to participate. Maybe whatever had happened to her at the temple had turned the tide. There hadn't been a general announcement about her transformation, but the news had obviously made it through the capital. Or maybe the people who weren't happy about it hadn't attended. She took Kai's arm on the way down, and Frankie followed them out. There was going to be a reception in an hour to give the staff time to set the room again, so Kai led them to the part of the castle that overlooked the ruins. More seats had been added, and there were refreshments waiting for them.

"When you said you were the heir to Atlantis's throne, I wasn't expecting this," Frankie said. "I guess I didn't know what to expect really, but this is something. You did the impossible for me, and the rational part of my brain realizes your people had to be advanced, but the part that needs a reference to something familiar is in awe."

"I'm glad you came, so you could see Vivien will be safe here." Kai put her arm around her when she sat and kissed her cheek.

"I trust you with that, but there's something else." Frankie sat across from them and reached up to open his collar. "I was going to a meeting a few days ago, and I thought I was having a stroke when a laser beam came through the window straight into my neck." He took his shells out and showed them to them. "They've both changed, and so has what was etched into the original one."

"Wow," she said.

"That's not the only thing that's different." Frankie seemed nervous as he tapped his fingers on his knees. The bouncing leg was new and strange. "It actually freaks me out."

"Gills?" Kai asked.

"I thought the light was a dream, but the gills in the shower were hard to ignore." He laughed but stared at them as if looking for answers.

"Let me tell you a story," she said, and Kai nodded. She told him what happened in the temple, and he seemed to relax. "The same thing happened to our shells, but Kai already had gills. I found out when we took a swim."

"What does all this mean?" Frankie asked.

"We're not really sure, but Oba and her priestesses are working on it," Kai said. "I'm not sure about Viv, but your transformation might've happened because of your connection through the shells I gave you."

"We have time enough to think about that," Galen said when she joined them. "Tonight's about celebrations."

"Yes, ma'am, and thank you for allowing me to come along for the ride." Frankie bowed over Galen's hand and kissed it.

"Oba will want to see you all tomorrow, so come by, and I'll escort you." Galen took Frankie's arm and went back to the reception. "There are some people who'd like to meet this one."

Vivien smiled at the people who came and wished them well. Kai had told her a cross section of the community had been invited to the event, along with the royal court, only limited by space. Their realm was based on equality and openness, so they had to be accessible to all their people.

"Thank you," she said to a young girl. She crouched and accepted a small bouquet of flowers the girl presented her. "I love your dress."

"Thank you, Princess." The little girl bowed her head, but it seemed to be more from shyness than protocol.

The small girl made her think of the baby that wasn't that far in their future. She glanced up at Frankie when he came and stood beside her. This was a one hundred and eighty degree turn from her life, and she took a breath to settle herself in the moment. This wasn't dealing with roughnecks and oil executives, and it was going to take time to adjust.

"You're doing great," Frankie said, taking her hand. "This is what you were born to do."

"I don't know about that, but I'm not giving her up." She looked across the room and saw Kai talking to a group of older women. It took a second for Kai to turn her head and make eye contact. That was proof enough that Kai would never leave her to deal with any of this alone.

"Would you like to dance?" Kai asked a minute later. "I don't think we've ever done that together."

She followed Kai to the dance floor and smiled when Kai bent a little and pressed the side of her head to hers. "I'm thinking we've never danced because you got my clothes off the first chance you got. We didn't take time for the dancing part."

Kai laughed. "You love me and skinny-dipping as much as I do."

"There's plenty of this and skinny-dipping in your future." The future was one she never could have imagined, and it stretched ahead of them like an undersea yellow brick road. "This has been a good day." She put her hands on Kai's chest and moved one hand over Kai's shell. "You are the best-looking thing I've ever seen, and you're hot in this uniform."

"You're the one everyone's staring at." Kai kissed her, and they smiled at the applause it caused.

"You're blind if you think that, but thank you." She followed Kai around the floor and felt the happiness that consumed Kai's whole being. It seemed to radiate out of her and put to rest any sense she'd had of rushing Kai into something she might not have wanted. Of course that had most likely been all in her head, but right now she couldn't dredge up a negative thought.

"Listen to me, okay," Kai said.

She had a way of forgetting that when she got lost in her thoughts, she was easier to read. "I'm sorry," she said and smiled. "Today is a special day, and not the time for my craziness."

"You're the one being rushed, if anything. I know kids weren't in your plans, and I should've been more careful."

"Honey, listen. Children weren't in my grand plan, true, but I'm happy. We made this kid—you and me—and I'm happy with the fact that we did. At the time I didn't realize what I do now." The middle of a huge party wasn't the best time to have this conversation, but with Kai she always felt she could say anything.

"What's that?" Kai's smile was like a gift wrapped promise.

"I've belonged to you from the day we met. It was right there, and I didn't want to admit it because of what that would mean. Then I thought you'd been killed, and I couldn't deny it." She squeezed Kai's shell and closed her eyes. "I love you. I always have, and it made absolutely no sense. At times it's made me crazy that I couldn't shake it."

"What's that?" Kai repeated her question about what Viv had come to realize.

"That no matter who I spent time with, was intimate with, it wasn't you. That day when we were children, it was like you branded me, and I couldn't get past it."

"It had the opposite effect on me," Kai said and appeared chagrined. "It wasn't until the day I saw you outside your parents' home. I went from not thinking of that day to not being able to think about anything else. Our connection was strong enough that after our first disagreement, when you came searching for me, I was able to lead you right to me by mentally showing you the way. I couldn't have done that if there was nothing there, and I'm sorry I didn't know it then."

"Don't do this, baby. I love you, and as much as I am yours, you're mine. All this that happened was supposed to, and I'm as happy about it as you are." She put her hands behind Kai's head and kissed her again. "You and I are going to be a team and have great sex." Her teasing made Kai laugh.

"You dominate my thoughts and dreams. Thank you for marrying me."

"Of course I married you after you asked me so nicely." She studied every feature on Kai's face and smiled. Kai was so good-looking it made her burn. "You're the most handsome thing, and I love you."

"How about my dancing?"

"Flawless." She laughed and tried to forget everything else except enjoying herself. Whatever happened at the temple wasn't normal and was something to think about, as was Galen's mention that the head of her guard, Laud, wasn't there. Kai hadn't shared anything to do with security yet, but Steve and his people were all dead. That Pontos and his people had gotten so close meant there was still danger, and she'd worry about it, only not tonight. There wasn't anything to be afraid of unless some human-world military found them. That, though, was unlikely tonight.

All she wanted in the months ahead was to enjoy the gift of loving Kai and what had come about because of that love. There was a lot to unpack that she couldn't begin to understand, like the physical changes both she and Frankie had undergone, and she wanted answers.

The one who had the answers was Oba. There was no way of knowing if the priestess would tell her the truth. It wasn't a matter of Oba's relationship with Kai, but one of trust. She doubted Oba trusted her yet, but she wasn't giving up until she had all the answers. She did at least want to try, since she had six months to give their daughter a future without any threat hanging over her. And unlike her parents, she vowed to believe her child if she had a story to tell, no matter what happened in her daughter's life, and she'd champion her in whatever battles she faced.

❖

Hadley turned the video on and nodded to Laud. Galen kissed the top of Hadley's head before sitting and smiling at the screen. "We missed you at the wedding," Galen said.

"I would've loved to have been there in person, but the team and I watched it. We're starting to make progress, though, so it wasn't the time to go." Laud split the screen, and she and Hadley saw Tanice sitting in her cell smiling and talking to one of Laud's team. The conversation was animated even without the sound on, and Tanice appeared happy.

Galen imagined for a second losing Hadley and what the grief would do to her. For all of Tanice's crimes, she was a woman grieving the person she loved. Their new technology made Tanice believe she was not only at home on planet Atlantis, but sitting with Pontos. After a moment of laughter, Tanice leaned forward and kissed her interrogator.

"I'm not sure how all this works, but she's really convinced it's Pontos?" Galen asked. There was no reason to listen in since they'd get the report shortly, but it was interesting. "Has she divulged anything useful?"

Laud nodded. "Pontos arrived with his team, which by all accounts was small, in three ships. He feared being trapped here if things went wrong, so the other two ships were backups. His sister was the one who set up the link between the Oberon family and our people. He didn't bring a large force because he had one here ready to follow orders."

Hadley tightened her grip on the arms of her chair and leaned forward toward the screen. "Tell me you have names."

"I'm sorry, I should've said, he *thought* he had troops who would do his bidding. Francesca Yelter overexaggerated the number of people with her as well as her military service and experience." Another screen came up, and she and Hadley saw a screenshot of the homepage for a site called *Devotion to Our True King*. "It's a closed site, but we have the names of all the members and a way to trace them."

"Are any still in the capital?" Hadley asked.

The wedding celebrations were still going on, and Galen felt a duty to go back, but she had to hear this. The new development actually made her want to run back and check on Kai and Vivien. If any enemies willing to kill them were still hiding within their walls, she needed to protect her family. She had to force herself to relax and take a breath. The sudden fear had squeezed the joy and air right out of her.

"My people are rounding up the ones in the city, and I called on Belm to take care of the most troublesome."

"Who?" Hadley asked.

"Cara Cosh." The minister of agriculture. They'd set aside acres of land to bring to fruition Cosh's ambition to expand their food sources. Cosh was also ambitious when it came to trying to get closer to Galen. "She's part of your court and can get close enough to do damage."

"Hadley," Galen said, looking at her consort. Cosh was at the wedding and close enough to her family to carry out any violence she'd been ordered to do.

Laud held up her hand to stop any panic. "We quietly removed her and her family, Highness. I wouldn't have bothered you today otherwise, but I didn't want to take any chances. My job now is to find the connections to Yelter, which will hopefully lead us to her wife and daughter." Laud exhaled as she switched off the view of Tanice. "I'll be returning tonight and leaving the team to finish here. Now that Tanice is talking, we should get all the information we need."

"Thank you, and report in the morning. I want to go with you when you question Cosh." Hadley sounded like she was having trouble containing her rage.

Galen would've called her on it, but she was having the same problem. That anyone was disgruntled enough to commit treason didn't make sense because of the lives they all led. Her subjects were free to pursue the things that gave them satisfaction, and no one was left behind. This was as close to the utopia humans talked about as you could achieve, and yet some craved the authoritarian rule of a tyrant.

"Safe journey, Laud." Galen turned to Hadley when the screen shut off.

"It's time to bring this to everyone's attention. We can't allow a few people to put us all in danger," Hadley said.

"We need to find them all first, love." Hadley was still upset but Galen softened her tone as she caressed her cheek. "We still have another wedding to attend, and I don't want anyone to take the chance to escape if we speak too soon. I also have to set the security forces to assure nothing happens while we're topside." She took Hadley's hand and motioned for the guards to open the door. "You owe me a dance."

Galen knew herself well enough to know she'd worry until all this was truly over. That she'd take care of some of these people with a very permanent solution wasn't a question. From her first day on the throne, a small group of women had questioned her strength and her ability to be firm when need be. They, along with everyone else, would find out the strength and willingness to kill to protect her child and her family wasn't going to be a problem. If they'd gambled on her running from conflicts, they'd lose.

CHAPTER NINE

Kai held Vivien against her and swayed to the music. This would be their last dance before they retired for the night. She'd planned a quick trip to celebrate their joining, but her mothers leaving for an hour meant there was a chance that wouldn't happen. Security would trump any honeymoon plans she had, and she'd have to agree. She wasn't taking any chances with Vivien.

"The best part of today is I get to sleep with you tonight." Vivien squeezed Kai's shoulders and smiled up at her. "I've missed you."

"Tonight, and every night, Mrs. Merlin, and the missing went both ways." She watched her parents rejoin the party and head out to the dance floor. Galen seemed tense and Hadley just seemed pissed.

"What's wrong?" Vivien placed her hand on her cheek and moved her head so she'd look at her.

"I'm not sure, but something's off."

"They didn't change their minds, did they?" Vivien glanced back and Kai's parents smiled at them.

"There's no chance of that." She moved them closer to her parents, and Vivien nodded, not having to ask when Kai handed her off to her mother Hadley. Now face-to-face with her mother Galen, Kai said, "Okay, don't make me torture it out of you."

"Laud gathered some information we'll have to deal with. I'm not keeping it from you because I don't want you involved, but because I want to give you and Vivien time alone. Take a day, and then I'll tell you everything."

"Can I take her anywhere?" She glanced at Vivien laughing at something her mom had said.

"Use the retreat, and don't fuss at the number of guards that'll be necessary."

"Give us the day and then come and join us. We'll have to figure something out since Vivien's family is expecting to host a wedding."

"And that'll happen," her mom said, pinching her cheek. "We need to see what we're up against, so we can put security in place. There's no chance I'll put you, Vivien, and her family in harm's way."

"Did something big happen today? I'm not naive enough to think that everyone would embrace my choice." She winked at Vivien when she found her glancing their way. "But this is getting ridiculous. Are these idiots reading some other history of Atlantis I don't know about? Poseidon and then the Oberons ruled with their boots on everyone's necks."

"Honey, you know that no matter what's going on, someone's not happy. Whoever's involved probably sees this as a power grab and is using the Oberons to get more than their share." Her mother kissed her cheek and hugged her as the song ended. "Right now, *you* have nothing to worry about. Go enjoy your first night as a married woman. If you hear any wailing, that'll be all the women who realize you're off the market."

"Not funny, Mama." They joined their mates and Vivien immediately took her hand. "Ready to go?"

"More than ready, and thank you both so much for this wonderful day. I loved it from beginning to end." Vivien hugged Kai's parents and followed them to the top of the dais. They had to stay for one more toast. Quiet fell over the room when her mother raised her hands.

"Parents dream of the day their child finds the kind of love you pray they will. Today is that day for Hadley and me. We raise our glasses to Kai and Vivien." Her mother raised her glass and smiled at them. "May the goddess bless you with happiness, wisdom, and long life."

Everyone followed her mom's lead and waited. When her mom took a sip everyone else did too, then cheered. That was the last duty performed that released them to go. She led Vivien back to her room and closed the door after placing the guards farther away than they'd wanted.

"Was there anything wrong? Hadley gave me no clue." Vivien came closer and unbuttoned Kai's jacket.

"Something happened, but Mama isn't talking. She did, though, offer her retreat that's a few hours away. It's in a series of caves, which made it possible to build beautiful beaches. They'll give us a day and then join us to tell us what's happening." She folded the jacket and dropped it over a chair.

"Good, but we don't need to talk about that right now." Vivien started on the buttons of her shirt next. "You know," Vivien said, leaving the shirt open but on. "Before I met you, I hardly ever thought about sex."

"Really? That's surprising." She glanced down when her pants dropped to her ankles.

"Why? When we met, the only person who was interested in me was Steve. Believe me, I never had any sexual fantasies about him. You came along, though, and woke up that part of me, and now I want you all the time."

"That sounds like a good thing. It puts us on the same wavelength. You're the fuel that feeds the fire in me." She turned Vivien around and unzipped her. "You'd think I'm a horny teenager, the amount of time I think about getting you naked." She gently bit Vivien's earlobe, enjoying the moan it produced.

"Horny's a good word for it," Viv said and laughed. "It's a good thing we only had to wait three days." Vivien pulled Kai's underwear off next and put her hands on her ass.

"Are you trying to tell me something?" Kai asked.

"There's plenty I have to say, but really it's more something I want from you." Vivien glanced between her and the bed. "Are you going to make me wait?"

She walked backward until she hit the bed after getting naked. Tonight she wanted to give Vivien everything she wanted and the freedom to claim it. Vivien lowered her head and kissed her. It seemed as if Vivien was frantic by the way she was trying to devour her mouth.

"Slow down, baby. We have time."

Vivien sat up, straddling her. She shook her head to clear her hair out of her face. "There's no sin in rushing the first time." Vivien wiggled her eyebrows as she said it, then cupped her breasts like she was trying to get her to fall in line. "You know you want to."

Kai ran her hands up Vivien's thighs to her waist. There were very few things in her life that she enjoyed more than touching Viv. She'd had relationships with a number of women, the most serious being Oba, but none of them made her this desperate. Vivien had turned her inside out from their first time together, and to prove the rightness of the relationship, she was sure they'd conceived that first time.

"I do want to," she said as she sucked in a nipple. The way Viv pulled her hair and moaned made her want to rush. She was turned-on, and the desire made it hard to concentrate on what she was doing. "I want you."

She moved down and kissed Vivien's abdomen next. She kept going down and put her head between Viv's legs. Viv pulled her hair a little when she kissed her sex.

"Are you going slow for a reason?" Viv raised her head and stared down at her. "Paybacks, honey."

The tease made her circle Viv's hard clit with just the tip of her tongue. She lifted her head slightly, and Viv followed by lifting her hips. "You are so gorgeous—especially like this."

Vivien opened her mouth to say something but let her head drop back when Kai moved to finish what she'd started. She sucked Vivien in and wanted to smile when Viv clamped her thighs together, trapping her in place. It was as if Viv wasn't taking any chances that she'd stop again for any other romantic declarations.

"Honey, go inside," Vivien said breathlessly. "I need you...I need...you." Vivien grabbed her hair and pulled. "Oh." Vivien was loud when she gave her what she wanted. The feel of Viv tightening around her fingers made her want to slow and enjoy the moment, but Viv had set their pace. "Ah, yes...don't stop." The stuttered speech made her thrust faster and deeper, and Viv arched her back. "Don't stop." She gave the command one more time, then went rigid.

She kissed Viv's sex before moving up. Viv reached down and circled her wrist. It was a silent plea for her to stay inside. "You okay?"

"I am now." The words sounded lazy and easy. "You've turned me into a hedonist."

"I come from a long proud line of them, so get used to it." She smiled when Viv moved to straddle her again without dislodging her fingers. "Show me how much you want me."

Viv blushed but cupped her breasts again and started to rock her hips. This time she went slower and looked down at Kai until she moved her thumb to her clit. That stopped Viv altogether, but it seemed to be a moment of enjoying where she was. Vivien closed her eyes as she pinched her nipples, and Kai wanted to melt into the bed.

"You make me crazy," Viv said as she opened her eyes.

Kai's hips started to move faster, and she smiled down at her. "I hope I always do."

"Yes…oh yes." The movements of Vivien's hips were smooth as she sped up. She didn't get jerky until the end. "Absence really does do something to the heart."

"Let's hope you don't get bored now that you're stuck with me." She held Viv when she slumped down on top of her. Viv felt warm and soft.

"Not possible." Viv raised her head and stared down at her. When Vivien lowered her head to reach her lips, the shell around her throat touched Kai's, and the same blinding light from the temple happened again, only this time it was in her head.

It made no sense, but whatever was happening obscured her vision. The way Vivien was blinking meant she was experiencing the same thing. She stared straight ahead as the brightness became bearable, and she saw Vivien, only now she was very pregnant.

Visions of the future weren't in Kai's wheelhouse, and she glanced around, trying to figure out why she was having one now. She concentrated on Vivien's face and moved toward her. Mentally she knew Viv was in her arms, but it was hard to convince herself of that from what she was seeing. It was all so real.

"Kai," Vivien said, holding her hand out.

She stretched out to take Viv's hand, but the darkness behind Vivien was like an avalanche. "Viv," she yelled and felt Vivien's fingertips skim her own as something ripped her away in a wave. "Vivien," she screamed again, but she was gone.

Vivien had been swallowed by the darkness, taking the baby with her.

Despair made her want to claw her skin to add to the pain she was in. She needed the other half of her heart to survive, and the shell around her neck went cold as if it too sensed the loss. The hard ground was biting when she fell to her knees, and all she wanted was to wake and see it was all a nightmare.

Her tears fell even though her eyes were closed, and they turned to sobs when she felt a hand on her cheek. It was as familiar as her own face in the mirror, but it didn't compute.

"Honey," Vivien said. Her voice was so compassionate Kai was desperate to believe she was truly there. "Open your eyes."

Vivien was there, safe, and that brought on more tears, this time, from pure relief. It flooded through her, leaving her cold and tired. "What in the world was that?"

"What did you see?" Vivien stroked her face, and it was calming.

"What did you?" She didn't want to upset Vivien if she was the only one who'd been affected by whatever had happened. "Did you see anything at all?"

"It was a rush of cold and dark that cut me off from you. I felt your fingers for a moment, like you were trying to save me but couldn't." Vivien wiped Kai's face and kissed her forehead. "I'm not sure what that was, but it wasn't pleasant."

"If this was the shells' idea of a wedding gift, I would've rather skipped it." She took a deep breath and tried to purge the panic from her head. "I saw the same thing, and I couldn't run fast enough to get to you before a wave of something evil ripped you away."

"Okay, you're right, this sucked." Vivien moved to lie on top of her. "I don't want this to replace our afterglow moments. If this is our wedding gift, a gift certificate to The Cheesecake Factory would've been nicer."

She couldn't help laughing. "That sucked the wind out of my sails."

"How about if I suck something else right out of you?" Viv slid down her body and ran her tongue over her clit before doing what she'd promised. She sucked her in, and it was embarrassing how quickly she came.

"Shit." She exhaled when Vivien came back up and kissed her chin before her lips.

"What? You didn't like it?" Vivien pinched her side and laughed. "That quick takeoff says otherwise."

"Don't remind me. It does make me look like a novice, doesn't it." She laughed when she got pinched again. "Or it could be I've been waiting three days."

"All you have to pray for now is that my mother won't make you wait longer than that." Viv completely relaxed against her. "And I hate to bring it up again, but do you think there's anything to what just happened? This isn't some obscure Atlantis ritual divorce proceeding that ends in me being taken away on a rogue wave, right?"

"My mom Hadley told me once that my devotion to the goddess would come when I had something to pray for. Up to now I've spent my life learning to defend my queen, my sisters, and the ideal of who we are." She ran her hands up and down Viv's back, and the sense of having the freedom to do so twisted something free in her heart. This was something new and wonderful, and she gave herself over to the kiss Viv started.

She'd never prayed to be gifted with a great love because she'd never met a woman who had conjured that up in her. Oba was someone she'd loved, but not like this. It was true she'd never prayed for it, but she'd been blessed just the same. Vivien's love infused her with a strength and happiness that she'd never take for granted.

"You'll never have to hide anything from me," Vivien said. "I'll love you when you're strong, when you're unsure, and when you're lost. You are my mate, and I belong to you."

She couldn't help the tears that welled up in her eyes. The fact that she didn't have to be strong all the time made her love Vivien even more. "You are the most important thing to pray for. If my mothers feel anything close to what I do for you, it explains why they're still so crazy about each other."

"You can tell me anything, and I promise I'll always listen."

"Thank you, and I've always participated in all the temple ceremony that's been required, but I haven't spent a lot of time there." It was an awkward non sequitur, but she was following a train of thought.

"I wouldn't say that, stud. You got the priestess in charge to sleep with you." Vivien's pinch was more pronounced this time.

"I did, but I didn't go over there to pray, and that's a dead subject. I'm happily married and in love."

"Okay." Vivien smiled and kissed her anyway. "What is it you're trying to say badly?"

"I wasn't as interested in all the religious teachings as I should've been, and maybe I missed some important lessons. It might explain

why I don't have a clue as to why I have no clue to what's going on."
She rolled them over and put her thigh between Viv's legs. "Right now
I can promise there are no dark waves or dangers lurking nearby."

"Are you sure?" Viv held on to her and pressed closer.

"Yes. Let's make sure there are no more visions in our future."

What she'd seen of perhaps an unknown future had scared her.
Her mom had a philosophy about that as well. Letting fear rule your life
was tantamount to completely giving up. Facing the things that scared
you was never easy, but it was the only way to rid yourself of them. If
what they'd seen was a warning, she wasn't letting Viv out of her sight,
and neither would the guards she'd assign to her new consort.

Vivien was someone to pray for, but not even a personal appearance
from the goddess would make up for losing her. Before, all she had to
gamble with was herself, and she'd been at times cavalier about her
safety. With Vivien and the baby, though, she'd leave nothing to chance
even if she had to sacrifice herself. She tried to put all that out of her
head as she lost herself in the passion. The battles could wait.

CHAPTER TEN

The next morning, Vivien walked along the corridor looking at the paintings that lined the walls. The collection the Merlins owned was phenomenal, and any museum would freak seeing some of the works long thought destroyed. She wasn't an expert on art, but the selection of old masters made you want to linger.

"Highness," a young woman said before bowing. The landscape Vivien was staring at was beautiful, but she glanced around expecting Galen or Hadley. She knew Kai was making preparations for their departure to the queen's retreat and wouldn't be back for an hour.

"Who are you looking for, ma'am?" Viv asked her.

She smiled when the woman and the others with her tried not to appear amused. It was obvious she had a huge learning curve when it came to all this and wondered if there was some etiquette class she could take. She was more of a roughneck than royalty.

"Highness, we meant you." The young woman pointed at her and smiled.

The title made her want to laugh. "Trust me, I'm just Vivien."

All the women just stared at her with not-quite disbelief, or was it shock? It didn't matter, but they all appeared to be trying to figure out if she was kidding or crazy.

"No, ma'am. You'll never be just Vivien again, Your Highness." The women bowed again as if to drive the point home. "We're glad Princess Kai has found you, and we'll be happy to help you with whatever you need. This morning we wanted to walk you to breakfast. This place is large and hard to navigate at first, and your brother's waiting for you along with the queen and her consort."

"Thank you." She followed but kept her eyes on the walls.

"It's a beautiful place to live and work," one of the younger women said shyly. "You might not have time today, but Princess Kai's grandmother Yara is the best docent to take you through here. She studied art history, and her mother was on the squad that found some of these after the great war. The other items in the collection have been in the family for generations. Our museum has an extensive collection going back to what humans consider prehistoric times. I'd be happy to go with you if you're into that kind of thing."

"Thanks for the tip and the offer. I'd like to get to know everyone here better. These really are magnificent." The same dining room where they'd eaten with Kai's family was where they led her. "I also appreciate you all keeping me on track. Don't hesitate to speak up if I'm about to mess up."

"It's our pleasure, ma'am. You make Princess Kai happy, and everyone has loved her from the day she was born. It won't take long before everyone feels the same about you. If you don't mind me saying, we're enjoying serving you."

"That's sweet of you to say, and I promise I'll take good care of her." She nodded to everyone around the table as her new friend pulled out her chair. "Did you sleep okay?" she asked Frankie. He had a huge plate in front of him and looked thrilled.

"Mari was nice enough to give me a quick tour. That kept me out late, but it was totally worth it." Frankie was smiling like a man content with the world, and Kai's parents appeared happy to have him there.

"We'll have to have you come back, so we can show you the rest," Galen said. "Anna, would you fix Vivien a plate, please? There's plenty we need to talk about, but I'd like to wait for Kai. She's getting the security team set up and shouldn't be much longer."

"Did Kai happen to mention what happened to us? That's what we'd like to talk to you about because of its bizarreness. Is there something new I need to know about?" She smiled up at Anna and repeated her name a few times in her head to remember it. There were so many people in the palace, and it was going to take time to learn all their names.

"Nothing that can't wait. And she's good at *not* mentioning things, so you won't worry," Galen said, pointing at Hadley. "She learned that particular annoying trait from this one. You might want to remember that and hone your interrogation skills. Sometimes you have to torture it out of them."

"Hey, I'm not that bad," Hadley said as Kai walked in.

"What'd you do now?" Kai kissed both her mothers' cheeks before sitting next to Vivien and kissing her lips. "We're set," Kai said to her softly.

"You're being accused of being too much like me." Hadley pointed her fork at Kai. "So fess up now before your mother starts throwing eggs at you. It's too late to keep quiet. Vivien gave you up."

"Let's eat and then we'll head to your office." Kai took her hand and squeezed her fingers. They ate and enjoyed each other's company, trying to leave the business alone until they were done. All the weird things Kai couldn't work out from their vision would keep them from moving around too freely when they doubled security around them. It was going to be tough being married to a national treasure, but she'd cope.

Their meal was nice, unrushed, and she got to see a new wing of the palace when they headed to Galen's office. The security offices were amazing with monitor after monitor of radar, monitoring all of Earth's bodies of water, land masses, and airspace. From what she was seeing, the human race as a whole was way behind technologically and they were lucky Kai and her people weren't aggressive. There was nothing Galen and her people didn't see and know, which meant their weaponry was probably advanced beyond human imagination. That gave Vivien some peace of mind, but she wouldn't completely relax until she had answers.

"This is incredible." She stopped and looked around at the monitors.

"We can see everything from here," Kai said. "We'd never attack anyone unless they attacked first, but we do need to stay vigilant to keep our secrets. There are countermeasures we can deploy if anyone gets too close, but mankind seems more interested in space than in the depths. There's not a whole lot on Mars, not like before, and it's been entertaining to watch those rovers send back pictures and everyone trying to guess what they are. As long as everyone's heads are in the stars, we'll be okay."

"Has anyone ever come close?" She saw Frankie studying the layout with the wonder of a small child. It really was like something out of a movie. "Close to this place, I mean."

"Not really. Like I said, there are very few people who've figured out how to dive this deep." Kai held her hand and pointed out a few things. "And it'd take some considerable luck to pinpoint this and our other settlements, even the very large ones."

"We've tried our best to stay clear of human affairs, but we have intervened on occasion," Galen said as she got them walking again to the inner office. "We've only ever ordered something like that when it was for the greater good. All this technology protects us from the topsiders, but mostly it's to alert us about someone like Pontos. Even with all this, though, we haven't figured out how he landed without raising any alarms."

She waited until they were behind the door of the large office that had another great view of the city. In the light of day, the city was even more impressive, and Vivien always found something new when she stared down at it. The construction was well beyond imagination, and it seemed well-planned. The city's grid pattern reminded her of Washington, D.C.

"Your family's ruled since Queen Nessa's arrival?" Frankie asked. He stood next to her and had that same awe-struck expression she knew she did.

"There have been challenges to the throne throughout the years, but none lately. We are a free people even if I have a crown. My sisters want what most people want—they fall in love, marry, and have children. Some are happy never seeing the surface, and others, like your friend Etta at Tulane, go on to have careers that they enjoy." Hadley invited them all to sit as she walked behind the desk. "I'm not sure why someone would think to throw away all that defines our way of life for something that will not end well for anyone."

"Did you capture all of Pontos's people? Maybe they can tell you something if you have them in custody." Vivien had noticed the patrols previously, and how they seemed to pass on a regular schedule, but there seemed to be more of them today. Maybe she was imagining that, but she wasn't sure.

"Right after Kai returned from her time with you, Galen received a transmission from Atlantis. Sol Oberon, the current ruler, was asking about his son. He had no idea Pontos was dead." Hadley spoke freely. "That, combined with Edil's crew rounding up the survivors, made us believe that chapter was done. If anyone had escaped, they'd have sent word back."

"Made you believe? Did something change your mind?" Frankie asked.

"There's no way to know for sure," Galen said. "What we do know is that Pontos got here and existed in this world without detection, with help from some of our citizens. We haven't found or even identified all those who were involved, although we're working on it."

She stared at Galen and was having a hard time believing that even with all these advancements they were still no closer to definitive answers.

"It's hard to navigate when you're in the dark about something, even with all this," Galen said as if reading her mind. She probably had, Vivien realized.

"So we wait until they attack?" she asked.

"We prepare as if their attack is imminent. Sitting and worrying while we pace isn't in our nature," Hadley said.

"We had a vision last night," Kai said as if she couldn't hold it in any longer.

Vivien wanted to throw up. It had nothing to do with morning sickness and everything to do with dread when Kai told them what they saw. Everything Hadley and Galen had said, or more importantly hadn't said, made her believe the danger was still out there. That would make the threat in the vision real, and how cruel would life be, to find everything she wanted only to have it ripped away?

"Both of you had the same vision?" Galen asked, glancing between her and Kai.

"Yes—well, sort of. It was the same outcome, but we saw two different perspectives. Kai thought we should talk to Oba about it." She wanted answers, but she didn't think it was her place to rush anyone.

"I'm sure she can help, and she will," Galen said, smiling. "Oba's started her fasting meditation to try to find answers about you and Frankie. Plenty has happened that shouldn't have necessarily happened, and I'd like to know why. Some in the temple want to wrap it in a bow of mystic happenings, but there has to be an answer besides religious magic."

"Anything we should know?" She tried to gauge everyone's reaction but kept her focus mainly on Galen.

"Vivien, sweetheart," Galen said with compassion. "You love my child, and I'm happy about that. I'm not trying to find fault in you or why Kai picked you. I happen to love my mother-in-law, and I want the two of us to get along in that same way. All I'm saying is you were with Kai in front of that orb when it changed you, and that sort of made sense. You seem to be the exception to our rules when it comes to our interactions with humans. But, Frankie, you do not make sense. Do you mind me calling you that?"

"No, Your Majesty, and for the record, I'm not upset with the changes." Frankie's smile was contagious.

"What's this record you speak of?" Hadley asked.

"It's a saying. He doesn't mean a real record, Mom," Kai said, smiling.

The joke finally loosened the grip of fear strangling her heart. "When will Oba be ready?" It was hard not to freak over the half answers they seemed to be getting, but Kai's parents didn't appear worried.

"In two days, maybe sooner," Galen said. "If I had answers, I'd give them to you. Our plan should be to wait until you and Kai get back, or we can come to you. That might be the better choice. The retreat will have fewer people around to overhear our conversations, and we can relax. All I need to know is if you can stay, Frankie."

"I'd like to stay, and you guys need to start your honeymoon. If we figure all this out, you can have a longer one after your next wedding." Frankie winked at her, and it made her happy that he was there. They'd been through so much together, and she didn't want him to think that would come to an end now that she was married.

"Good," Kai said. "We'll see all of you tomorrow afternoon. Make sure you call ahead to make sure I have pants on."

"Kai," Vivien said, closing her eyes. Her blush must've been spectacular by the way Kai chuckled.

"What? It's our honeymoon, sweetheart. Frankie said so." It was the first time Kai had used his nickname. "Call if anything comes up."

They moved to the spot where the *Salacia* had been docked, but this time it held a smaller vessel that only had room for two. She was going to enjoy having Kai all to herself even if it was only for the night. Kai brought her fist to her chest and saluted as one of the soldiers closed the hatch for them.

"Edil and the others have our bags, so we're ready to go." Kai kissed her before turning her attention to the control panel.

"Where exactly are we going?" The view out the large window gave her a closer view of the city as Kai took them over it. She noticed all the areas outside the city grid were a dull gray, devoid of plant life. After diving all over the world, it was strange to see such a barren landscape. Within the city, even outside the domes, there was plant and fish life that shouldn't really be able to survive here. "And how did you get parrotfish to survive at this depth?"

"There's a kind of invisible dome over the area, like a force field. That protection regulates not only the pressure but the sunlight as well, so we can grow plants as well as stock the area with fish that are both edible and decorative. It's how Ivan and Ram along with some of their friends are able to swim here. I've also trained them not to attack the guards and to stick to the fish in the area."

"And they know to stay in that perimeter?"

"Think of an electric fence for a dog. Everything swimming back there gets a friendly reminder when they're about to leave the safe zone. We'd have made it bigger, but it'd be hard to explain why a large part of the ocean is as bright as the sun."

"All this is going to take a while to understand fully."

"Not really. All you need is a little history. The original city we built in the water was closer to the Greek Isles, but long before mankind could develop the technology to find us, it was moved here." Kai picked up speed, but their escort kept pace. The region they were entering was much darker, but the floodlight from their vessel illuminated enough for her to see the canyon walls at either side. The ravine they were in was massive.

"Your ancestors were smart."

"I find it strange that humans aren't more curious about their own planet. Only five percent of the oceans have been explored, but on the flipside, that's lucky for us." Kai pointed to the canyon walls. "These trenches are rich in minerals and gems but deep enough to keep us safe. The gold and diamonds we've mined are how we've purchased large shares of companies on land we thought important."

"Lucky for us you did." It'd been Kai's family's vote that had reverted the controlling interest of their company to her father.

"Pontos wasn't wrong when he picked oil as the easiest way to bring mankind to its knees. Control the main fuel humans are dependent on, then add the takeover of communications systems, and it wouldn't take long."

"Let's not waste time talking about him. Tell me more about this place."

"When the original settlers picked this area, they scoped out the best places for the city, the palace, and for further expansion. In those searches they also found the series of caves we're headed to. Surprisingly even at this depth there were air pockets."

"The depths are beyond human capability to explore, and I'm glad no one has found this place. People have a tendency to destroy what they don't understand." She put her head on Kai's shoulder but didn't shift her attention from outside. "I've been thinking about our future. Our baby will one day take over for you, and it's important to always keep this safe. I want her to enjoy her childhood like you did, without having to worry that someone is after her."

"There's a nation willing to fight to the death to keep you, her, and their sisters safe. The vision we had is something we'll figure out, but I don't want you to worry too much. Oba will come through for us." Kai turned left, and they seemed to be diving deeper. It was amazing that they weren't being crushed like a beer can from the pressure. "She's not talkative sometimes, but after my mother gets through with her, she'll cooperate."

"Why wouldn't she be talkative?" Great, now she had to worry about a jealous old girlfriend on top of everything else.

"The most important part of that thought is *old* girlfriend," Kai said, leaning over to kiss her. "You're going to have to accept that I'm madly in love with you, and I'm planning to be sappy about it until we're old and I'm too feeble to chase you."

"I promise not to move too fast." She had to laugh at her inexperience with someone plucking all her thoughts from her head.

Frankie had been able to do it at times, but not with the accuracy Kai had.

They slowed as the area around them seemed to brighten as if Kai was sailing to an oasis of light. The cave entrance wasn't huge but big enough to see what was inside when Kai surfaced for a moment. Palm trees under the rock dome were swaying, as if a tropical breeze was moving through the space. It was beautiful, and she was on sensory overload.

"This is unbelievable." She glanced at Kai before turning her attention to their destination again. They'd bled off speed, and unlike at the palace, where they'd docked at the domed structure, here the docking station appeared freestanding.

"We could go all the way in with the shuttle, but I like swimming in. Would you mind getting wet?" Kai's question made her laugh.

"Oh, honey, I'm planning on being wet until it's time to go, then way beyond that." She loved being able to laugh with Kai like this. It was freeing after a life of no romance because she'd never found anyone to let go with. Being in love was so far the greatest adventure of all, and Kai was the reason.

"Cheeky," Kai said, waving to the two women who were anchoring their vessel. "I like it. Are you ready, my love?"

"Definitely." The rush of cold water when she dove scared her at first. She held her breath, but the gill system she now had took over. Her throat seemed to close to keep her lungs clear, and her vision seemed better as well. The wet suit Kai had given her immediately regulated her body temperature even in the areas not covered by the thin blue material.

She took Kai's hand and relaxed as Kai pulled them along with powerful strokes. They were heading away from the entrance toward the canyon wall. The carvings were well lit, and she stared at the two women forever captured in the stone.

Queen Nessa and her consort, Jyri. Kai's voice was clear in her head. Next to the women were strange writings, but their meaning was as clear as the day Oba had spoken to her in the temple. *Their reign will last for an eternity.*

In so many ways it had. These brave pioneers had only tried to make a home when they could've done so much more. Those who'd come after had gone on to expand what they started and were still happy with the parts of the planet they'd claimed as their own. It was the definition of nobility.

"Let's go," Kai said, pointing to the entrance below the carvings, and guided them through the maze of tunnels. There were more carvings of women as they went. "It's a hall of modern queens."

Vivien smiled when she saw the ones of Kai's grandmothers and mothers. "It's amazing," she said as Kai headed up. It didn't take long for them to break through the surface to a gorgeous beach with aquamarine water. "I have no idea how all this is possible, but it's the most beautiful beach I've ever been on."

Kai held her hand as they walked onto the shore, and the soft white sand was warm under her feet. There weren't many buildings here, making the beach house surrounded by vegetation stand out. Vivien watched as the seagulls and other birds flew above them and through the trees, and if she wasn't hallucinating, there were also monkeys and other wildlife.

"Your Highnesses," an old woman said, bowing. "Welcome. We prepared everything you asked for, so if there's nothing else, I'll leave you in peace."

"Vivien, I'd like to introduce you to Nicole Shep. She's in charge of this place, and she and her crew live about a mile down the beach. Nicole took over this post a year before I was born." Kai let her go to kiss Nicole's cheek and the woman appeared thrilled with the affection.

"Welcome, Princess," Nicole said, taking her hand, "and congratulations. You're free to relax here. There's only one way in and out, and Edil's team will be on guard. The others are far enough away that your privacy is assured. I hope you enjoy your night and will visit again for longer next time."

"I think our wise friend is trying to tell you how much I enjoy skinny-dipping," Kai said, making her shake her head.

"You have your hands full with this one, Highness." Nicole laughed and waved as she started walking down the beach with the two women who'd exited the house.

"Want a tour?" Kai asked.

"I'd love one."

The house wasn't overly large and, like the temple, had an open feel to it. There was food on the kitchen counter with a note that dinner would be served on the beach that night whenever they were ready. The bedroom had thin curtains hanging from the ceiling that didn't obscure the view of the water, and there wasn't much else in the room aside from the large bed.

Kai stepped behind her and kissed her neck. "How about a bath?"

When she turned around Kai was naked. Vivien had always been athletic, keeping up with her water activities as well as working out with Frankie in the gym to keep his upper body strong enough to maneuver his wheelchair, but she didn't resemble Kai at all. Kai was muscular without being bulky, and she was perfect.

"Do you have one clue how sexy you are?" She stood still as Kai peeled her suit off for her. Her nipples hardened, and she groaned when Kai knelt and sucked one in.

"I'm glad you think so," Kai said, gently nipping the other nipple with her teeth. "Come with me."

She stood in the large tub and waited for Kai to join her after helping her in. The water had flowers floating in it and it smelled like lavender. It was all very decadent, but she wanted to rush through it so they could move to the bed. Need ratcheted to a painful level when Kai moved behind her again and cupped her breasts. Never in her life had she begged someone to fuck her, but that might change today if Kai didn't move faster.

"You're so perfect," Kai said. Her hands moved down her body to the top of her sex, then back up where she pinched her nipples to the brink of pain.

"Jesus Christ." Her knees were weak, so she turned around and wrapped a leg around Kai. "Don't tease me." She tried to find someplace on Kai she could rub against, to quench her need.

"I'm going to keep touching you until you're completely mine."

Kai sat and had her straddle her lap. She held on as Kai touched her everywhere except where she needed her. The frustration made her want to demand release, and then she saw the expression on Kai's face. She was looking at her as if this was their first time and she didn't want to rush through it.

"Baby," she said, and Kai smiled. "What are you thinking about, aside from making me crazy?"

"I remember that fire in your eyes the first day you saw me standing in your parents' yard, and you found out I was taking your job." Kai's hands went down past her hips to her thighs. "I couldn't take my eyes off you."

"I saw you earlier in the coffee shop and couldn't figure out what was wrong with me. It was so out of character for me to openly stare, and I couldn't stop myself. After I saw you at Etta's, I ended up following you to the aquarium. I did get mad when I found that you were taking my job, but what you made me feel didn't change." The talk brought her pulse down, and she slowly started touching Kai. "That'd never happened to me before. When you finally touched me, I was lost."

"Never again, my love. We've both found our place with each other. Now, feel me, listen to my heart, and let me love you."

It took a second to climb the peak again, and this time Kai was relentless in how she touched, caressed, and kissed her. Vivien was so wet and turned-on she thought she'd pull a muscle if she didn't come soon. Kai stroked her, and she couldn't form words as her hips jerked. She was about to complain when Kai reversed their positions and pressed Vivien's back to the side of the tub.

"Oh God, yes...fuck," she said when Kai's head went under the water, and she put her mouth on her. Kai flattened her tongue on her clit, then sucked as her fingers slid in. "Baby, please don't stop. Oh, oh...ah." She was yelling, and she grabbed Kai's hair and pressed her closer. This was like being connected to a live wire that you didn't want to let go of.

"I'm coming, like that...I'm coming." Her orgasm was so intense it came close to knocking her out, and Kai didn't give her a chance to recover when she surfaced and moved her to the side of the tub.

"I can't wait," Kai said, water droplets sliding over her bronzed skin. Vivien spread her sex when Kai came down on her. It was hard to explain, but they seemed to click together, and Kai's need reignited her own. It was as if she hadn't just come with an intensity that should've sated her when Kai started thrusting. "Fuck," Kai said, and all she could do was nod.

"Yes, holy fuck, yes." She wrapped her legs around Kai and raked her nails down Kai's back. If this got any better, she was going to have an out of body experience.

"Come with me," Kai managed to grind out before she stiffened in her arms.

She swore she saw stars as she squeezed Kai's ass and let go.

It didn't seem possible, but making love to Kai seemed to get better. "That was unbelievable."

"Yes, it was." Kai sounded exhausted, and she rolled off her with the grace of a drunkard. "And you're incredible. It's never been like this."

Vivien hadn't had that many lovers, but none of them made her want to chew through their clothes and demand they touch her. "You've woken me up to what making love is supposed to be. The fact that you can breathe underwater is an added bonus."

Kai laughed before helping her back in the bath. "I have all kinds of hidden talents. I'll need them to keep you happy."

"All you need to do is wake up every morning to do that, honey. Thanks for bringing me here." She sat between Kai's legs with her back against her.

"I don't want you to think I'm not doing my best, and I did promise your parents I'd do everything in my power to make you happy." Kai rested her hands on her abdomen, and it felt right. They hadn't been together that long, but they were a family.

"You may not know it, but you're my father's idea of the perfect in-law. You're successful, you love me, and you saved his ass." She laughed, remembering all the times her dad had told her the same thing about Steve. Except for the saving his ass part. "That last part really made him love you."

"When I came home hurt and broken, I didn't care about the shot Pontos had taken. What made me hurt more than anything was having to leave you behind. I couldn't let you lose your company as well. It was a poor substitute, but it belonged to you and the family." Kai's hands started to move, and Vivien sighed when her nipples got rock hard again. "I think his company is important to him, but I read his mind. You and Frankie are at the center of his thoughts."

"Was it as hard for you when you left as it was for me?" It was the one thing they hadn't talked about yet.

"My life isn't exactly all my own. Leaving made me face some hard truths, and I couldn't reconcile the things I had to do with the things I wanted. With time I don't think I could've left you completely."

"That's what scared everyone, wasn't it? That you'd choose me over your duty?" She'd heard about this prophecy, but her logical mind couldn't accept something so ludicrous. The words that had been written made sense, but that someone had foreseen their relationship thousands of years ago sounded like a children's story.

"It was, but they got that wrong. You're part of me, Vivien Palmer Merlin, and the only way anyone can get me to deny it is to kill me."

"Not while I'm around. With my luck I'm going to have a kid who's going to act just like you, and I have a feeling you were hyperactive. That means I'm not going to chase this guppy all by myself, sexy." She turned to face Kai and pinched her cheeks. "You're the love of my life, and you put a ring on my finger. No leaving me early."

"Don't get me wrong, I'm thrilled about the baby, but that's not the main reason I love you." Kai moved her hand in a small circle on her abdomen and it made Vivien warm. "You did that, and I'd fallen in love before I knew about this little girl."

"The prophecy was real, though, and it makes me worry about our vision. I found the impossible, and I refuse to let it go. Whatever that was in our vision, it was powerful, and it hated us." That was the emotion she hadn't been able to pin down before. It was hatred, personal and deep.

"I pray that those with Bella Riverstone and her mother don't know about the baby. You have to promise me you'll do everything you can to survive if something goes wrong. Even if that means going back to your life and forgetting all this until it's safe to return."

She turned around completely and pulled away from Kai. That Kai could even say that made her angry. The heat of her fury rose from her chest to her head, and she had to take a breath to keep from screaming. Their vows had been different than what she'd imagined saying, but devotion and honor were part of the deal. Running at the first sign of danger had nothing to do with that.

"Let's clear up a few things right now. I am your wife." She poked Kai in the chest and took another deep breath after saying the last four words slowly and with plenty of force. "That means I'm not going anywhere. Don't make me say that again. If I'm going back to land, you're coming with me." She put her hand up when Kai opened her mouth to speak. "Maybe you're used to all the bowing and scraping everyone does around you, but you picked wrong if that's what you were expecting from me."

"Bowing and scraping?" Kai asked, clearly trying not to smile.

"You know what I mean, and don't try to charm me. I'm mad at you."

"I'm sorry—I was only trying to take precautions to make sure you'll be okay. Let me make it up to you."

Kai carried her out of the tub and laid her on the bed. She was still a bit angry, but seeing Kai in the light streaming in from outside was starting to soften her. "I know you love me, and you're a slow learner, so repeat after me. We're a team." Kai dutifully did as she asked. "Good, now get over here."

In her previous life, she'd only had responsibility for Frankie, her job, and in a way her parents. All that wasn't perfect, but it was simple. The weight of what she'd taken on with Kai could be heavy, but she hadn't gone in blind. Their first night together, when Kai had come back to her strong and whole, Kai'd told her the truth of who she was and what it meant to stay with her. The lessons she'd begun would help her to be a good consort—the good wife part, she and Kai would figure out together.

She was sure Kai would've sacrificed both their happiness for her commitment to her mother's throne. That would've killed something vital in both of them, and she ached at the truth of it. It was also what attracted her to Kai to begin with. Knowing someone was willing to put the welfare of all her people ahead of her own happiness spoke of her noble heart, and Vivien was blessed that it hadn't come to that.

"This life of ours will be built on how much we love each other, and there's room enough for all of it. You'll be queen one day, and I'll pledge myself to you then like I have now." She spread her legs for Kai and saw the same gold thread between their shells as before. It appeared fragile, but it would take death to sever it. Of that she was sure. "You're mine."

"Totally," Kai said, coming down on her again.

She kept her eyes open as Kai made love to her, and she felt nothing but relief. It wasn't from the act but from the sense of coming home. Whatever was threatening their future scared the hell out of her, but she wouldn't back down. Kai's fight belonged equally to her, and she'd face it with the same intensity with which she loved her mate.

The goddess might've foretold their bond and produced the visual proof of it, but she and Kai had the free will to accept that future or turn their backs on it. There was no question they'd both simply accepted it and would do what was necessary to save Atlantis. It was also a fact that the love they shared was theirs, no one else's.

Her die was cast, and she found strength in the truth of who she was in Kai's life.

CHAPTER ELEVEN

Daria stood on the bridge with Frem and stared at the terrifying hole that seemed to be alive and hungry. On their approach she'd watched as everything from meteors to stars went in, but nothing satisfied the monster's appetite. They were now caught in its gravitational pull, so there was no turning back even if she wanted to, and she'd vacillated between wanting to turn back to speeding them up. If they'd miscalculated, the end would come quickly.

"What are you thinking?" Frem asked.

"I have the great Queen Nessa on my mind. All my life I've been taught what a weakling she was, but fuck..." She spoke softly, not wanting to be overheard by the hypervigilant crew. Every one of them appeared scared and nervous, and it proved they weren't stupid. "She sought this out and went into that willingly. I can see now why it took so long for anyone to follow her. This might be suicide."

"What choice do we have? There's nothing to go back to, and we both know it. If we die, the poets will sing about it for the little time we have left."

"Recheck our course before it's too late." She gave the order and tried to keep her voice steady.

The ship started to rattle, making her wonder how Pontos the coward had really handled this. Her brother had needed propping up all his pampered life, which was something she believed he'd inherited from their father. When Pontos insisted on going instead of her as had been planned, she'd prayed for his failure. Like all prayers and sacrifices to the goddess, it was in vain. If the bitch had ever existed, she was long dead along with her water orb. Pontos *had* failed, but in her father's eyes, his downfall had been because of her, not his own stupidity. She hadn't prepared Pontos enough to win the war he'd been supposed to wage.

They went in at an alarming speed, and the lights flickered and then died along with their engines. She cursed and screamed for someone to reset everything. There was no way of knowing how long they'd been in this deathtrap, but just as her panic was about to choke her, she was blinking into the sun's brightness through the deck's observation window. The planet in the distance was like a bright blue jewel waiting to be taken.

She laughed when the crew cheered, and she let them have their moment. "Set the course to land," she said to Frem. "Once we review our plan, we'll make plans to move forward."

Earth disappeared from view when they landed close to Pontos's three ships on the dark side of the moon. She opened the communications line to see if Pontos had left anyone on board. The silence meant they were the only true Atlanteans left. Her brother had left no one behind. She wanted to feel grief, considering he was probably dead, but all she could dredge up for him was disgust. Pontos had been all about himself and what power he could grab no matter the planet, and his greed had gotten him killed.

"Send a group to see if there are any other shuttles left aboard any of those cruisers," she said to Frem. "We might need them to add to our numbers."

"Do you want to send word home? We have the frequency Pontos used open and ready." Frem bowed as she spoke, as if setting an example for the others.

Their trip had been long enough for her to know some of her troops had residual resentment over what had happened to their dead commander. They knew she'd killed him without a trial, and some were having a hard time hiding their contempt. She was trying her best not to have to repeat that action, because of the small number of crew, but it was possible she'd have to rip out a few more eyes to assert her power. The idiots who were openly hostile didn't know who they were dealing with.

"Send a short message to Bronti and tell her to share our first triumph publicly. Report that we've arrived and that we're planning for an attack. Maybe the crew won't be so irksome if their families know they're safe." She stopped talking when one of her men handed her a comm unit. "What?"

"One of the men ran a sweep of Prince Pontos's ships and found this."

She pressed the play button. "This is Bella Riverstone. My mother and I are part of the resistance and we need help. We've had to run and have no contact with our people."

The message was repeated on a loop, but Bella sounded more desperate in each new transmission. "When was the last one sent?" She handed the unit back and sat.

"Three days ago, Majesty."

"Can you answer it, or did she send it on a closed circuit?" Bella had discovered she was distantly related to the Oberon family and had used her position with Galen to contact Daria. Daria had leveraged that contact to start what Pontos had tried to finish. Bella had been promised a joining with Daria, so she could ascend to Nessa's throne as her consort.

Bella Riverstone would have the answers Daria needed about what had happened here.

"She used the prince's private channel. You can contact her if you like."

"Good," she said, nodding. "Lead one of the teams and personally search my brother's quarters to see if you find anything that'll lead us to him." She waved the man away and retired to the commander's office. The security code to the channel Bella had used was the same for the whole royal family. She listened to the message again and replied in a coded text.

Her contact with Earth had started with Bella, but she got what she wanted from Francesca Yelter. Not everyone in Galen's little paradise was happy with the little they'd claimed of this planet, and it'd been her luck to have found someone who wanted to crush Galen and rebuild. That kind of ambition she understood and could exploit. That Yelter was familiar with Galen's military force and defenses had been a gift from the goddess.

"Do you think any of them are still alive?" Frem asked when she joined her. They were both staring at Pontos's ships.

"I doubt Galen's forces could've defeated all our people. But Pontos is most certainly dead. He wasn't much of a warrior except when it came to bragging about being one, but the trainers always had to hold back so as not to bruise his ego along with his body. Right now, all I care about is finding Yelter and her family, as well as Tanice." She laughed at how easily Tanice had manipulated her brother into commitment, making him think it was his idea. "If anyone was smart enough to survive, it was that bitch."

"When do you want to head down?"

"When I'm ready. Galen will outnumber us head-to-head, so we have to be smart about how we do this. I want our first blow to send them scattering and not give them a chance to regroup." She tightened her fists and laughed. "The new Atlantis will be built on the ashes of Nessa's throne, and her ideas will end with her people because they'll either surrender or die. You'll be at my side ruling with me."

"What about your promise to Bella?" Frem sounded jealous, and it was humorous.

"She'll do as a number two wife, but you have my heart." As much of her heart as she knew how to give. "Let's get ready. I'm anxious to begin."

Chapter Twelve

K ai opened her eyes to the cloudy day and could smell the rain in the air. It was a perfect day to stay in bed and enjoy the peace that would inevitably end. She'd only been married a day, and she'd already learned plenty about partnerships in that short span. It'd been interesting. Before now, nothing she did for the realm and herself called for a lot of advance consultation with anyone else. Having a wife would change that dynamic.

She smiled and closed her eyes when Vivien hummed in her sleep. They had until that afternoon, and she wasn't wasting a minute. The rain started coming down in sheets, and she heard the thunder in the distance. She'd always loved playing in the rain as a kid, but now it made it easy to drift back to sleep.

"Hey," she said a few hours later. Vivien was facing her, tracing her eyebrows with her index finger. "Have you been up long?"

"Just enjoying watching you sleep." Vivien leaned in and kissed her. "It's hard to believe it's raining outside. How is that possible?"

"The atmospheric technology is amazing. It uses ocean water, obviously, but it filters and desalinates it so it won't kill the plants. The thunder is created using the cave's natural echo system. But we're not in control of it, as such. It self-regulates, just like the weather topside." She moved to reach Vivien's lips again. "As much as I'd love to explain all that to you, it's raining, we're in bed, and we're naked."

Vivien had the best laugh, and she blushed beautifully. "That's all true, and you can add that I'm deliriously happy. Sometimes I can't believe this is my life now."

"I feel the same way. You're so perfect for me, and I can't help but fall in love with you over and over. And I'm glad you agreed to come here with me. This place is special." She held Vivien closer when the wind picked up. It was blowing through the thin curtains, dropping the temperature of the room. "You have to ask my mother about it. It's special to her for more than the obvious."

"Excuse the intrusion, Highnesses." Nicole kept her eyes down as she entered with a tray. "The queen ordered breakfast."

"Of course she did." She smiled at her mom's hint to take care of Vivien.

"Thank you, Nicole. You can leave it if you like," Vivien said. She pulled the sheet up and smiled at Nicole. "Please thank everyone for dinner last night. It was lovely."

"My staff will love hearing that, Highness. This is one of the most sought after jobs in the realm, so they try their best." Nicole appeared as taken with Vivien as everyone else who met her. "Please let us know if you require something else."

"Perhaps move lunch to the dining room," Kai said. "I doubt we'll be able to use the space outside today." She felt Vivien's hand on her stomach, and it reminded her of the clock. Their time alone was running out.

"Her Majesty the Queen called this morning. She wanted me to tell you they'll be arriving earlier than she mentioned. There have been new developments."

"When?" she asked, not believing the timing of all this crap.

"In an hour. I hated to bother you, but duty calls." Nicole smiled, bowed, and left.

"Don't be mad. We have a lifetime of mornings and it sounds important." Vivien rolled away from her and poured them some coffee. She looked beautiful in the morning light, and Kai wanted nothing more than to touch her. "Stop, we don't have time," Vivien said, winking at her. "I'm not greeting your parents reeking of sex."

"Then put some clothes on, or get over here."

"We can come back, right?" Vivien stacked the pillows behind Kai's back, so she could straddle her lap and share the cup. "I know Nicole and the others are here, but it seems so private."

"Anytime you want. Being related to my mother has some pretty good perks. Now eat something before my mother gets mad at me for not taking good care of you." They shared breakfast and then a shower, so they could sit on the covered veranda and wait. "Here they come."

It was still raining when the small shuttle broke to the surface. "They don't like swimming?" Vivien asked.

"I'm sure this is Mom's way of easing Frankie into the world under the surface. Eventually he'll fall in love with it like you did, if he hasn't already." Kai walked out and greeted the party leading them inside.

"Highnesses," Vivien said, bowing.

"Please, Vivien, no need for formality when it's just family," Galen said, hugging her.

"What a beautiful spot," Frankie said. "How far down are we?"

"Speaking in miles, about fourteen," Kai said smiling. "Don't let it freak you out."

Nicole greeted Kai's moms with hugs before inviting them to lunch. "Whenever you're ready, Highnesses."

"Thank you, my friend," her mom Galen said. "We'll catch up once we're done. It's been too long since our last visit." They followed Nicole to the hall, where lunch was already laid out and ready. There was little formality about the seating, which Kai was grateful for. It was enough to have that in the city—she didn't want it in a place they were meant to relax.

Kai shook Laud's hand and knew her being here had to do with more than protecting her mom. Laud was one of the most loyal people she knew, and it comforted her that she was at her mom's side when she and her mom Hadley weren't. The head of her mother's guard had been one of her trainers from the time she was old enough to hold a trident and had taught her to stay calm in every situation. Those lessons were the only thing that had kept her alive when she'd faced Pontos.

"Did you have a good day, Vivien?" her mom Hadley asked.

"We did. Kai treated me to dinner on the beach with Nicole's help. The weather was beautiful until early this morning, but despite that, this really is paradise."

Her mother Galen smiled and nodded. "It is, and I promise I'll order a long vacation for you and Kai in the future. It's not really fair that this is happening during a time that should be all about happiness and celebrating the future."

"We'll have time for that, but not until we know everyone is safe," Vivien said, making both Kai's mothers smile. It was clear Vivien might not know all their ways, but she understood the importance of service.

"What did you find out?" Kai asked, not caring who answered.

"Laud has Tanice Themis talking, so we know how they got here," her mom Hadley said. "It took the scientists on planet Atlantis time to figure out Nessa's route. They'd believed for centuries that they'd taken a more conventional path. I can't believe Sol would've gambled with Pontos's life by sending him into what's basically a time warp."

"From what Tanice said, their world is in bad shape, and Sol's reign has sped up their decline. They had no choice but to try what Nessa had," Laud said. "From their calculations, it's not a total planetary collapse, but their current situation will kill approximately ninety percent of their population, if not more."

"They've been in that situation for eons," Kai said. "They waited until now because the catastrophe is imminent?"

"Everyone always thinks they have time, but the people left on Atlantis are starving and sick from their contaminated waters," her mother Galen said. "Our genetic makeup and preferences from a home we only know through history books hasn't changed. Water makes us strong, and it's in our blood. Nessa and Jyri started on land here, but they always stayed close to the water because they understood that fundamental truth. What's happened on planet Atlantis is tragic, but they can't be allowed to repeat their mistakes here. This is our home, and we'll protect it until death."

"This is our home, but it's different, isn't it?" Kai said.

"What do you mean?" Vivien asked.

"Earth is larger in size, has more species of land mammals and fish, and there are humans. Even though our Atlantis here is more advanced than the planet of our ancestors, Atlantis and Pontos's people are more advanced than the human race." Laud said it so calmly that Vivien simply blinked. "From what Tanice admitted, Pontos's plan was to enslave everyone on Earth once he'd destroyed Queen Galen and the rest of us. After he'd taken the throne, his plan was to bring their entire population here. The cycle of abuse would've started all over again."

"Is that why he tried to kill you?" Vivien asked.

"We're what stood in the way of what he wanted, but he's dead." She tried to sound reassuring for Vivien and Frankie, but there had to be more to this. Pontos was dead, and the survivors of the people he'd brought with him would never be free. But the tension in everyone's eyes was clear. "Did some of his people escape?"

"No, our conversations with Tanice have been productive toward figuring out who was involved from our end. Bella Riverstone played a much larger role than we thought. It seems she's convinced she's related to the Oberons, albeit distantly," her mother Galen said. It wasn't often her mom sounded disgusted, but the betrayal of her trust was evident in her tone. "That's not a heritage I'd think anyone would be proud of, but she used her clearance through my office to start communication with planet Atlantis. She covered her tracks well enough that no one here figured it out. Not until it was too late."

"Does Themis know where Riverstone is?" Kai asked. She'd been trying to remember if she'd had any contact with Riverstone aside from a short greeting when she went to visit her mother. The woman hadn't been very memorable, but she definitely had some grandiose plans.

"Neither Pontos nor Tanice ever met with Bella or her stepmother, Yelter, while they were here. They did communicate from the time he arrived through the comm boxes you found throughout the Gulf, but it was more important for Bella to keep her place with the queen. Leaving the city to meet with him would've possibly been detected." Laud handed over a full report. "Bella was to blame for leaking the queen's schedule."

"Our objective is to find Riverstone and her traitorous mother. Yelter got off easy." She smiled at Vivien and sent her a mental message. They were sitting across from each other, but Vivien gazed at her and smiled so she'd heard her. *From the sound of it, Riverstone is the head of the snake. Find her and we find the body.*

"That *is* a priority, but not our only one," her mom Hadley said. The way she exhaled made Kai's heart speed up, and she wanted to run. Not from fear exactly but from a need to keep Vivien and her family safe. "Pontos's plan failed, and his ships are still sitting on the dark side of the moon. He brought three."

"Three cruisers?" she asked in shock. "There's no way we eliminated or captured all his men if that's true. Three ships means thousands of people. We need to find that bitch Riverstone and apply whatever pain it takes to make her want to tell us everything."

"Kai," her mother Galen said, her tone sharp. "You know better than to think any situation, no matter how dire, will make us resort to torture. That is not who we are." Her mom's admonishment was clear. "Pontos was more of a worrier and an egomaniac than he was a tactical genius. His force was small, and the three cruisers were more for backup than a massive invading force. His girlfriend had the information to back that up."

"So he was a chickenshit on top of being an annoying son of a bitch." She was still angry at herself for not figuring out what the asshole's agenda was.

"Honey, how in the world would you have figured that out?" Vivien pushed her plate away and rose to stand behind her. "Everyone in the world simply thought he was an asshole, including me."

"Is the new development the knowledge of his ships?" She threaded her fingers with Vivien's when Frankie traded seats with her.

"We're not so much interested in the ships here, but the ones still available on Atlantis. Pontos found the route, which means others can follow," Laud said. "When he arrived in our solar system, he took small shuttles to the surface. Those had enough cloaking to fly under our radar."

"Even if we'd noticed them, our technicians would've reported it as meteor activity," her mother Hadley said. "That was the one smart move he made."

"If Tanice is telling the truth, there's only one ship left on their planet. When Pontos didn't report in, he'd been classified as missing. Finding him might be enough of an incentive for his father to send that ship out. If they're better prepared and don't come alone, we could potentially be facing a force of seventy thousand." Laud not only always sounded calm, but she also never sugarcoated anything.

"That's not what worries me," her mother Galen said, her eyes on Vivien. "Bella knew enough about you, Vivien, to report to Pontos. That worries me on two fronts."

"Two?" Vivien asked. Kai tried to be comforting without trying to shield Vivien from what she needed to know. "What does she know about me that would be damaging?"

"She understood your growing relationship with Princess Kai. Bella was careful about how often and what she passed on, and didn't contact Pontos with that development, at least not at first." For once

Laud sounded almost as disgusted as her mother did. "That's the only reason he didn't attack you sooner."

"If her goal was to take over or at least be elevated in status under Pontos's rule, not saying anything doesn't make sense," she said.

"Once she knew your relationship with Princess Kai was serious and understood how it could be leveraged, she passed word of it on. Which is why Francesca Yelter, Bella's stepmother and one of Queen Galen's biggest critics, was killed trying to assassinate Princess Kai. According to Tanice, a message was sent to Pontos, identifying you, but it came from Yelter and not Bella." Laud was as compassionate as Kai had ever heard her, and she was angry at herself that she hadn't prepared Viv better for all this.

"That doesn't make sense, if Bella was their contact within the realm." Kai had to smile despite the situation when Vivien moved closer to her.

"That's what Tanice thought as well. Her theory was that Bella was in contact with them through the comm boxes, but her real master wasn't Pontos. It was someone still on planet Atlantis." Her mother Hadley stood and poured two cups of coffee, handing her mother Galen one.

"Bella was taking orders from Sol?" she asked.

"I doubt it. If Sol was her true master, there's no way he wouldn't have told Tanice and Pontos who you were. You remember how concerned Sol was after it was all over," her mother Galen said. "Asking about Pontos was tantamount to admitting he has a small, useless penis. I'm sure that's true, but no man will ever admit it."

"What are you worried about?" Vivien laughed at the description but still appeared worried herself.

"What Laud and the rest of us are worried about," her mother Galen said, taking Vivien's free hand, "is simple. There were very few people who knew about you and Kai aside from Hadley and me. There was Oba, Laud, and Kai's detail. The news of your pregnancy is only known by Laud and Oba."

"You think someone close to you betrayed you?" Vivien seemed horrified. "Besides this Bella woman?"

"There's no way it was Laud or any of my people," Hadley said. "It can't be Oba either, so where does that leave us? It's not so much a betrayal to pass on the information that you're pregnant, but that they passed along *any* information about you. To know such intimate details of your life as well as ours means someone close to us is working against us."

"Oba will be here when she's done with her duties." Her mom Galen stood and headed for the covered veranda. "And before your thoughts run away from you, Oba would lay down her life before she betrayed us. Any of us."

"It has to be someone close to her then," she said. One glance at Vivien proved her wife might not agree with that assessment.

"Let's wait for her, and she'll answer your questions." Her mother Hadley's statement closed discussion for now. "Let's enjoy the quiet until that happens. Right now, that's all we know, and there's no sense in driving ourselves to distraction while we wait."

Vivien and Frankie stayed with Kai as the others left. The retreat was meant for relaxation, but the offices on the other side of the house close to her moms' bedroom were fully equipped to run the realm no matter how long they stayed. She pointed Frankie in the direction of the restroom when he asked before she faced Vivien.

Before she had a chance to speak, Vivien said, "I know what you're going to say, but it's going to take time for me to trust her. I know what it is to love you. There's no telling how I'd handle losing you." Vivien rested her head on her shoulder and sighed. "She had you when you left, and she lost you to me. That couldn't have been a cakewalk, no matter what she says."

"Oba's one of our youngest head priestesses, but my mother has complete faith in her. What I shared with her wasn't something she wanted long-term, and I didn't know any better. My fate was to marry and have children, but I never thought I'd find what my mothers share. Their relationship is special, so being with Oba was easy and convenient." She spoke as Vivien pressed the side of her face to her chest.

"Still, honey, a woman might say one thing and mean something else. Oba might've been nonchalant about it, but I get the impression it wasn't easy to let you go."

"Finding you made me see what love is supposed to be, and I'm planning on a life with only you." She held Vivien, knowing that only time would heal the doubt she bore because of her upbringing. "Oba is someone I love as a friend, but a betrayal of this magnitude wouldn't be forgiven, especially by me. The penalty for this kind of treason is death. Oba knows that as well as she knows her prayers to the goddess."

"I'm sorry—you're right. Let's blame my stupidity on hormones."

"I do that, and you'll pulverize me." They laughed and didn't separate when Frankie came back in. "You're the center of my world, my love. There's nothing I wouldn't do to keep you with me and safe. No one will ever be more important to me than you."

"She's a keeper, sis," Frankie said and stared outside. "My bet is on one of Oba's priestesses. I have no idea where that thought came from, but I know it's true. This upgrade to my shell has done interesting things to my head." He wiggled his hand and laughed. "Last night I could tell you two were really happy, until you weren't."

"Oh my God. Tell me you can't sense when we're having sex." Vivien pulled Kai down to sit next to her. "If you can, go ahead and lie. I'll be totally okay with that."

"No," Frankie said shaking his head. "Eww, no. It's more like I can feel extreme emotion, which wasn't uncommon for us before all this." Frankie pointed between himself and Vivien. "But now I can feel Kai too. At first the happy made sense—it was your honeymoon night after all—but then it made no sense. I sensed fear and anger…and darkness." He closed his eyes and laughed. "Maybe the pressure from being at the bottom of the ocean is getting to me, and I'm going mad."

She kissed the top of Vivien's head when she pressed against her. Frankie having ominous visions about them wasn't a good thing. "Like we said, we had a vision, and that made no sense. But it sounds a lot like what you felt."

"Then why is it happening? A dual vision isn't common no matter what world you're from, let alone a triple vision." Frankie shrugged as if that should be apparent. "Maybe we need to pay attention to what you saw. It might be a clue about what could happen. I'd rather be prepared if that's the case."

"I'm not ignoring it." She held Vivien against her and wasn't ready to let go of the fear even if she didn't want to admit it even to herself. "All I know is if there was a betrayal, it wasn't Oba."

"Thank you for your faith in me, Your Majesty." Oba came in and knelt before her and Vivien. "I've dedicated my life to the goddess and to my queen. It was an oath I took seriously, and I love you too much to break it."

"I believe you," Vivien said before Kai could say anything.

"Who, then?" Kai asked, not moving.

Vivien glanced at her before turning her attention to Oba. From her expression Kai realized Vivien could tell that Kai didn't quite believe Oba, despite what she'd said, not yet. There was a simmering rage in her, and she couldn't understand it, much less control it. All she could guess was it stemmed from being in the dark, and it made her feel vulnerable.

"Honey?" Vivien put her hand over her heart and kissed her cheek. "Breathe, okay?"

"It's just a question, Oba, so answer it." Her tone made Oba flinch.

"When you left for your quest, I spent time in the temple. I knew what was waiting for you even if you thought it was a joke. The goddess had shown me the prophecy so many times it was a part of my soul, and the only thing I didn't know was who Vivien was."

"Any old human would've done, huh?" Vivien asked and laughed.

"There was and is only one match for Kai, never believe otherwise," Oba said to Vivien before turning back to her. "I loved you even if you think I didn't, and I spent the time in prayer healing myself of your loss." Oba's eyes filled with tears. "My weakness opened my mind and my heart. Someone used that to get to you, and that I allowed it to happen fills me with shame. You know I'd never do anything to hurt you or those you love of my own free will."

Laud entered, leading a woman in cuffs with a hood over her head. "Kneel or I swear I'll make it so you can't stand." The woman dropped to the floor, and her head moved from side to side as if she was trying to hear something.

"I asked for your forgiveness even though I don't deserve it." Oba spoke softly and placed her hands on Kai's knee. "I will love and serve you like I have your mother, but I'll also go if you ask it of me."

"Oba?" the woman on her knees said. She sounded scared and anxious. "Why am I here?"

Kai motioned to Laud, and she took the woman away. She had no need to see her just yet, especially when she was still so angry. She leaned forward, letting Vivien go, and placed her hand on Oba's cheek.

It was an intimate move, and it made Oba's tears fall faster. She sensed Vivien wanted to stop her from doing anything else, but all that was left between her and Oba was a friendly affection and nothing more.

"There's nothing to forgive." She wiped Oba's face with her fingers and kissed her cheek. "Nothing."

"That woman read your mind, didn't she?" Vivien asked. Whatever was happening had brought Frankie closer, and he sat on the other side of his sister.

"I was meditating. That's how I communicate with the goddess. In a moment when my defenses were down, Susan tapped into my thoughts. By that time, you'd found Vivien, and the prophecy had begun to unfold. I'm the one who first realized you were expecting when I went back to vote on our stock, giving your family your business back." Oba looked at Vivien and Frankie, and Kai could feel Vivien's struggle not to have any anger toward her old friend. "Susan gathered information as a way to gain power by siding with Bella. I'm sure she traded what she was able to get from me for the promise of being the wielder of the water orb and the head priestess, once their plan was complete."

"Then you did nothing wrong," Vivien said, kissing Oba's other cheek. "Can you do to her what she did to you?"

Kai's shell warmed at Vivien's suggestion, making her think of something else, and she saw Frankie touch his too. "Let's forget about Susan for now. Oba, do you remember the ways of the ancients?" It was something she'd learned as a child when she'd begun her lessons about the goddess. The first priestesses would often join forces as a way to sharpen their conduit to hear the goddess's voice.

"Sit in a circle and have your knees touch," Oba said, moving out of the way so Kai, Vivien, and Frankie could sit close together. "Now hold hands."

Kai could already see the thin gold thread that connected her shell to Vivien's and wondered if Oba and Frankie could as well. Their connection had changed from that day in the temple, and it had changed again when they'd had the same vision, albeit from different perspectives. Now she thought it'd transform again given how easily Vivien was able to make the connection, and it would only get stronger with time.

"Close your eyes and concentrate on our physical bond," Oba said, holding her hand out to Frankie and nodding at him to take Vivien's hand. "You might not have grown up with the goddess as your guiding force, but open your heart and mind to her now."

Oba's voice was getting faint, but Kai could still feel everything around her. Vivien did as she was told, and Kai saw the thread thickening between them, and then it extended to Frankie. They formed a circle of light, so she took a breath and let go. It was like falling, only through time and not from a high place. In a moment they flew through space to a place she didn't recognize, yet it felt like coming home.

CHAPTER THIRTEEN

K ai studied the area but wasn't worried because both Frankie and Vivien held on to her as they too looked around. Oba, in charge of holding the vision in place, wasn't with them. The worry of being able to find their way home crossed her mind, but she needed answers before they started searching for a way back. Wherever they were, it was beautiful, with its open spaces backed by mountains and jungle. It had a wild, primitive feel to it as if it was untouched and pure, but there were people here.

"There." She pointed behind them. The structures were massive, and the sound of construction beyond that reached her ears.

It was strange to see spaceships sitting on the ground in a formation she instinctively knew was for defense. They were out of place, but not really. Without them where would she and her sisters be now? They had to be witnessing the first people. Queen Nessa's people.

"No, there," Vivien said, heading for the replica of the temple she knew. This one was made of wood, as was the statue of the goddess, but it was beautiful.

They walked side by side, and their surroundings seemed so real, yet she could still feel Vivien's and Frankie's hands tethering her to their world. The chanting was unfamiliar when they entered, since it was in the old language. It was beautiful, and she smiled when Vivien placed her hand on her stomach.

"The baby seems to know this place," Vivien said, whispering.

The chanting stopped when a young woman bowed before the altar and said a soft prayer she couldn't quite make out. "Come forward," the woman said.

She glanced at Vivien because the woman seemed to be talking to them. They walked forward, and the woman bowed.

"Welcome, Highnesses. I've prayed for a long time to see your faces."

They followed the woman to the fire burning at the center of the building. Kai noticed how young all the priestesses surrounding them were. If this was in any way an accurate picture of who had followed Nessa, it was true that only the young and brilliant had made the trip. She could sense their devotion not only to the goddess, but to the queen they served. What they lacked in years they made up for in loyalty.

"What time is this?" she asked, and the woman smiled.

"I see Jyri's impatience is still strong in her line. No greeting, just business." The woman laughed and Vivien joined in. "This is the second year of our coming." The woman waved them to sit before she did the same. "Much has happened in our time here, but it is now a moment for celebration."

"Why?" Vivien asked.

"Our queen led us here, and we have made it our home. The land and the water are untouched, and we've enjoyed exploring since our arrival. After our life on planet Atlantis, you can smell the freedom here, and we praise the goddess for it. Now, though, with the help of the Consort Jyri's breakthroughs, our queen is close to giving birth to our heir. She waited until she could carry her mate's child, just like you have. It comes much sooner than your child, Princess," the woman said to Vivien. "The goddess was true in what she showed me. The bonding shouldn't have worked, but her love for you has made it possible."

"I love her as well," Vivien said.

"I know that, as does the goddess. We pray to her, but she understands the importance of finding your match. She has also found the same for herself among the gods, if you read all her teachings, and the love of her children is what has kept her faith in us through the millennia." The woman bowed again, as did all the others.

The two women who entered made Vivien gasp. "She looks so much like you."

"I think the proper order is *she* looks so much like me," the taller of the women said, pointing at Kai. She smiled as she helped her very pregnant companion sit on one of the cushions.

"If the goddess only allows me to see one glimpse of the future,

I thank her for this." The pregnant woman was beautiful, and she had kind eyes. Kai had seen paintings and pictures of her, but seeing her now made a sense of love flow through her.

"Queen Nessa," she said, lowering her head in respect. "Consort Jyri."

"Please, Kai," Nessa said, "we're family, so look at me and let me be happy that what we did was not in vain."

"Your realm is vast and thriving, and you and Jyri are still celebrated. What you did laid a foundation that's guided every queen who's followed you." She wished her mothers could be here to see this. Nessa and Jyri were legends, and while they had video images of their life, seeing them in the flesh was an exhilarating experience.

"She's a wise woman, my wife," Jyri said. "See? I told you they'd never forget you." Jyri kissed Nessa's temple and smiled. "And the bond we have is also hereditary, from what I can tell. Vivien, welcome to our world."

"Thank you, Highness," Vivien said, reaching for her hand.

"The sight of you makes the craving to hold our daughter that much stronger." Nessa spoke directly to Kai. "Your mate is right. You resemble my love, and it's good to see the family line continues still."

"My mother Hadley actually looks a lot like you, so I got my dark hair and height from her. We must have a thing for pretty blondes," Kai said, and Jyri laughed.

"Ah, you sound like Jyri too, but now let's talk about what you need to know. That the three of you made it here means the goddess has blessed you, and you figured out how to use those blessings. You'll need them to defeat the coming darkness." The priestesses started praying in a low voice as Nessa spoke, and it sounded like humming in the background.

"What do you mean?" Vivien asked.

"The prophecy written by our priestess was not complete. I thought giving the whole thing away would give an advantage to those who'd do harm to our family." Nessa leaned back against Jyri and rubbed her middle. "I didn't believe what they told me at first, but I also didn't want to take any chances. Our people deserve to be free and happy in this world."

Kai glanced at Vivien. She couldn't remember the names of every queen they'd had, but this is where they began. Nessa and Jyri were the base of their family tree, and she was proud to have come from these brave women.

"That's what my mother believes as well, and when our Priestess Oba told her she'd given birth to the one who'd bring about the prophecy, it worried her a little."

"Kai, you might not believe us, but we've been with you from the time your mother carried you."

"It's true," Nessa said. "You have nothing to fear from the prophecy, and neither does your mother. What was written was a sign of the changing, but a change that will only strengthen our line."

Jyri nodded and continued, "What we started has grown and evolved, and we have rested in peace as we watched our people do great things." Jyri placed her hand on Nessa's and smiled. "Our people have known their purpose as they did in our time."

"Will you tell us what that is?" Frankie asked shyly.

"Welcome to our family, Frankie." Nessa smiled at him. "We have watched you and Vivien from the day Kai first found you. Little did you know you were part of such"—Nessa tilted her head and tapped her chin—"*spooky* things," she said, having obviously plucked the expression from his head.

Frankie laughed. "That is how I've thought about it. All this is out of our norm."

"If things were balanced, you would only know Kai as your family and nothing more. Sometimes, though, the past won't let us go so easily even if it takes eons to come back to haunt us." Jyri spoke, and Nessa looked up at her with an expression of adoration.

"The chance we took was to build the history you're a part of," Nessa said. "The purpose we taught and wanted our children to carry forth was that of service. It wasn't about lording over anyone or using our position to dominate. *Our* history contained plenty of that," Nessa said of her and Jyri. "When we joined, I took Jyri's name as a way of erasing my father's cruelty. The vision we shared made it paramount for us to leave when we saw no future in our old home. My father would've never allowed it."

"The Oberons' rule, as you know, became much worse than your father's, and because of their quest for power, planet Atlantis is on the precipice of extinction." Kai had watched her mother's meetings with Sol, and the man was unhinged. It seemed not much had changed in the years since Nessa and Jyri had led their people to freedom. "Sol Oberon sent his son following the same path you did to kill me, and I'm sure Vivien would've been on his list as well when he found out about the baby."

"Your death would've ended the dream we had for the new Atlantis. These people who have fallen under the sway of the Oberons do not follow Sol. His rule is over, and it's his heir who wants what you have. *She* will kill to get it, so you three must work together to stop the darkness that comes. The realm needs you both, Kai and Vivien, but your bond with Frankie will be important as well. It needs you all and the child you carry to continue our rule."

"Believe me, I'll do whatever I need to in order for Vivien and our baby to survive." She took Vivien's hand as well as Frankie's.

"Don't be so quick to sacrifice yourself." Jyri's eyes bored into hers. "I look at you, and I see myself, the same drive to keep your mate whole and happy. I'm the one who found the way here, and those who followed us wanted the same things you do. They wanted to join and love who they chose and not have someone choose for them. Keep your word and the vows you made. Your child, like ours, will need you to teach her the responsibilities of her future and the self-sacrifice it takes to be a good queen."

"The best way to show your people the way forward is to live a good life, love your wife, and cherish the years you have together," Nessa said. "The greatest blessing I was ever given was growing old with my love, and we want the same for you."

"Look to the past, and you'll find the rest of the prophecy," Jyri said.

"There's a record of it?" Vivien asked.

"Our head priestess followed our wishes and left what you'll need to prepare. Once you know all of what the goddess promised, you'll be ready to face what you must." Nessa reached out for Vivien's hand and held it between hers. "You are the strength she'll need to wear the crown. Like Jyri is to me and Hadley is to our daughter Galen, you must accept your role and the crown. Don't be afraid to claim that which is yours."

"Will she win?" Vivien's tears appeared ready to fall, and Kai put her arm around her gently, not wanting to disturb Viv's connection to Nessa.

"Nothing in this life is promised, but one thing," Jyri said. "Her love for you is so legendary it was written about in our time. You come not directly from our line, but you belong to us, nonetheless. The goddess has fulfilled the other things she promised when it comes to you and Frankie. It's been ordained. The changing of your shells at the temple started the wheel of fate you must complete."

"So she won't win?" Vivien released a sob and fell against Kai.

"That's not what she said at all," Nessa said. "The wielder of a trident fighting for power and fame will make them seem invincible, but the one who wields the trident for love *is* invincible." Nessa leaned forward and wiped Vivien's tears. "What was shown to us, at first I thought a curse, payment for some of the changes we made here like letting our male citizens die out, but that's not it at all. You were made for each other and destined to meet."

"So the goddess is on our side, then?" Vivien asked, but Kai was thinking the same thing.

"What you have are the choices you made. Something can be thrown in your path, and every one of us has the choice to walk by, ignoring it. When you saw Kai emerge from the water as a child it was fate," Nessa said. "It started the prophecy, but had you not truly fallen in love, the prophecy would've had to wait for another generation."

"As prophecies go, this one's been good from the start," Kai said, making Nessa and Jyri laugh.

"Remember all that we've said before the connection is lost," Nessa said.

"Thank you." Kai wanted to talk fast, so as to not leave with just a promise of the danger headed their way. "Can you tell me where in the past to look?"

"Think of your childhood, Kai," Nessa said. She turned and stared at Jyri. Something was silently decided between her and Nessa, and Jyri took her jacket off.

The tattoo on Jyri's bicep was intricate, and Kai stared at the design. It niggled something in the back of her mind, but it was like fog. She'd seen it somewhere but had no idea where.

"The answers lie with us," Jyri said. "Finding what we left will teach you to work together because it's only together that you will find the strength to win."

"Find your answers, and don't forget to lean on each other. The three of you have a trust that will never be broken, and it must always be so," Nessa said. "Until we see each other again."

The blinding light came like before, and when Kai opened her eyes, they were sitting in the room where they'd started. Both Vivien and Frankie held her hands tightly and seemed disoriented when they turned their attention to her.

"What in the hell?" Frankie took a deep breath and let them go.

"That was different," Vivien said, falling against her chest. "At least it wasn't as disconcerting as our first foray into group visions."

"You'd think they could be clearer if it was a damn vision. Teamwork is great and all, but I'd rather have them give us an X marks the spot." She sat back against the couch and made Vivien comfortable. "I have more questions than answers."

"Will you tell me what you saw?" Oba appeared calmer, as if she'd used the time they were mentally away to compose herself.

"I'll be happy to, but let's go get my parents. Then I want to talk to the priestess you brought with you. I want to know who she gave the information to besides Bella Riverstone, and what exactly she passed along. I'm going to do whatever I have to, to keep my family safe, and if that takes ripping the answers out of her head, then so be it." She held Vivien closer and noticed Frankie didn't move too far away.

Laud and her mother Hadley were right outside the room, and they seemed to be waiting until they were done. Hopefully they hadn't started questioning the woman without her. What Nessa and Jyri had said about Frankie meant she'd keep him with them until all the danger was done. Given that he'd been able to join them in the second vision, he'd be the best ally to keep Vivien safe.

"Did you get anything?" her mom asked.

"Plenty, but let's wait and talk about it in a minute. Where is our guest?"

"The queen is waiting in the grotto, Highness." Laud led the way, and Kai was glad the rain had slackened a bit. The spot Laud had mentioned was outside through the back, where the foliage started to get thick.

The grotto was a cave within the cave they were already in and had been incorporated into the landscape. Her grandmother had commissioned a small statue of the goddess, and it stood above the natural pool that was heated by some source deep in the ground. She smiled when she saw her aunt sitting with her mother near the entrance.

"Congratulations, stud. I didn't have a chance to talk to you last night to tell you how happy we are for you." Clarice kissed her cheeks before putting her arms around Vivien. "Sorry all this came up now. I swear our family isn't this drama riddled all the time."

"Thank you, and thanks for the great gift." Vivien had received a book of old maps after Kai had told Clarice about how much Vivien loved diving old wrecks.

"Where is she?" It was time to get this over with, so they'd have time to discuss other things. She didn't see the priestess, which might be a good thing since she was ready to drive her trident right through her skull.

"By the pool with Edil, and we sedated her to keep her from reading anyone else's mind. Susan seems to have a special talent for that." Her mother Galen had her arms crossed over her chest.

"Did she read someone's mind? She's only been here a couple of hours, so I hope none of you meditated around her," she said, and Clarice laughed. It was the type of laugh that was the definition of taunting your sibling.

"You might want to add daydreaming to that no-no list." Clarice chuckled, and her mother glared at her sister.

"What does that mean?" Kai knew how much her aunt loved tormenting her mother, so she could imagine what happened.

"Let's just say this Susan woman will have a new appreciation for your mom," her aunt said and smiled as she pointed at her mother Galen.

"And before you think of teasing me," her mother said, "think about the random thoughts that pop into your head when you look at Vivien. I'm sure they're not all about flowers and chocolates."

"It's a wonder you're not in therapy," Frankie said in a soft voice. "It's an even bigger surprise you're an only child."

"It's not from their lack of trying," Kai joked. "Did she see anything besides the wonders of your sex life?" She had to laugh despite the seriousness of the situation.

"Not much, so I thought this was the best place for her until Laud transports her up north to join the other prisoners." Her mom walked over and patted her chest. "I thought the quiet and the darkness might make her want to have a chat. A lifetime of this would drive even the most devoted to madness, and I think she knows that."

"Can I try before she's taken away?" She wanted answers, but if the woman was a talented mind reader, maybe waiting would be smart. Giving anyone an edge in finding what Nessa and Jyri left would be a mistake that could lead to defeat.

"Waiting would be the smart move, but we need to try," Vivien said as she started walking.

She shook her head and followed, since Vivien seemed to know where she was going. There was something different about Vivien, and Kai was mesmerized. It was as if each day she spent in the kingdom, the more confident she became. Not that Vivien was weak before, but now she had an inner strength that made Kai ready to follow her anywhere.

That was the type of relationship her mothers had, and it was misunderstood by many because of the public image they seemed to portray. Her mother Hadley was the trained warrior, but her mother Galen wasn't weak. She was actually the one her mom Hadley leaned on, yet her mother didn't hesitate to make the hard decisions that came with sitting on the throne. Until Vivien, Kai never realized that's what she wanted. Someone she could count on to carry the weight of her worry and love her anyway when it threatened to swamp her.

She *was* worried, but whoever thought to face them would have to kill her to take what was hers. As for the priestess Susan, she hoped her mom would banish her, alone and forgotten in the frozen waters of the north. That's, after all, what Pontos and his followers had planned for their people. The Oberons were a sickness that left destruction in their path, and it was time to rid all worlds of them.

"Is that you, Princess?" Susan lifted her head and appeared to know exactly where she was. "Did you bring the disease that will sicken and kill all of us with time?"

"Do you mean me?" Vivien cocked her head slightly and studied Susan, clearly thinking of something. For the first time since they'd met, Kai couldn't make out one thought in Vivien's mind. It was closed to her, and she hoped that meant it was closed to Susan. "Is my humanity going to be what brings the realm to its knees?"

"It's already been written. You will bring about the end, and Kai knew that and brought you here anyway. I can't allow that to happen." Susan spoke with authority but didn't try to break her bonds.

"So you're justified in your actions. How many more did you use your little trick on, besides Oba?" Vivien was doing a great job, so she and Frankie stood back and let her go.

"You were easy, which makes what you're trying to do now laughable."

"Really? Go ahead and read my mind. Tell me what we're going to do next and how we're going to gather all the people working with you up and lock them away until every one of you is forgotten." Vivien got close enough for Susan to feel her body heat. "Go on, tell me."

"Are you sure you want me to know?" Susan laughed but lunged forward, falling on her face when Vivien put her fist around her shell and ripped it from her throat. "Give it back. It belonged to my mother, and you have no right."

"Stop talking, or you'll lose more than the shell." Kai motioned for Vivien to put it down before whatever power the shell had could infect her. "Tell me what you reported and to who, and I promise I'll eventually let you go free."

"You Merlins know how to lie, so I won't tell you anything."

"Are you sure? Or is it that you haven't done anything with the information now that Bella has run?" She got as close as Vivien had and tapped her finger against Susan's forehead. "Tell me, or this will be your reality for the rest of your days."

"I'll never betray my people like you have."

"So be it. I'm not lying when I tell you I'll win with the goddess's blessing, and my love for Vivien will be written about as much as the love Nessa and Jyri shared."

"You speak blasphemy."

"I speak the words of the goddess, and you will choke on the truth of it when all this is done. Take her away."

Kai couldn't sense anything from Susan, and it was often like that with women of true faith. When they devoted themselves to the goddess so completely, even when it was misguided, it was hard to break them. As with Tanice, that would take time and finesse.

The guards dragged Susan away as she screamed for her shell back. "Now what?" Vivien asked.

"Now we try to finish by finding what was left for us, and we need to do that quickly."

Vivien nodded. "Something and someone are coming. I can feel it, and I sensed that in her when I ripped the shell from her neck. We need to be prepared."

CHAPTER FOURTEEN

Daria waited four days, and finally a response came through from Bella. The shuttles were ready, and she'd sent out the second wave of them in a random pattern throughout the night. She'd looked at the coordinates Bella sent, and they would land them in North America downriver of a place called New Orleans.

"Is there something on your mind?" she asked Frem.

"I'm not sure I understand how you know all you do about Pontos and some of the other information you have. From the beginning, Bella made wise moves that kept Pontos ahead of the game until *he* cut off contact." Frem sat across from her and stared out into space. "That was his first mistake, but if what you say is true, *her* mistake was not telling Pontos that Kai Merlin is Galen's heir. Why do you think that is?"

"Because I asked her not to." She admitted one of the things she'd held back. Bella was sending her messages even after Pontos had arrived. "Before you think to condemn me for his death, think about where we'd be if Pontos had succeeded."

"You set him up for failure?" Frem appeared more amused than upset.

"He told me had he won, he would've never allowed us to come here. This would've been his realm, and the women of Galen's kingdom would've been his slaves as well as his harem."

"You know I had no love for Pontos, but some might hold that—as well as what will happen to your parents—against you."

"My brother was a bastard, and my parents helped perfect those traits in him. Now they can face their loving subjects with someone else in charge of their fates. My only wish is to talk to them before the crowd tears them apart, so they'll know it was me. I'm the architect of their downfall, and it started with the failures I assured for Pontos."

"Was Kai in this New Orleans?" Frem asked.

"It's where she met Vivien Palmer. To me it shows how weak Galen's line has become. That her heir has chosen a human is shameful. Pontos went on and on about what feeble stupid creatures humans are. Why would you pollute your bloodline by mating with one?"

"Surely it was simply for the sex." Frem had to laugh.

This new world was full of people that looked like them, yet were inferior. Pontos had spent a few years on the planet and had sent back regular reports of the surface dwellers as well as the world they'd created, which had hardly moved beyond their Neanderthal forebears. If Galen's subjects had mixed themselves with theses mongrels, they'd be even easier to defeat. "It's even better than that. Kai got this human pregnant."

"How is that possible?"

"I need to talk to Bella about that, but that information might be useful." She understood the power that came from the body-stone connection, but procreation still took a man and woman. That she'd need help on that front when she did join was something that infuriated her. "Our first priority is to find Bella and her mother. Once we have them, Francesca Yelter will have plenty to answer for."

"The troops who've already gone down are in position, so we'll be ready within the hour. The best place to land will be at the mouth of the great river. Send Bella a message, and have her wait with transportation. The humans use crafts that float on the surface, so we'll need some if you want to go undetected for now." Frem gave her a picture of the vessel.

"We'll need more than boats, and your landing area won't work. There's too much traffic there. We need to move somewhere with more open water." She pointed to an area to the west of where Frem had picked.

"I'll make it so." Frem left her, and the silence was overwhelming.

It made her heart race, and she clenched her fists. She was ready to begin what she needed to do, and she sighed at the truth she didn't like to face. The fact was, she was alone. Once her parents had Pontos, they should've stopped, but she'd been born two years later. Her mother had given her away to be raised by staff, but that had made her strong. Once she started this, she wouldn't be tethered to Pontos's incessant need to please their father.

"I hope you live long enough to see what you threw away," she said out loud. The message was especially for her father. She'd never made it a secret how deep her hatred ran for her father, and this would be her sweetest revenge. "I could've given you everything, but you threw me away for Pontos."

She stood and straightened her uniform before heading down to the shuttles. There would be a skeleton crew left aboard, an escape route for anyone who wanted to return to what they knew, assuming they could find another black hole that would allow them to return. For her, it'd either be success or death. There'd be no going back.

CHAPTER FIFTEEN

Honey, you need to relax, or you're never going to figure it out," Vivien said. They were back at the capital, and their talk with the priestess working with Bella Riverstone had been useless. Plus being in her presence felt like someone was clawing the inside of her brain to get information. Frankie, God bless him, had put "99 Bottles of Beer" in the woman's head, derailing her attempts to gain more information from them. Now he'd gone back topside with guards to protect their parents and Marsha.

Not finding the answers they needed from their second vision was making Kai crazy. Jyri had been cryptic to protect the answers, but maybe she'd been too cryptic. That made no sense to either of them, but there was no way to know what was going through the mind of Atlantis's first rulers when they hid the full prophecy. If finding the answers drove them to madness, maybe it wasn't the best team building exercise. Kai's moms had been none the wiser about the symbol they'd been given, nor had Oba. It was painful to watch Kai try to squeeze it from her memories, and so far nothing had worked.

"Sorry, my love." Kai sat next to her. "It's like I can feel someone right behind us, and I can't slow them down."

Once they'd returned to the capital, she'd spent time with Galen and with Kai's grandmother Sibyl, learning about her new responsibilities as Kai's wife. Loving her was easy, but it seemed their future would also revolve around running a nation with way more people than she would've guessed. It was bizarre to think this much was happening under the water, but Kai told her it'd be no different than running a company.

"The thing we need to do is what Oba said." The priestess had tried her best to make her feel at ease and had apologized numerous times for Susan's betrayal. She laughed at Kai's expression throughout the process of her trying to navigate a friendship with Oba. "Relax and let me join your thoughts."

"The answer's in that tattoo. Body art is not something we do often, but some of the warriors have inked some of the old runes on their body." Kai drew random patterns on her shoulder as she talked, and despite their unsolved mysteries, she was enjoying these quiet moments.

"I've always thought of getting one but it's hard to choose something I'll have forever." She turned her head and shifted to kiss Kai's neck but missed when she stood abruptly.

"You're a genius, sweetheart." Kai stripped off the linen pants and shirt she had on and reached for her wet suit. "You want to come with me?" Kai held up Vivien's suit and smiled.

It was a cloudy day, but there was enough light outside to see the ruins west of the palace. They reminded her of something she'd seen in Greece, only these appeared more desolate and paradoxically more well-maintained. Kai led her to one of the airlocks that led outside, seeming to be in a hurry. Edil led the guards outside first and moved into position so they'd be surrounded no matter where they swam.

The water was cold momentarily, but she gladly followed Kai to the area that the guards patrolled. The spot reminded her of a gazebo, only the columns were carved out of marble, and the spotlights that shone day and night set it apart from everything else. The open dome had stars carved into the arched ribs that made up the roof, and she swam up and ran her fingers along them. It was the medallion at its center that caught her attention.

"It's been years since I've been here." Kai traced the design Jyri had on her bicep. "This was their original resting place. It was constructed in the shallows off the Greek Isles, and when we moved, it was brought here intact."

"Why not move this to be with them if it was already moved once?" She moved down to where the two tombs had sat. There were two indentions in the stone. At the center of one was the same design of Jyri's tattoo, and the other had what looked like one of the constellations.

"It's a sacred site, but so is this one, which is why it's still guarded.

Why they did that I don't know, but I've always found this spot special."
Kai swam closer and looked at what she'd pointed out. "That's Pisces."

It made sense that it'd be a sign of water. "Why is it here?"

"It's not often seen by the naked eye in the sky, but the constellation has a galaxy at its center. It's the gateway that leads to Atlantis. It's the only bit of home Nessa kept. It's part of our royal crest."

"It has to be here then." She glanced at the medallion then the stone.

"Look to the past is what Jyri said." Kai pointed to the carved constellation. This was their past—the place they'd left behind but that still mattered to them even though it was millions of light years away.

"What does the symbol Jyri had tattooed on her arm mean?"

"I remember asking the same thing one time when I swam here with Laud. She told me it was the DNA strand of Nessa and Jyri's baby. In a way, this is their past and their future."

"Then this is definitely the place. The royal crest they developed and the sign of their child—the past and future that hold the answers. We'll go through all the combinations."

"Ready," Kai said, placing her hand on the medallion, while Viv placed her hand on the tomb base. "Press."

She felt the click in her fingers, and she opened her mouth and tasted the salt from the water. The square of the constellation rose, and there was something underneath it. Kai swam down and took the package. Seeing it gave Vivien a sense of calm, and she smiled at Kai.

"You're the love of my life." She wanted to say that before they read whatever this was. The world of prophecies and visions was new to her. It made her think she was being set up for failure no matter how devoted she was to Kai. It was hard to accept being different and being the first of her kind, and that's who she was in this new world.

"You worry too much. Simply believe your place is with me," Kai said, taking her hand.

It sounded like something that was written as law, but Vivien knew her acceptance by the nation would take more than a prophecy from thousands of years ago. She was sure that more than one person believed the same thing Susan did—that she'd be Kai's downfall.

"I love you, and that won't change."

It was weird to cry while swimming, but Kai's kindness had a way of undoing her. "You're sweet."

"You bring it out in me, so let's go see what we found." Kai took her hand and swam back to the palace.

One of the guards followed them to the airlock, and Edil ordered her back to her post. The woman hesitated, and Vivien wondered if the opposition group was larger than they imagined. She glanced back once before they went through the lock. The woman smiled, and she didn't sense any aggression from her, so maybe she was letting her imagination run away with her.

She slicked her hair back as she swam up to the edge and grabbed Kai's hand for a boost up. It didn't surprise her to find Oba waiting. The great priestess seemed connected to Kai and came running when she felt she needed her. She repeated the mantra that she wasn't jealous a few times before putting a smile on her face. It made her laugh when Kai smiled at her and touched over her heart before kissing her.

"Do me a favor," Kai said with her lips pressed to her ear. It made her shiver but in a good way.

"Anything."

"Remind me later to get you naked and touch you until you scream." Kai had her back to their escorts, and she put her hands on Vivien's ass and squeezed hard. "Think you can remember that?"

"I won't forget."

They followed Oba and their guards to the queen's office at the center of the palace and sat to wait. Kai's mom Galen was busy in meetings but told them to call if anything came up. Hadley was already on her way back from the training grounds, where they were preparing their troops for battle no matter where they had to fight it.

"Do you want to be alone when you open it?" Oba asked, breaking the silence.

Kai shook her head. "Are you ready?"

"We need to know." There was no sense in waiting.

Kai opened the packet and took out a stone tablet about nine inches high by four inches wide. It wasn't large, but there was a lot on it. The tablet was the same shape as the Ten Commandments were represented in popular culture, only smaller. The markings on it seemed to be laser-etched in the old language, and if they were as old as Nessa and Jyri, they were in remarkable shape.

"*She will turn from the path set by the first, and that will bring about the end of our world as we know it*," Kai read.

The first line sounded familiar since it was what Kai had told her when she'd first started the story of who she was. This was the line that was supposed to signal their doom.

"That's the prophecy we have," Oba said.

"It is, and we need to get your parents here to hear the rest." Vivien placed a sheet of paper over the tablet and accepted a towel from Kai for her wet hair.

"What are you thinking?" Kai asked, helping her dry off.

"It's probably stupid, but I have a gut feeling your moms should hear this too when we read it. Once the words are spoken out loud, we should find a way to lock this away somewhere it'll be safe until our battle is fought." She reached up and pressed her hand to Kai's neck. "Nessa and Jyri kept them hidden all this time, so let's not give it all away now."

"I'll call to see if they'll be much longer," Oba said, leaving them alone.

"Can you believe no one has found these before us?" She entwined her fingers behind Kai's head and pulled her down for a kiss.

"It is pretty shocking, but maybe this means we'll be prepared to beat whoever lines up against us." Kai kissed her, and she closed her eyes, trying to enjoy their time before everyone was in puzzle-solving mode. It was easy to lose herself when Kai kissed her like this.

"I'm glad you married for love and not for anything else," Galen said when she came in and caught them.

"After seeing you all my life, did you think I'd marry for any other reason?" Kai pressed another quick kiss to Vivien's lips before waving to the desk. "Look what we found."

Kai's mothers came closer and studied the tablets before waving Kai to read on. "*Her path will now have one foot on the land and one in the water. The love she'll find will give our people a way forward as they embrace fully our new home. They will find that love can bridge worlds, and their heir will be the first of her kind. A new Atlantean.*"

"It's amazing they saw the baby that long ago," Galen said. "She'll bring about change, and that'll only lead to better things." She looked thoughtful. "But we already knew we were bridging the worlds with this child. What else does it say?"

Kai continued to read. "*Someone will come to take what we have built. It begins with a quest for power but will end by a love born of*" *misguidance. Search where the love story began, and lure the darkness out. Destroy it, and clear the realm of the danger that waits to tear it down.* Where our own love story started, or someone else's?"

Kai tapped her finger on the desk until Vivien covered Kai's hand with hers to get her to stop. It was one of the little hints that she was giving birth to a hyperactive kid since she was starting to feel constant flutters. Kai was seldom still no matter what they were doing, and this kid was going to be a carbon copy of her.

"The vision convinces me it's ours, and where it began could be one of two places." She turned and put her arms around Kai's waist, but they stared at the tablet, trying to figure out if it held any other clue.

"Two?" Hadley asked.

"The beach house where we met or the waters where Kai worked for our company. We spent more time out there than we did in the office, so that makes more sense." She had a feeling it was the work option. "The beach is memorable and our start, but I fell in love on a sailboat in the Gulf. It was like my heart had come home, so let's start there."

"You're a poet, my love, and you're right." Kai kissed her, not seeming to care who was in the room. "We need to go back."

"Are you sure that's a good idea?" Hadley asked.

"Clear the room," Galen said. Oba and the others walked out in front of Laud, and Galen asked her trusted guard to stay. The door was locked, and extra security measures were put in place to make the room private. "Do you know what your plan is going to be?"

"There's only one option after reading that. We all know it, so it's time to get started. We have to be out in the open to draw these people out. No one can fight a battle in the dark, so it's time to show ourselves and trust in the people we place at our backs." Kai walked Vivien to a chair and sat next to her. "We need to move quickly, before our enemies get better organized. I think we have to assume they're already here and in motion. They've probably learned from Pontos's mistakes, so we need to eliminate all of the threat."

"Are you leaving Vivien here?" Galen asked.

"Mom, I won't place Vivien in danger, but I can't force her to stay behind if that's not what she wants."

"And I don't want. My place is with Kai. I think if I stay here, I might be safe, but no one will respect me going forward." She didn't have to say it, but she believed they all knew it was true.

"What's your plan?" Laud asked. "I've got an idea of what it should be, but I'll follow your lead."

"Simply, the plan is to fight, and I need to bring the fight to me. Viv's right in that we can't hide here and expect anyone to follow us once the crown is ours." Kai locked eyes with her mothers, and they were all quiet for a moment. "Pontos wanted me, Bella Riverstone targeted me, and whatever or whoever is coming wants to take me on. They need to fight me and beat me if they want to take over the realm. My loss will be seen as the downfall of your reign. That means I need to put myself out in the open, available to whoever it is coming for us."

"I'm not disagreeing with you, but don't complain about the extensive security going with you," Galen said. "The moment something happens, I'm sending in everything we have. I don't care if it makes the national news."

"I wouldn't expect anything else." Kai made Galen laugh and stood so they could hug as Hadley put her arms around Vivien and hugged her as well. "Promise me you both will stay here, though. We need to find all the idiots who are helping these people, and I don't need to be worried about you two. You stick close to Mom," Kai told Galen. "Don't make me ground you for not following orders."

"We'll see," Galen said, which Vivien took to mean they probably wouldn't. "Be careful and take care of Vivien. Don't let her take any chances." Galen opened her arms to Vivien and kissed her cheeks. "She's a little compulsive sometimes but we love her anyway, so start practicing your mom voice."

"I'll put her on a leash if I have to." She felt the heat in her ears once the words left her mouth, and she laughed along with Kai's parents.

"As my younger staff like to tell me," Galen said with a smile, "TMI, sweetie."

They spent the afternoon packing, and it didn't take much time to prepare the *Salacia* for travel, with Ivan and Ram accompanying them. Laud had sent out word and was in charge of deciding who would accompany Kai and Vivien onto land. Whoever she sent needed to be ready for war, like any military would be when there was an attempt at a power grab.

Galen and Hadley had come down to see them off, and she wasn't surprised to see Oba with them. Oba closed her eyes and appeared to be saying a prayer. She stood next to Kai and waited along with the guards going with them. A prayer or two couldn't hurt anything.

"Highness," Oba said, stepping forward. She lifted her hand slowly, and Vivien didn't stop her when she placed it on her middle and closed her eyes for another prayer. "Have faith in what you have with her, and rejoice in the life you carry. It means your reign will last for a thousand years."

"Thank you," she said, smiling at Oba when she offered her the small book in her hand. The blessing wasn't one anyone in the realm made lightly.

"It was my mother's," Oba said. "It's the story of the goddess and the basic prayers. You'll need to know those when Kai becomes queen."

The comment rang of a rock-solid faith that their future would be everything she wanted. A life focused on Kai and their children sounded in no way progressive, but they could be that and so much more if given the chance to live. "Thank you, and we'd appreciate your prayers while we're gone."

"That would be my honor, and if the goddess blesses me with any visions of the future, I'll be in touch."

"You're a good friend to her, Oba, and I hope we can be the same."

The airlock closed behind them, and she glanced around, glad to know all the guards riding with them, but this time there were quite a few other ships tagging along. Each of them was filled with guards and advanced weaponry. That made her feel better and she lay in Kai's arms as they watched the bleakness outside whiz by. She called Frankie to let him know they were on their way back, and he invited them to dinner at Marsha's.

"It sounds like things are going well," she said when she put the phone back on the side table. The way Kai inhaled and let it out slowly made her smile.

As passionate as they were, she was glad they could be quiet together. It was what she'd wanted when she actually spent time thinking about the kind of relationship she wanted. Kai held her like she wanted to be with her and because she enjoyed having her close. She didn't go through the motions because she wanted to gain something from her she wasn't willing to give. It sounded simple, but that hadn't been her experience up to now. Her family's wealth had always been a factor when she allowed anyone into her life.

"It's a good thing he can follow directions." Kai laughed as she combed her fingers through Vivien's hair.

She lifted her head and smiled down at Kai. "Do I want to know what you're talking about? I always pushed Frankie into having a love life, but I don't know if I want the blow-by-blow."

"He was worried he'd drown that night we went skinny-dipping, so I told him to just stop overthinking it and jump in. His body would know what to do." Kai reached up and ran her thumb across her lips. "I think he figured out that translated into more than just swimming."

"You're giving romance lessons?"

Kai laughed again. "When you're madly in love, you want the whole world to join you. This is so good it'd be selfish not to share."

"My life would be so empty without you." She bit Kai's thumb gently and rolled on top of her. "Swear to me that you won't take any chances that'll leave me alone."

"Baby—" Kai said, moving her hands to her back.

"No, you promise me. I spent my life looking for the meaning of the shell you gave me, and I'm glad I never gave up. It led me right to you and this world you've opened up to me, but it'll mean nothing without you. Promise me."

"I promise, my love. It's why we have all these people with us, and after some real estate purchases, they'll be close by. I'll never leave us exposed to any kind of danger." Kai moved her leg between Vivien's and kissed her. "It's amazing the goddess saw how much I would love you, and I don't think she'd go through all this to have it end too soon. All we need to do is have faith in each other."

"Yes, but you're the first one to run toward danger. I saw it when you faced Pontos, and it scares the hell out of me."

"My life will be about loving you, but I can't turn my back on any threat that will try to destroy what we stand for." Kai held her close. "I've never understood the allure of taking total control of a people. Once you do, what's next? What else is there? I mean, look at what's happened on Atlantis. Something like that never ends well."

"You have a good heart, so you'll never understand that kind of thinking. All I want is for you to come out of this whole. I have plans for you." She kissed Kai and slipped her hand under her T-shirt. The warm skin made her smile.

"I'll follow wherever you lead."

Kai touched her with such gentleness and devotion it made her want to weep. She saw the love in Kai's eyes, and it awed her to the point she couldn't look away. "I love you so much." She rested her head on Kai's shoulder and sighed. "I feel very lucky."

"You aren't the only one, and it makes me sound sappy to say this, but I can't stand to be away from you for a minute. I'm sure you'll be sick of me before too long."

"As if." She pinched the skin on Kai's side and laughed. "See, everyone thinks you're this big macho warrior, but I'm glad I get to see the softer side of you." The way Kai laughed made her happy. There was a joy in it that lightened her like nothing ever had. "What exactly are we going to do when we get back? It's been home for my entire life, but it doesn't feel like that anymore." They hadn't stopped to discuss their future in more practical ways. Where would they live? Would Vivien keep working, or did being part of the royal family mean her job was under the sea now? The questions had been in her mind for a while, but now they finally had some time to talk it over.

"It'll be what you make it. I'll never keep you from your family, so we'll spend time with them, but the job you have now might have to change." Kai ran her fingers up and down her back, and it made her shiver. "We have plenty invested in that field of business, and we might reach a point where we'll share more of our technology that'll move humans away from fossil fuels. That'll take a lot of debate, considering what happened last time."

"My father will be thrilled you're putting that off for now." Winston Palmer's identity was wrapped up in the company their family had founded. She and Franklin had been groomed from the very beginning to continue the Palmer legacy, and her father had given them little choice in the matter. "In our own way we have a lot in common with your people—my father won't let go of the old ways easily. We also have to talk about the fact that he's having trouble reconciling his memories of what happened to you. I doubt he's stopped thinking about it since we left."

"Frankie will come into his own at the helm, and with our help, he'll lead Palmer into a new way of doing business." Kai's hand moved under her waistband and stopped.

"Is that why you picked us?" She'd never thought to ask. Their company was profitable, but nothing compared to the big boys in the industry.

"Buying stock with an eye to changing major companies is basically a quagmire of red tape that got us nowhere. The big boys, when it comes to oil production, move with the speed of dinosaurs, so a company like yours is perfect. Palmer is a good size to be an agent for change, and proven changes within your operations that yield results could steer the industry. Like the land expanders I installed. The board thought they were a waste of resources until they weren't."

"You're a smart egg, honey." She smiled when she felt Kai's hand move to her butt. "You're also sexy as hell."

"It wasn't all my idea, and you're the sexy one here." Kai reached between them and unbuttoned Vivien's shorts.

She lifted her hips and sucked on Kai's neck when Kai pulled her shorts and her underwear off. "I'm rapidly losing interest in this conversation."

"Good." Kai kissed her as she put her hand between her legs, then encouraged her to sit up.

She hoped no one could see in the window when she came down on Kai's fingers, but even an audience wouldn't stop her right now. It felt incredible, and she could feel how wet she was as she moved up and down, taking Kai in. "I love you, and I love being with you like this." It was all she could say as she moved faster. "I'm coming, oh, I'm coming. I can't…hang…on." She hated that the orgasm overwhelmed her before she had a chance to really enjoy herself, but she was too lethargic to care.

"Should I beat my chest now?" Kai held her with her free hand, and the joke made her snort.

"I'd say you're full of yourself, but you can totally beat your chest."

She sat back up and took her shirt off with Kai's eyes on her the entire time. "If anyone saw you like this, they'd know why I go all head over heels for you."

"No one can see in here, right? We have enough people with us that we could be entertainment for a few Peeping Toms." She glanced at the window and tapped on it.

"No, I'm not a sharer. The window's tinted, so this is a private view."

She enjoyed the way Kai always watched as she got naked. That intense gaze made her feel beautiful. Kai sat up and pressed their bodies together and started touching her again. The slowness of it was magical, and she moved against Kai as she kissed her. Kai's tongue in her mouth made her soar, and she stiffened as she moaned.

"I think I've said this before." She pressed her forehead to Kai's and squeezed her sex around Kai's fingers. "The things you do to me are wonderful." Her phone buzzed, and she wanted to ignore it but picked it up when Kai said it was Frankie. "Don't think about any funny business," she said to Kai. "Hey, did you forget something?" she asked Frankie. She put him on speaker and tried to move away from Kai, but Kai shook her head and kept her fingers right where they were.

"You guys are being summoned to the big house," Frankie said, sounding upbeat.

"We're about two hours from the mouth of the river, so we should make it," Kai said. She moved her thumb over Viv's clit, and she widened her eyes while shaking her head. "We have a boat waiting to take us to the platform, and we'll hop a helicopter from there, so we won't be late."

Kai's thumb pressed and stroked a little harder, and she bit her lip, trying and failing to hold back a moan.

"Viv, you okay?" Frankie asked.

"I'm fine, just moved wrong." She pinched Kai's earlobe, but that smile was chipping away at her resolve.

"Okay. Get ready for a night of planning. Mom's taking your comment about getting married before you're hugely pregnant seriously. With luck and no glitches, that'll happen in two weeks." Frankie laughed, and she came close to groaning. "And don't groan. I'll run interference for you with Marsha's help."

She inhaled sharply when Kai's touch became firmer. "You're reading my mind now?" She couldn't help lifting her hips slightly and coming down again.

"If I did that, I'd be blushing badly." He laughed, and Kai smiled as she wiggled her eyebrows. "I'm kidding, but I know you two. A long trip with nothing else to do means you're killing time doing something else."

"Okay, stop teasing Viv. Let your mother know we'll be there." Kai laughed and Frankie hung up.

Vivien dropped the phone on the floor with her clothes, not caring who else called them. "*You* are a huge troublemaker." She would've continued, but Kai stroked up again, and it made her stop talking. "Do you want me to touch you?"

"I need you to kiss me and let me have you," Kai said. She never let up moving her hand and pressed her lips to the side of Vivien's neck.

The desire ratcheted up, and she couldn't help but move with Kai as she filled her up and drove her insane. There was no way to hold back when Kai kissed her and moved her hand faster.

"Ah," she grunted out, unable to breathe, much less form words. The orgasm rushed through her, and she took a deep breath when her body finally let go. "You make me crazy in such good ways that I don't have a way to adequately describe it." She spent a long moment kissing Kai and threading her fingers through Kai's hair.

Kai lay back with her on top and smiled up at her. "Like I told you that first night I saw you. The thing I thought first was how beautiful you were. I couldn't take my eyes off you, and I'm lucky I get to touch you like this. You are so much more than that, though, which really does make me lucky."

She touched Kai and enjoyed the way she responded to her touch. Kai was wet and ready, and it didn't take long to get her to come as hard as she had. They had time for a nap when they were done, and she smiled when Kai woke her up by kissing her all over her face. It was nice to be quiet for a bit and enjoy the feel of Kai against her.

"Let's take a shower. We should be close when we're done," Kai said, helping her up.

They were standing in the galley when Edil gave the command to surface. The area around them was clear of any boats or air traffic, and she watched as Ram and Ivan swam lazily around, having been released before they surfaced. The Palmer boat Isla was navigating pulled alongside them, crewed entirely by women, and she had to guess Palmer now had more than one of Kai's people on their payroll. It'd be the easiest way to guard them without arousing suspicion.

"We're closer to the port, so I thought we'd take off from there," Edil said.

"That's good," Kai said. "How long before the rest of the team is in place?"

"We sent a squad ahead, so you'll be fully guarded by the time you get home."

The ride took less than an hour, and Vivien raised her eyebrows when she saw the new helicopter with their company logo on it. "Have you been shopping?" she asked Kai.

"Security is a bear sometimes, but it's necessary. This is a gift from Mom and her paranoia, but she's a good tactician, so I trust her instincts when it comes to all things military." Kai held her hand as they headed to their new ride. "It's also for Frankie and your family if they have to come out here. The guards won't just be a reality for us."

"That'll be hard to explain."

"Not really. Trust me," Kai said as she climbed in after her. Edil and five other women got into the helicopter with them, and an hour later, they landed at the heliport next to the Superdome. The women didn't look armed, but Kai assured her they were fully capable of fending off anyone.

"It feels like forever since I've been home," she said, resting against Kai in the car. The world felt so ordinary now compared to where'd they'd been for the last week. "Are you sure you don't mind going to my parents' place tonight? With everything going on, wedding plans seem like a waste of time."

"Marrying you isn't a waste of time, and I want to see what your mom has planned. If I *marry* you"—Kai made air quotes and laughed—"I'm thinking that'll get your dad off my back about getting you pregnant. Though I doubt he's put that one together yet."

"I'm sure he thinks I messed up somehow, and you're being noble about it." There was something in her father's expression at the beach that she hadn't been able to decipher yet. It was as if he was pleading with her to tell him the truth about the jumbled pieces in his mind.

"I don't think that at all. Your dad's mind is like a volcano spewing one crazy thought after another, only he doesn't have enough information to know they're not crazy at all."

"What are we going to do if he starts asking questions again? You don't know my father well yet, but he's not the type to let something like this go." She slipped her hand under Kai's T-shirt, needing to feel her.

"I talked to my mom about it," Kai said, and Vivien instinctively knew she meant Galen. "This is new territory for all of us, and I told her we needed to make some concessions."

"What exactly does that mean?" They turned into her driveway, and she thanked the woman who'd driven them before handing the keys to Kai to unlock the door. The small flashing units at the corner of each room made her curious, but she wanted to finish their conversation about her family first.

"Frankie's transformation shouldn't have happened, not according to all the scholars who've studied the prophecy for as long as there's been a prophecy. Don't get me wrong, I'm happy that what happened did, but some of our people are freaked about it." Kai went to the kitchen and poured herself a glass of milk, offering her some.

"If it's a gift from the goddess, why would they be upset about it?" She shook her head and grimaced thinking about milk in her mouth. The only reason it was in the refrigerator was because Kai liked it.

"I don't think they're upset—it's more like they're surprised in a really big way. There hasn't been a male Atlantean on Earth in thousands of years, but by definition, there is one now. What happened to Frankie can't be undone, no more than I can stop being who I am." Kai moved to the couch and put her arm around her when she joined her.

"I think it's good, since the changes mean he can visit us when we have to be home for longer periods of time."

"I think it's a good thing too, baby. The changes have bigger implications, though. If Frankie ever has children, and I have no doubt he will, Marsha doesn't seem the type to be happy being kept in the dark, and if she has a kid with gills, she's going to do serious damage to his manhood."

She laughed so hard at that she snorted. "You haven't known her long, but that's Marsha in a nutshell. What exactly are you going to do about that?"

"We'll wait and see how tonight goes before we make any big decisions. It's not like they're pregnant already, so we have time."

She moved to sit in Kai's lap so she could see her face. "What exactly about that worries you?"

"We've never procreated with humans because we didn't think it would work. Then you proved that completely wrong by getting pregnant before all your nifty upgrades. It happened with us because of the bonding of our shells. Frankie doesn't need the shell to get Marsha pregnant, so like I said, little kids with gills will be hard to explain." Kai seemed relaxed as she ran her hand up and down her thigh but didn't stop there.

The baby bump was getting harder to hide, and she had a renewed energy that had eluded her at the beginning, when all she did was throw up. Thankfully, it really had become morning sickness, and once it was over the rest of her day was pretty uneventful. The sensations she got from having Kai this close to her gave her hope to dream about their future.

"Our baby will be like us, right?" Until Kai had mentioned Frankie, she'd assumed their child would share Kai's genetic makeup. There was no scientific reasoning for that, but her gut knew it to be true.

"Stop letting your brain skitter off to dark places, my love," Kai said, moving her hand back up to cup her cheek. "Our child will be the first of her kind. I'm not sure what that means, but one thing is clear. She's our heir. Our heir gets the throne when I'm too feeble to remember my name and can't make decisions any longer."

"But what if—"

"There are no what-ifs in this scenario. That's how it's worked for thousands of years, and it's not making a radical change now." Kai kissed her gently at first before pressing more firmly against her. "I'll promise you as many times as it takes that it'll be okay. It'll be so because we conceived her right over there." Kai pointed to the spot in front of the fireplace. "The bonding worked, and our child will be no different than any other child born in Atlantis. She'll be born, and before she's introduced to the nation, we'll carve her a shell that she'll wear forever." Kai touched the shell around Vivien's neck and smiled.

"You make it sound so easy."

"It will be, I promise. One day when she finds the woman she wants to spend her life with, she'll do the same for her. It'll have the history of our dynasty in those lines, and my prayer is that she finds a love as deep and perfect as I have."

"Should I see a human doctor? Or an Atlantean one?"

"One of the people in the house to our right is Dr. Jac Dalton. Jac will invite you over there for a full exam tomorrow, and she's prepared to stay at your side until the baby is born. My mother assures me Jac's the best obstetrician we have. Her mother took care of my mother when she was carrying me, so we'll think of it as a family tradition."

"Thank you for not thinking I'm totally crazy." She turned and kissed Kai as a way of showing how much she cared.

"I am totally crazy—about you," Kai said, smiling. "Let's get dressed before Frankie and Marsha get here and find us naked on the floor."

"We never finished talking about my father."

"Like I said, I talked to my mom. The mind manipulation Edil and the others did as they took me away wasn't a complete hard reset."

She nodded and didn't complain when Kai rubbed her back. "You've said that before, but I'm not totally sure what that means."

"Think about what Pontos did to your father. That day we found those comm boxes attached to your rig and I was close enough to him, all your dad could think about was a wedding between you and Steve. I don't know much about human men, but in most cases, I don't think they sit around all day thinking things like that, so someone manipulated his mind by putting that image on a loop in his head." Kai's hands went under her shorts, making her smile.

"He was pretty persistent when it came to that asshole. Little did he know I had the hots for you."

"I'm sure he was, and I took the chance to break that chain of thought. Fortunately, I didn't break him in the process, and he started to see the truth of what was happening around him. The day I was hurt, Edil did the same thing for everyone except you. I was too imprinted on you to erase me without doing serious damage." Kai kissed the top of her head when she rested it on her shoulder. "The thing is, Edil gave them the choice to forget, or not. And to pick and choose which of those events not to forget."

"Why wouldn't they want to forget?" She unbuttoned her shorts and began to take them off, motioning for Kai to take her shirt off. "What? We have to get ready, you said."

"There was a lot to process, love. An attack team doesn't usually show up and blow stuff—and people—up in your yard. Your dad was present in his surroundings and in his feelings for you and Frankie once I broke through what Pontos had done to him. He let the things in his heart that've always been there flourish and grow like they were supposed to."

"What things?" She stood for a moment to get Kai out of the rest of her clothes and briefly glanced at the bank of french doors on the far wall. "I think it's the room. It's making me hot, and if there's anyone in the yard watching us, they're fired."

"Your dad loves you and Frankie. He's your father, but he's also your dad. I think what's happened is that he saw how much pain you were in when I left, and it touched that paternal part of his heart that craved making it better." Kai lay down so she could straddle her, and she could tell Kai knew what was on her mind.

"My broken heart made him remember?"

"Your broken heart had to have stemmed from something, and he made the conscious choice to remember. He did that because he's your dad, and he loves you."

"Do you think my mom did?" She lifted Kai's hands and placed them on her breasts. "And I'm not sure what the hell is wrong with me, but I'm horny as hell."

"I'm not complaining, and I think your mom was ahead of the curve on this one. Their problem is not having a point of reference they find acceptable, so I talked to my mom about it. She thinks we should be honest with them if they ask. We shouldn't force the truth on them if they're not ready."

"Thank you for doing that, honey. Now can we trade places?" She remembered their first time together in this room and how Kai had awakened her to what she truly desired in this life.

It was hot, passionate, and totally consuming when Kai had pressed their sexes together and made love to her until she'd gone mad. That day she'd thought she'd imagined the connection with Kai was way more than sexual, as if all of who Kai was had opened to her. The bonding had given her a piece of her mate that her body had readily accepted. The crazy thoughts didn't start until a few weeks later when she'd taken that pregnancy test.

"Want to go upstairs?" Kai asked as she got on top. "And this works with you on me if you'd like to try it."

"I figured, but there's something about you pinning me down, making love to me, and showing off these muscles that makes me crazy." She squeezed Kai's biceps and moaned.

"Show me," Kai said, holding herself up.

She reached down and opened her sex, feeling how wet she was. "I want you right here."

Kai gave her what she desired, and she wrapped her legs around Kai and hung on. Sex like this was so intense, and she felt full even if that was impossible. It was good because she could look at Kai's face and see how close to the edge she was and how much she wanted her. They might be married, which gave some people ideas about their sex life now, but this was better than anything she'd ever experienced.

"Yes, baby, don't stop now," she said as Kai started to sweat and pump faster.

"Fuck...ah," Kai said loudly. The muscles in her chest and arms were tight, and Vivien ran her hands up Kai's arms until they were behind her neck.

"Come with me, baby—I can't hold on." She spoke slowly, but the orgasm hit fast and hard. She let the last of the ripples of pleasure go through her before she let her legs fall open as Kai held herself up by one arm. "I'm beginning to think there was something wrong with me until you came along. I've never craved sex this much."

"Trust me, neither have I. It's like you're putting out some kind of pheromone that's making me turn into a horndog." Kai rolled to the side, so most of her weight was off her. "I'm thrilled we're in the same boat."

"It's time to share a shower before our ride gets here. Marsha can go on for days if she finds something to tease you about."

She watched Kai gather all their clothes and offer her a hand up once she'd wadded them all together. "You know I love getting wet with you."

The joy Kai brought into her life was something she wanted to celebrate for the rest of her life. She'd never seen this kind of thing in her parents' relationship, but Kai's parents still appeared wild about each other. It proved that those kinds of relationships did exist. As long as they were together, whatever fears she had flew from her mind.

"Are you ready to get married again in a few weeks?" she asked as Kai adjusted the water temperature in the shower.

"I'd marry you every week if that's what you wanted. That way the honeymoon will always be something to look forward to."

Yes, Kai Merlin was a definite keeper.

CHAPTER SIXTEEN

Daria stood on the deck of the boat her people had guided her to and studied the shoreline. From here it appeared to be lined with some sort of vegetation, and there seemed to be dwellings of some sort in the distance. The dwellings were raised on poles, making her think these people were afraid of the water.

"None of them live in the depths?" she asked the woman who'd picked them up after landing. Some of her people had been in the area for days.

"No, Highness. There is very little under the water, from the small amount of research I've done," the woman said. "If we stay in the shuttles, we should be fine."

"Do you think we've come here to hide like cowards?" She stopped herself from slapping the woman, but her arm tensed. Right now, she needed everyone rallying around one goal more than she needed the gratification of punishing the stupid. "Where's Bella Riverstone?"

"She's close, ma'am. She and her mother have been staying in New Orleans in one of the land dwellings."

She waved the woman away and went back to her study of their surroundings. This place had such a different feel than Atlantis. The water here was brown but didn't have the layer of sludge that'd started to kill their fish. There were also strange trees and flying things Pontos had called *birds*. She'd been studying the reports Pontos had relayed home about the year he'd spent trying to learn what he needed to fit in. It was interesting to see this place in person.

"Highness." The young woman who came aboard bowed deeply and kissed her hand. "I'm so happy you made it safely."

"Bella, you've done well." She stared at this woman who was supposed to become her wife. "Wilma," she said, getting the other woman to straighten up. "You've both done well."

"Thank you, Highness." Bella smiled.

She found her attractive. Bella's light hair and eyes were mesmerizing, and she felt desire flare for the first time in days. Maybe there'd be time later to break Bella in to what she liked. "I'm surprised you've come alone." She was expecting at least a team of warriors to be traveling with them.

"We had no choice but to run when…well…," Wilma said.

Daria tightened her fists and went inside when it started to rain. Bella and Wilma followed her silently. Whatever was about to come out of Wilma's mouth wasn't going to please her, and she didn't need everyone witnessing the consequences of her displeasure. "I'm here to finish what my idiot brother couldn't. If you want to stay in my good graces and not be thrown back at Galen's feet, tell me what happened to Pontos. Then you can tell me when Francesca will arrive with my troops."

Bella and her mother looked at each other before Bella started talking. "Like you ordered, I never told Pontos who Kai was. In his mind, Kai was simply another Palmer employee who'd taken a job on what they call an oil rig. Kai decided to complete her quest to promote fish and land conservation, and to improve the way the people here produce oil."

"What's this *oil production*?" She poured herself some liquor she'd brought from home and took a large gulp.

"Almost every human machine runs on oil, which is converted to fuel. The structures over the water are how they set up a sort of drill to extract it from the earth. At times spills can be damaging to the environment, and Kai took an interest in improving how they extract oil, to make it safer."

Bella was soft-spoken, and she couldn't tell if that was her normal way, or if it was from fear. "She's more of a weakling than a warrior is what you're saying." Daria watched as Bella and her mother exchanged another look. "Stop stalling, and tell me the rest."

"Pontos's plan was to go through a human joining to gain control of one of these oil companies. If he'd been able to control more of the oil market, he would've been able to start to bring the planet under his control." Bella was wringing her hands, and her voice was getting even softer.

"You mentioned his whole plan hinged on this woman who hated him. That sounds like Pontos and his weak mind."

"Vivien Palmer wasn't interested in him. Pontos had been at it for over a year, and it took Kai less than a month to get Vivien to fall in love with her. It infuriated Pontos, but not as much as Mr. Palmer turning against him. It wasn't until the night that Kai led her people to send out a neutralizing pulse that destroyed the comm boxes, as well as any comm units using our frequency, that he figured it out. Pontos knew immediately who Kai was and went to the Palmer house to challenge her."

"Kai Merlin killed Pontos?" That didn't surprise her. Pontos hadn't been much on their training grounds and being killed by a woman must've been humiliating. She came close to laughing.

"Yes, Highness. She killed Pontos, and her team took the few who survived. Where they were taken I don't know, but I haven't been able to make contact with anyone. The priestess Susan gave me the information after Mom and I had to run." Bella lowered her head, but Daria doubted it was because of respect. "Kai was injured in the fight with Pontos but has since recovered. That's all I know because we've lost contact with Susan as well."

"My order was to attack. When I arrived, I was expecting Galen's forces depleted and ready for the killing blow. With my small force and Francesca's people we would end this." She flattened her hand on the table. "Where is Yelter?"

"Francesca's dead," Wilma said, closing her eyes. It was like she was expecting a blow but didn't want to see it coming.

"Francesca's dead," she repeated, clipping the two words. "When did this happen?"

"Three days after our last contact," Bella said. Both mother and daughter appeared frightened, and she did nothing to quell that. "She left with her main team to kill Kai while she was alone on a mission for Palmer. Francesca's plan was to strike and kill Kai so they could return to the capital and start the insurrection. With information she got from me, Francesca went to a remote area miles from here and tried to ambush Kai while she was alone."

"Kai Merlin must be someone to fear. She faced Francesca and her army, and it was Francesca who was killed. Is that your explanation?" She lowered her voice since she was having trouble with the rage that was closing her throat.

"Francesca lied to us, Highness," Wilma said, crying. "She only had a few friends who shared her beliefs about Galen. Francesca told us she'd served in our forces and had a full contingent, but Bella found out that wasn't true. By the time we knew the truth, we were in too deep. We were afraid to share the truth with you."

There was a guard posted inside the door, and Daria moved fast to rip the trident out of his hands. It was sticking out of Wilma's chest before she could shed another tear. The expression of shock was frozen on Wilma's face, and Bella's hands were quickly covered in blood when she went to hold her mother.

"Get her out of my sight, and prepare her for questioning. I'll see what else she's been holding back from me."

The guard bowed and took the sobbing Bella out. She stared at Wilma and wished she could revive her only so she could kill her again. Did these idiots have any clue what a dangerous game they'd been playing? The luckiest one had been Francesca Yelter. Her daughter Bella would pray for a quick death once she was done getting information from her. That the little bitch thought she was somehow related to her was laughable.

Frem entered and waited for her to speak. "Have someone get rid of that." She pointed to Wilma. Frem removed the trident and handed it back to the guard. She watched as two of her soldiers threw Wilma overboard so they could get on their way. To where, she had no idea. There had to be a plan going forward, but she damn well couldn't think of one.

"What happened?" Frem asked. The story she told made Frem pale, and she was grateful at last someone understood the shit they were in.

They were here with a limited force, which would in no way be enough to go against Galen. She'd trusted Bella and her family, and she'd underestimated Kai Merlin. Galen's spawn had not only killed Pontos, but everyone with him. That was not the weakling Bella had described in her messages. It would, though, make the victory of killing the princess that much sweeter. That part of their mission hadn't changed. They'd left their home to make this one theirs, and there was no other option.

"What do you want to do?" Frem asked.

"Find a place to anchor, and send the others to find suitable boats. I need to spend some time with Bella to plan our attack. This planet might be primitive, but it's vast. We need to know where Galen and her people are before we can decide how to kill them." She sat and watched the coastline disappear. "Assemble a team and send them on a hunt. There has to be something edible in all this water."

"As soon as we anchor, I'll make it so." Frem left, and Daria could hear her giving orders.

This might be paradise compared to home, but her father would laugh at the joke of her dying here. If she did, it wouldn't be long before he was back in charge, and if any of her crew survived, there'd be no going back—she'd lied to them about that. Once they'd committed to this voyage, their fate was sealed for good or bad.

The only thing that would make this work and worth it was victory, and she'd kill everything in her path until it was won. It would take more time, but it was the only way forward. That'd been the most valuable lesson Sol had taught her. Kill and don't stop until the world falls at your feet.

❖

Kai stood at the large tank and watched Winston's fish swim through the fake rig legs. She placed her hand on the glass and sent a call out to the small shark she knew was in there. Her first time in the house she'd sensed his despair and tried to comfort him. She smiled when she saw him swim from the top to tap his nose against the glass like an eager puppy.

Vivien came and stood next to her and placed her hand to the side of hers. They both stared at Vivien's hand when the shark moved and repeated the playful actions. It made Kai believe that Vivien had been given some of her own gifts as well as the other changes she'd undergone. Ivan and Ram interacted with Vivien now as they did with her, and her mate had lost her fear of the big sharks. What other gifts would make themselves known over time?

"He's still a little loony, but he doesn't act as crazy," Winston said, tapping the glass. "He's actually started being more sharklike and eats one of his tankmates every so often."

"That's his nature," she said as Vivien took her other hand. One day, maybe she'd get him to let the little shark swim into the wild.

"Your mother's dying to go through her list. You might want to sit with her and whittle it down before Kai runs out of here. She doesn't look like the wedding-planning type." Winston kissed Vivien's cheek and waited expectantly. Vivien hesitated before kissing Kai and joining her mother.

"Thanks for starting the process, sir. Viv was thinking about her to-do list when we went to visit my parents, and it was making her nervous even if she wouldn't admit it. Hopefully Cornelia kept it somewhat small."

"Trust me, she's bitched about how hard it was to cut the guest list, but she said the ones left are necessary. It's your job to convince our girl that is indeed the case." He laughed and slapped her on the back. "How about you and Frankie join me in the study."

"Kai already agreed to marry Viv, Dad. You don't need to coerce her," Frankie said.

They followed Winston into what was obviously his domain in the house, thanks to the teak walls, oil platform pictures, and massive oak desk. He poured drinks for her and Frankie and tapped his finger against his glass as if nervous about something. She liked Winston, and after she'd gotten rid of Pontos's manipulation, he'd become a good father. Frankie and Vivien were certainly starting to enjoy his company again.

"Whatever Vivien and Cornelia decide is okay with me. All I need to know is where to show up." She sat next to Frankie, and they glanced at each other. What was going through Winston's mind made it easy to understand the jumble he was trying to unravel. From his expression, Frankie understood as well. "I love her and our baby, so you have no worries about my commitment. Whatever kind of wedding she wants is what we'll give her."

"I know that about you," Winston said, his voice cracking slightly. Some of his good humor was gone, but he did smile. "I don't worry about Vivien's happiness and future at all."

If she needed proof of Vivien's ability to use her shell, it came when Vivien, her mother, and Marsha walked in. Frankie moved to sit with Marsha, so Vivien could sit next to her. She mentally asked the siblings if they wanted and were ready to start answering questions. Since they both agreed, she planted the permission in Winston's mind to voice what he needed to know.

"Everything ready? You didn't change your mind, did you?" she asked Vivien, making her laugh. She needed to bring the tension down if this was going to work.

"You're stuck with me, honey." Vivien pressed against her and smiled at her parents.

"This is the time to speak up if you're not sure," Cornelia said, pointing at them. "All we want is you two to be happy."

"We are, Mom, and it's okay if you have questions too." Vivien held her hand and seemed to be trying to reassure her parents.

Winston steepled his fingers under his chin and sighed. "You've done a good job for us, Kai, and you brought in a ton of new business. For the life of me, though, I can't remember where you went for all those weeks right before we got the company back. I keep trying, and what pops into my head doesn't make sense. Whatever it is isn't as important as you knowing how miserable my daughter was when you just vanished."

She gave Winston her full attention and felt her shell warm. "You mentioned something before about what happened that day and where Steve had gone. Isn't that where your questions begin?"

"What happened to that obnoxious asshole?" Marsha asked. Her question made everyone in the room glance her way, except Kai, who kept her eyes on Winston.

"Kai, do you want us to step out?" Frankie asked. They'd talked about Vivien's parents but not Marsha being privy to what Kai was going to say.

"You're fine." She finally broke eye contact with Winston and sent Frankie a mental message about Marsha. There was no reason for her not to know, but that decision she'd leave up to him. Letting her stay said more about what kind of commitment he'd want with Marsha than Kai's comfort level in sharing the truth with her.

"Yes," Frankie said out loud, and she almost laughed.

"Yes what?" Marsha asked, taking his glass away from him and finishing his drink.

"Tell me what you remember," Kai asked Winston.

"You were here," Cornelia said, cutting her husband off. "You'd spent the night because you were hurt, but the next morning I woke up when Vivien's truck exploded. It was burning, and Steve was down there screaming something."

"It gets fuzzy after that but there were so many people, and then he hit you with something and you were dead." Winston's eyes got glassy, and he stopped talking to take a sip of his whiskey. "After that you were gone, and it was like you'd never been here. The only thing that proved to me that you weren't someone I'd made up was Vivien. She appeared haunted and sad, and it killed me that I couldn't make it better. It was the kind of sadness you know in your gut someone is going to carry for the rest of their life, and I wanted to hate you for doing that to my child."

"Then after that we got the company back, and we stopped talking about that day," Cornelia finished. "It wasn't because we didn't care about you, but the pieces didn't fit. None of it made sense, and it sure as hell doesn't now. Talking about it wasn't going to make it better because there was no plausible explanation."

Kai composed her thoughts, working out how to say things so they wouldn't be overwhelmed. "Let's start at the beginning. Do you remember the girl Vivien and Frankie told you they'd seen that day at the beach? They told you this wild tale about her and how she swam right toward these huge sharks." She saw she had their attention now, and Vivien moved closer to her, so she put her arms around her. "They were so sad when you didn't believe them, and that started a fissure in your family it took years to undo."

"I wasn't proud we didn't handle that better," Cornelia said. "There was never any proof, but still, we should've handled it better."

"The girl they saw was me."

"You gave them those shells, didn't you?" Cornelia asked. "They've never taken them off."

"The shell Vivien wears is the one she threw into the water because of the story you told, that if you throw a treasure into the sea it will give you something more valuable back. I felt bad for getting them into trouble, so I came back that night. The carvings have... let's say, *enhanced* the bond they share as siblings." She could see her explanation was only confusing them, but Frankie and Viv stayed quiet.

"You made them?" Winston asked. "I'm not sure what in the world you're talking about."

Maybe being more direct was a better option. "Everything Vivien and Frankie told you about that day is true. My true name is Princess Kai Merlin, heir to the throne of Queen Nessa, first queen of Atlantis." She smiled when Marsha let out a laugh.

"Sorry, but that sounds insane," Marsha said. "Like, totally insane."

"It's sounds crazy, but she's telling the truth," Frankie said. "The sharks Viv and I saw that day are still alive and are massive. Their names are Ram and Ivan, and they know to protect because they're spirit bonded with Kai. I was able to join them for a couple days in the kingdom of Atlantis, and it was amazing."

"I'm having…having a hard time processing this," Winston said. He leaned forward with his hands on his knees and took a few deep breaths. "This can't be true."

"Princess Kai?" Cornelia asked, her eyes narrowed. "So you're telling me there's a place under the water, like in the stories?"

"That's what I'm telling you. I know it's a lot to take in, but what you should concentrate on is that I love your daughter and will spend my life devoted to her happiness."

"How in the world can this be true?" Cornelia massaged her temples and couldn't take her eyes off Vivien's abdomen. "That means you're taking Vivien somewhere we can't get to her."

"I'd never do that. My family is important to me, and I know how Vivien feels about you, Winston, and Frankie. You're her family along with you, Marsha, and I'd never keep her from you. As I've told Vivien, I personally have plenty of investments in this area, so we'll be here more often than you think." She tried to project calm, but every one of the three who were hearing this for the first time appeared ready to run from the room to keep from hearing anything else. "Vivien was going to talk to you about her transition as far as Palmer Oil, but my devotion to her and our child is everything to me."

"Marsha's right," Winston said. "This is absurd."

Now that the door had been opened, she needed them to walk through it. Otherwise there was the possibility of a rift they wouldn't be able to repair. Intuitively, she held Vivien's hand and offered Frankie her other hand.

The shell at her throat warmed, and she felt Vivien and Frankie tighten their hold on her. She projected the truth of their history, so Cornelia, Winston, and Marsha could see what the truth was, all that had happened, in a quick montage of memories, from the time Kai had come back into Viv's life. She projected images of their home and kingdom, and they saw it like they were gliding over it, before she cut the link.

"Oh my God," Winston said when they were done. "You're completely serious."

"Atlantis." Cornelia said it almost like a prayer.

Winston shook his head, leaning forward like he was trying to recapture what he'd seen. "People who live underwater." He turned toward Kai and really looked at her, as though trying to see how she was different.

"I'd never joke about something like this." She sat and gave them a minute to come to grips with what they'd learned.

"Frankie," Cornelia said, walking to her son and kneeling next to the sofa where he sat. "You can walk."

The one thing about opening their eyes to the truth of everything, was it opened their eyes to the truth of *everything*. They now remembered the world as it had been and saw what it was now. Marsha was also staring at Frankie's legs and shaking her head. When they started their life together, she doubted Vivien thought her future would include things like this. Had she fallen in love with someone from her world, there'd be none of this drama. "If I'd fallen in love with someone else, I also wouldn't be carrying their baby, and Frankie wouldn't have gotten his dream," Vivien said. Viv pulled her head down and kissed her until her father cleared his throat. "You keep telling me you love me, so believe me when I tell you I feel the same."

"This is something, and it's really unbelievable. My God, the mistakes we've made, starting with the day Viv and Frankie first saw you. I've been such an idiot, and I compounded it with Steve. It would've been easier for you to tell us the truth, and it's eye-opening that you were able to shield us from it," Winston said. He stared at Frankie. "It's like a miracle."

"It's time to stop blaming yourself for something that was really on me," Kai said. "My mistake was popping out of the water, but I'd do it again and again given the opportunity because it led me back to

Vivien." Kai smiled and tried to ease his guilt. "As for Frankie, he wasn't less of a man in the chair, but it was his dream to know the sensation of running. We were able to give that to him."

"It really is a miracle, and you're right. Frankie is a better man than I am."

"I can never fully repay Kai and her people for what they've done for me, and I was able to walk with Viv when she and Kai joined in Atlantis. But hey, for the wedding up here, that's your job, Dad."

"Please accept my apology about that," Kai said. "We should've had this conversation sooner, so you and Cornelia could've attended. I can tell you my mothers will be here for the ceremony you're planning." She reached into her pocket and took out the three shells she'd brought with her. "I talked with my mother Galen, and she wanted me to tell you the truth because you deserved it. The other reason is that what happened with Pontos, or Steve as you know him, might not be over. You have to be aware of the danger you might be in until we figure out what that threat is."

Winston still looked bemused, and she waited for Cornelia to move back to her seat.

"I remember looking out there and thinking Steve had lost his mind. The thing he shot at Vivien's truck was something I couldn't wrap my head around, and then he did the same to you. It killed something in me when I thought you were dead because I knew how my child felt about you." Winston sounded so sincere, and she could see what kind of father he would've been without her intervention in their lives.

"Honey, come on, stop already," Vivien said.

"What are you talking about?" Marsha asked, appearing more than bewildered.

Vivien explained how she and Frankie had learned by trial and error how to use the shells and how that had changed once Kai came back and taught them how to channel the power of the bond. Marsha listened, glancing at Frankie every so often as Vivien explained how much better that connection became when you found your mate. She could read Kai's thoughts as easily as having her own.

There was a long moment of silence as all they'd said settled in. There would be a million questions, and Kai was happy to answer them. But she'd provide information as it was asked for, rather than dumping it on them all at once.

"What happens now?" Cornelia asked.

"We're trying to pinpoint the threat, but what'll happen next is our ceremony here in New Orleans. I'll have to ask one thing, though," she said, showing them the shells she'd taken from her pocket. "This isn't about not trusting you, but we need to take some steps to keep who we are a secret from the world."

"And those will do that?" Marsha asked, looking at the shells with some suspicion.

"They'll do more than that." She looked into Marsha's eyes and put a few things into her head about her childhood. "You can learn to do that if you allow me to give you this gift."

"What else will it do?" Winston asked.

"It will shield you from saying something you shouldn't. Like the shell around Frankie's neck shielded you from the truth of his healing. He's still the same man, only now he can walk. It hasn't changed who he is, but the legs would be hard to explain to anyone who's not cognizant of our advances." She waited to hear if they'd agree. If not, she'd have to leave it to Oba and her team to do something that would prevent them from saying something that would put them all in danger.

"Will we be able to communicate with you like that?" Marsha pointed at Kai's head, then hers. "Will I be able to hear Frankie's thoughts?"

"With practice you will, and I'm thinking Frankie will help you with that. Each shell is unique to the person, and it holds different gifts. How you expand those gifts is up to you. These will be your connection to Vivien, Frankie, and myself." She closed her fists over the shells and felt their mental agreement. "If you need us, all you need to do is send out a call with your mind. I promise you, we'll hear it."

"All we want is for Vivien and Frankie to have a good life. This isn't exactly what I had in mind," Winston said and laughed. "Not one thing in my life would've made me believe something like this existed. I've given you my blessing, though, and I'm not going back on that."

She nodded, handed Frankie a shell, then opened her hand so Vivien could cover the other two with her hand. Frankie held her other hand and Marsha's shell. They'd reviewed how to carve the shells, and this time it was important to have Vivien and Frankie put themselves into the lines because this was their family. Like their shells, the three they were making would have to have a strong connection with the siblings for them to truly work.

They spoke the old words, and their connection, the golden lines, was again visible from shell to shell. When they were done, Frankie threaded a leather strap through each shell, knowing instinctively which one belong to whom.

"Don't ever take them off," Vivien said.

"Thank you for sharing all this with us," Cornelia said, holding her shell in a closed fist.

"I hope you know how sorry I am I wasn't able to share this sooner. My vow to my sisters, as well as to my mothers, is important to me." She was prepared to answer all the questions they had, but Winston shook his head, almost as if he'd read her mind.

"I'm just glad I wasn't crazy. Let's eat, and you guys can go home so we can all think about all this. Tomorrow, we'll get through the wedding list. When are your parents getting here?" he asked. He looked at Cornelia and shook his head. "The queens of Atlantis."

"They'll arrive a few days before the ceremony, and we'll put them up. I'm sure, though, that they'll enjoy spending some time with you, so maybe I can put together a family dinner."

"Let me do that," Cornelia said. "Our place is bigger, and they can bring whoever they like. We'll be family, after all." She took a deep breath. "I assume they can be here, like you? On land?"

"Thank you for asking. Yes, we can all be on land without an issue." She felt Cornelia's relief. "My aunt and grandmothers are also coming, so I'm sure they'd love to join in. Thank you."

They sat down to dinner, and the only one who seemed a bit pissed was Marsha. It was like she couldn't accept she'd been cut off from the truth, and it made her angry. But her anger seemed to be directed at Kai, not Vivien or Frankie. Once they were done, she invited Marsha outside to sit on the side of the fountain where they'd first met.

"What's the problem?" She put her hand up and shook her head. "It'll be easier if you cut the shit and tell me."

Marsha crossed her legs at the ankles and frowned. "You know how I feel about Vivien, and I'm in love with Frankie. Why in the world would you not tell me all this, especially if you've put them in danger? If you knew that you were putting them in that position, why'd you come back?" Marsha was nearly yelling, but Kai didn't stop her. What

Marsha was going through wasn't resentment against her, so much as her worry for the two people she loved.

"You're right, and that's why we've given you the shells and let you in on a secret that has kept my people safe for thousands of years. You all need to know there's a threat, and now that you do, we can protect each other." Kai smiled when Marsha looked a little mollified. "I came back because I fell in love with your best friend. Doing that wasn't what anyone wished for me, but my heart chose her. She's my match, and because I love her and she loves me, we bonded and created a life that'll be the beginning of our family." She spoke from the heart and sent Vivien a message not to come out as she was getting ready to do. "If I thought for one minute leaving was what was best for Vivien, I would've, and she'd have never seen me again. The heart is a funny thing, though, right? We wanted a life together, and I couldn't deny either of us when it came to that."

"We've known each other since preschool. She should've told me."

"It's a few months too late, but we did. If you want to be mad at someone, pick me. Viv doesn't need the stress."

"And have her hand me my ass for getting mad at you? I don't think so. Viv loves you, and I'm glad she does. It's something that she's been looking for proof of all her life, and I think it's because of that afternoon she saw you as a girl. It changed something in her, and her best explanation is she'd found the one person who saw her for who she is. I believe with everything I am that's true, and I'm glad you're here. You'd better do everything you can to keep her safe. My godchild deserves to know both of you." Marsha poked her in the chest and wasn't gentle about it.

"You can count on it. I love Viv more than life, and I'm going to give her everything I can to make her happy." She smiled when Vivien ignored her and came out. "She's lucky to have a friend like you."

"That's what people always say when they're trying to calm someone down. I hate that, and if you step out of line, or something happens to Vivien, I'm going to kick your ass."

"There's the Marsha I know and love." Vivien walked up behind her friend and put her arms around her. "The same threat goes to you, sunshine. If you hurt Frankie, you won't find a place to hide I won't find you. I'm just glad that my two favorite people ended up together."

"I'm glad too. Frankie might be a few years younger than us, but until recently I never knew he realized I was alive. He's the most handsome thing I've ever seen, and he has a heart to match. We're both lucky."

"He didn't want to burden you before, but he's always been in love with you. Now take him home and tuck him in, so Kai can do the same with me. Remember not to take this off," Vivien said, tapping the shell.

"Got it, and you'd better talk Frankie into getting on one knee. After all this I'd better get a ring out of it. I've been waiting for years for him to get with the program."

Kai had to laugh and thought about Marsha meeting her family. Her aunt Clarice was going to love her. "Good night, and we'll see you tomorrow."

They went back in for a minute before the driver took them back to Vivien's. There wasn't a lot of talking as they undressed each other and went to bed. She had to admit she felt better after sharing who she was with Vivien's family. It had seemed disingenuous to marry Viv without them knowing the truth.

"Let's hope that's all the crap we have to go through until we go home," Vivien said as she pressed up against Kai.

"They'll be fine. I think people do better when there are no secrets. When you try to hide something, it only gets more complicated. It's not like we could say we were moving to Florida or something when we had to go home."

"What happens if we have another battle like the one Pontos brought to my father's door?"

"I've been thinking about that, and I don't really have an answer. If Sol sends someone else, we'll face them, and I'll do my best to keep it as controlled as possible. If we lose control, it'll have far worse consequences than people knowing we're here." She kissed Vivien, then pressed up behind her and put an arm around her. "Losing control means we might be losing the fight, and humans will have a lot more to worry about than the truth that we've been here for centuries."

"Do you think they'll be okay with what we said tonight?" Vivien sounded tired.

"It's going to be fine. Go to sleep, baby, and trust that my moms aren't going to stop until they have answers."

She closed her eyes and decided to wait to call her mom in the morning. The sense that something was coming to hurt them was growing. The visions alluded to it, and she had to have faith in who she was and her ability to protect her nation. Her prayer to the goddess was simply that her trident should be true if it came to that. For now she joined Vivien's dreams through their link and enjoyed the calm waters they were swimming through.

CHAPTER SEVENTEEN

B ella moaned and hung her head as Daria stood in front of her with the small whip she'd been using for hours. Daria didn't doubt Bella would've told her everything she needed to know without the torture, but she wasn't giving her that out. Pain was always an excellent motivator, and she'd allowed some of her team leaders to watch. It was good that they understood how she operated.

"So, tell me again."

Bella took a shuddering breath. "Vivien Palmer lives in New Orleans. It's north of here, and that's where her family is as well. If Kai is still with her, that's where you'll find her. Let me live, and I'll show you. Grabbing anyone in the Palmer family will draw Kai out if she's not there."

She drew her arm back and brought the whip across Bella's chest. "Do you see yourself in a position to give me orders? If I ask you where she is, you're going to tell me. What I do with the information you give me is not up to you." She hit her three more times and had to lift her head up by her hair to deliver a final slap. "Tell me."

In a broken voice, Bella gave her the coordinates and an explanation of how they had to travel to get there. She hung by her restraints when Daria was done with her, and she signaled someone to take Bella down. "Clean her up and feed her. If she thinks this is over, she's wrong."

She went to get something to eat. The fish here tasted so much better than on Atlantis, and she was enjoying the meals. It was an inane thing to think about, but she was going insane thinking of only the coming battle.

"Find out where this place is that Bella mentioned," she said to Frem. The meal was laid out, and Frem stood to serve her.

"It's not far from here, and if you want to go, we can start tonight."

"Set a course, and make sure our people know to keep Bella alive. It sounds like she ran with a few other people, and it's time to make contact with them. We can use the numbers, even if the force is minuscule. We'll also need them to fit in. I don't want to arouse suspicion until it's necessary."

She finished eating and went out on the deck. There were some boats in the distance with nets attached to their sides, and she dismissed them as simple fishermen. It would be easier to hunt in the water and drive the fish into their nets, but these weren't an evolved people. Right now, simple sounded good. If she'd been born to a fisherman or a servant, her life would've been shit, but at least it would've been cut-and-dried. She'd have gotten up every day and done the same damn thing until someone like her came along and killed her. It was hard to remember all the people her father had killed for some small perceived slight. Big fish ate little fish. It was the way of things.

She'd take over this planet or die trying. She didn't have enough backing, and while the humans weren't advanced, Pontos had said they had some military capability. Faced with that and having to defeat Galen and her people, she felt as small as one of those pathetic servants who waited for the day her father would put them out of their misery.

That was the last thing she could admit to anyone, especially Frem, but the old fears still crowded her head like eels. It was either win or run, but where was there to run? She went back in, then into the room where they'd put Bella. The room was quiet except for the whimpers Bella still had the strength to make. One of her eyes was swollen shut, and the shirt they'd put on her was wet with blood from the cuts the whip had made.

"Tell me about her." Her voice made Bella flinch.

"About who?" Bella didn't face her and didn't add her title. It was an outright provocation to kill her, she was sure, but Bella wasn't going to get that lucky.

"One of the things my father taught me…" she said, pressing her finger into one of the cuts. Bella tried to move away, which made her press harder. "Was that if you were patient, you could do this for months, and the person wouldn't die. They would wish for death, but death could be put off if the person was young and healthy. You're young, and you seem healthy enough, so release is a long way off."

"I'm sorry," Bella said, breathing hard.

"Are you?" She laughed and sat on the bed, lifting her hand off Bella. "The other hard truth is when someone displeased him, my father would keep them alive and slowly strip away their pride. That led to begging. That never worked, so eventually the person started to hate my father, and in a strange way it made them hang on longer." She laughed again at the thought of some of those prisoners, who seemed to cling to life only to hurl curses at her father while he skinned them. "I promise you, Bella, that you'll come to hate me, and you'll cling to life so you can curse my name."

"All I wanted was to please you. Francesca wasn't my mother, so I didn't know much about her when my mother Wilma joined with her. You didn't even ask my mother before you drove a trident through her." Bella cried fresh tears, but Daria wasn't moved.

"Tell me about Kai."

"Kai is Galen's only heir—"

"Only heir? Why?" That was interesting.

"The queen had complications after Kai's birth. Our doctors are good at their jobs, but they couldn't stop or reverse what had happened, so Kai is an only child. She's been trained by the nation's best warriors, and she's good with a trident, but she's also highly intelligent." Bella wiped her face and stared up at her. "She is beloved by my sisters, and from what the priestess Susan said, she drove a trident through Pontos's chest."

That really made her laugh. "Are you trying to provoke me?"

"I'm doing what you asked. Princess Kai is the daughter of Consort Hadley. Before her marriage to Queen Galen, Hadley was on track to be the leader of the queen's guard and leader of the queen's forces. She and her friends poured everything they know into Kai, and my sisters know she'll be the best protector of the realm they could hope for."

Bella's regretful tone was irritating. "How did you get out? Or a better question is why did you get out? If Galen and her spawn are such wonders, why leave?" She already knew the answer, but she wanted Bella to admit it.

"Francesca came into our lives, and she hated Galen and Hadley because she thought them to be weak. She was the one who found the connection between our families and told me I'd be a fool not to pursue it." Bella cried as if the story of her life was too much to handle. "I found out later, when Francesca's friend came to tell us she'd been killed, that she'd previously been imprisoned for theft. Francesca had been turned down from military service, even though they have no need for soldiers, and didn't want to work at anything else. She was bitter and wanted revenge for the perceived slight." She choked on a sob. "But I believed her. That the royal family weren't doing the best for our people."

"And that's who you sold me on? What a fool you must think I am. How did you get out?"

"We took a shuttle. Then had to swim the rest of the way. Someone must've figured out the shuttle was missing, and they can be controlled from the palace. We got out just in time before it was destroyed remotely."

"What are the coordinates to the city?" She doubted Bella had that in her head, but it was worth asking.

"I have them at our place in New Orleans. We went there thinking it was the last place anyone would think to look for us. If we were caught, we would've told Queen Galen we were scared of being blamed for the attempt on Kai's life." Bella closed her eyes and appeared to be finding a comfortable spot on the cot.

"We're traveling there now, and you're going to guide us. Try anything, and I'll make you regret your entire life."

One of their medics came in and closed all of Bella's lacerations and gave her something for the pain. Daria stood outside as they moved up the river, and she got her first glimpse of human civilization. The dwellings were close to the water, but they seemed constructed to avoid the water. It was a strange notion. Their vehicles also appeared clunky and slow, confirming what Pontos said about their backwardness. These humans seemed used to hard labor, and that would serve her well once her battles were done. They could build the world she wanted, and they'd come to worship her after they'd come to fear her.

The sun had completely set by the time they reached the city, and her navigator found a place to tie up while they searched for a vehicle to take to Bella's dwelling. As they neared the city, things started to change.

As a man drove them along wide streets, one thing she noticed was how loud the city was. It was late, but there were people in the streets playing music, drinking, dancing, and laughing. Perhaps they had arrived on some special celebration day, but she'd ask about that later.

Some of her people followed behind, and Bella assured her she had enough to pay the drivers. They had to climb stairs to reach Bella's place, and it was tiny compared to the palace back on Atlantis. Bella kept it neat, so she sat and snapped her fingers. Bella gave her the folder where she had all the information.

It took Daria until the sun rose before she finished reading, and she had a plan. "Go back to the ship and tell the warriors to wait. Attack and kill anyone who comes near them, but do not let them leave the ship. I'll send Frem when I'm ready for you," she told the man before he ran out the door.

"What are you thinking?" Frem asked.

"When you slay a dragon, you rip out its heart and show it to your enemies. Once they see it, they'll drop to their knees and cower in fear." She tied Bella's hands behind her back and placed her in a small windowless room that was full of clothes. She went without struggle and seemed to slide into the pile of clothes gratefully. Daria closed the door on her. "I plan to rip Kai Merlin's heart out and show it to her mother and her people."

"Galen will surrender?" Frem pointed to the information Bella provided before following her to the bedroom and removing her clothes.

"I don't really care what Galen does. What I want is for the sisterhood she has in the depths to see it. If their mighty protector Kai can be taken down this easily, then the rest have no chance." All she had to do was bide her time and wait for Kai to show herself. She doubted she'd be armed in this city, and she'd exploit that with an ambush. Winning when the odds were so heavily not in her favor would make her legendary, and that would fill all those empty places in her soul.

❖

"I'd take you out for a last night of fun before you become an old married woman, but you're already an old married woman," Marsha said as they sat in Vivien's backyard. Marsha drank wine, while she stuck to juice. It had been a quiet couple of weeks, and Vivien was starting to let some of her anxiousness go when their lives seemed almost ordinary. Over the weeks, they'd had conversations with Galen and Hadley, as well as Laud, to put plans in place for when the attack came their way. But the plans were only theoretical, since they couldn't be sure where the attack would come from. Kai felt that as warriors they'd come for her head-on, and so the plans were laid accordingly.

"Don't knock it until you try it, poopsie. Kai is many things, but boring is not one of them." She smiled at the thought of their sex life lately. If anything, it'd become more intense, and they had tried pretty much every surface in the house.

"All right already, I get it. Don't rub it in."

"I'm sure you have nothing to complain about in that department. To tell you the truth, I'm shocked you're not running away from Frankie to get a break." She laughed and tapped her glass against Marsha's.

"What do you mean?" Marsha seemed to idly play with the shell around her neck as if not realizing she was doing it.

"He's been alone for a long time because of some noble self-sacrifice, and now he finally has the girl he's dreamed about since he was old enough to realize he was crazy about you. I'd think he'd be all over you." All those times they'd spent time together, the three of them, she remembered getting glimpses of where Frankie's thoughts were when he looked at Marsha. It was love before Frankie fully realized his feelings.

"I'm only kidding you, and you know me. I haven't exactly been a nun all these years, and I've been so tired of that for so long because I thought love wasn't real." Marsha shook her head and sighed. "I look at my parents and wonder, why the hell even try. They're still married, but they don't like each other at all and have their own lives. It was my choice to be single because I asked myself why be married if all I was going to do was what I was already doing."

"I know, I didn't date as much as you did, but I still wondered if I'd find someone. We could've always married each other and not had sex," she said, laughing.

"Dream on. I've never been interested in women, but after getting an eyeful of Kai, I would've made an exception." Marsha smiled at her sweetly, making her laugh.

"She's hot, so yay, me."

"As for Frankie, I am a little tired these days but pleasantly so. He's like a rabbit, but he must've read some books because I'm seeing stars on a regular basis. Don't tell him I said that. He's hot, but he's kind of shy."

"Your secret is safe with me." They sipped their drinks while waiting for their partners, who were at the Palmer offices going over some new projects her father was interested in pursuing, and he wanted both Frankie's and Kai's input. "Do we have anything left to do for this weekend? If I miss anything on my mother's to-do list, she'll put a hit out on me."

"Everything is done, so we can relax and drink wine. Well, I can drink wine, and you can relax. When do Kai's parents get here?"

"Tomorrow, along with the rest of her family. They're really nice, and I'm sure all the wedding guests will wonder about the large number of women on Kai's side, but that can't be helped." They hadn't known each other long, but she'd come to love Kai's parents as well as grandparents. Hopefully the upcoming second wedding would proceed without any humans voicing something that would mortify her—not that she didn't think Galen and the others could handle it, but she wanted them to feel welcome.

She heard the back door open and smiled when she felt Kai kiss the top of her head. "Are we taking over the oil industry?" she asked when Kai sat at the end of her chaise.

"Frankie is, and your father is thinking of cutting back. He said he's taking your mother to Tahiti to work on her tan." Kai wiggled her eyebrows and laughed.

"Did he have a fever?" she asked, reaching for Kai's hand.

"No, and it shocked the hell out of me," Frankie said, kissing Marsha when she stood up. He sat and Marsha sat on his lap.

"Tell him if he thinks you're going to spend as much time at the office as he does, to think again. Your job is to keep me satisfied, and I'd hate to drop by the office just so I can strip you naked. The secretaries will never get over it," Marsha said, getting Frankie to blush. "See, I told you he was kind of shy."

"Please tell me you're not telling my sister about our sex lives." Frankie sounded mortified.

"More like I was bragging about our sex lives, baby, so relax. And

I wasn't kidding about what I said. Think about what your secretary would think when I'm screaming your name while riding you like a bronco."

"She's, like, eighty, so I'm sure it'd give her something to think about," Kai said.

"Do you two have to go back?" she asked, pulling Kai toward her.

"Nope, so we're taking you two to lunch and then I have to come back and go through some stuff with the guards. I was reminded that I haven't worked out in days."

"I wouldn't say that," she whispered into Kai's ear.

They ate close by and came home to find Edil and Isla waiting in the backyard to train with Kai. The way they went after each other with the tridents made her think they'd have to run to the emergency room after they were done, but she enjoyed the way Kai moved. Kai was strong, but when she worked out like this, her muscles were really visible. She laughed when she saw Marsha's expression as one of the other guards taught Frankie the beginning steps of using the traditional weapon.

"Gives you a whole new meaning of hot, doesn't it?" she asked, and Marsha nodded.

"Excuse me, Highness," one of the women in the team said with a slight bow. "There's a message for you."

"Thanks, Cori." She took the folded note and read the message from Etta Sinclair.

The Tulane professor had been a good friend for years and had never given a clue that she was actually from Atlantis. Etta had helped her with the maps she'd found that had led to some of her finds. Etta was the realm's gatekeeper when it came to piecemealing information to humans, in order to keep Atlantis secret. Vivien could've dived for years and would've found only what Etta wanted her to find. It was easy to understand why Etta did as she did, but it tweaked her just a little.

"Anything important?" Marsha asked.

She read the short note and smiled. Etta had found another clue in Kai's search for the shipwreck she'd been after for years. Kai had actually brought her along on one of her dives when they'd first met, and while they didn't find anything that would've helped her with the find, she did experience the joys of skinny-dipping.

"Etta found something Kai's been looking for. Want to come with me to pick it up while our warriors finish playing?" She stood and stretched, feeling lethargic. The morning sickness had eased, but the need for a nap a zillion times a day was taking its place.

"Sure, I've heard you talk about this professor, so I'd like to meet her. Do you think there are any other of Kai's people in town we had no idea about?" Marsha waved to Frankie and followed her inside. Viv had told Cori to let Kai know where they'd gone if they finished ahead of schedule. "Given how you've described the capital, why would any of them want to live in this mess and have regular jobs?"

"I guess I'll eventually figure out all their secrets, but I'm glad to find Etta is part of the realm." She grabbed her keys. "We've been focused on other things."

"Is it weird to have people call you *Highness*?"

"It's totally surreal, but Kai assures me I'll get used to it." They went out, and she got in the truck Kai had gotten her as an apology for the last one she'd owned, which had been blown up. "When I'm with Kai, we're like any other couple, but in the back of my mind I'm aware of what and who Kai is, and that there are conflicts we may have to face. I'm glad she's going to be the next queen, and I'm glad she's introduced me to people like Etta."

"You've known Etta for years." Marsha threw her purse in the back seat. "We've got a crowd behind us."

"I've never been a royal family watcher, but I have sympathy for them now that we've always got guards with us. And I have known Etta for years, but it turns out I didn't really *know* Etta." It didn't take long to reach the campus since her house was so close. Etta's office was toward the back, and she walked with her arm threaded through Marsha's, trying to ignore the plainclothes guards forming a perimeter around them. This had been their experience during every outing, and she doubted she'd ever be able to sneak out again.

They entered the building and walked past a few students as they took the steps to the second floor. Etta was a popular professor and usually had a line of them coming and going from her office like a paper tornado. When she knocked and entered, Etta stood and bowed, smiling as if glad to see her.

"Highness, to what do I owe this special visit?" Etta came closer and hugged her before she had a chance to introduce Marsha.

"Please, Etta, we've known each other too long. It's still Vivien to you." She pointed to the one chair in the place, and Marsha sat to one side of it so they could share. "And I'm here to pick up the information you have for Kai."

Etta's eyebrows came together in a perfect expression of confusion. "I'm sorry. What information?" The protocol was for Etta to stay on her feet until Vivien sat down, so she joined Marsha in the wingback chair. "I just recently returned from attending your joining and visiting my parents in Atlantis, so I haven't put anything together for the princess."

"I received a message less than an hour ago from you about the *Valhalla Sun*. We haven't done any more investigation of the last spot you sent Kai, but I'm hoping once we have a little time we could do that as part of our honeymoon." A sense of foreboding caused a shiver of worry to flutter through her.

"Please believe me, I wish I did have something else, but I think there's been some kind of mistake. I'd say it's someone's idea of a joke, but it's not funny." Etta lost her smile and tapped nervously on the desk. "It was signed by me?"

"I'm not sure—" The words died in her throat when she heard the noise from outside. It sounded like a riot, and one look out the window confirmed there was trouble—a crowd of students ran toward the courtyard outside Etta's office.

Her fear rose when the lights went out, and Etta put out a call for help on the phone that connected her to Edil and her forces. Hopefully the call was to Kai or someone else who'd be able to handle this better than campus police. The vision she'd had on her wedding night came back in nauseating clarity, and she gripped Marsha's hand as they stood in the dark. If this was it, Kai was nowhere close enough for her to be able to grab her hand. She could taste the bile at the back of her throat at the truth of never seeing Kai again. Never being able to say good-bye would be cruel to both of them, but especially to Kai.

"What's going on?" Marsha asked, standing next to her at the window.

Vivien watched as a woman leading a group—their distinctive dress made it clear they were together—made her way inside the building, and Vivien was desperate to come up with a place to hide. "Honey," she said loudly into the phone, not yet trusting her shell to communicate from this distance. She had a few minutes, tops.

"Someone overpowered our guard and is coming up to Etta's office now." The shell was almost uncomfortably hot against her skin, and her vision dimmed.

"Viv, do you have time to head away from Etta?" Kai was panting and sounded cornered.

"I don't think—" She stopped when the door splintered inward. A tall blonde with dark eyes stared at her with a feral grin. "Kai, find me."

It was the last thing she said before the phone was wrenched from her hand and thrown against the wall. Whoever this was held a trident, but unlike Kai's, this one was golden and had a visible current running across the tines. It was like the one Pontos had, and that current had shot the kind of pulse that had almost killed Kai.

"Princess Vivien Palmer," the woman said. It wasn't a question, and she spoke with the authority of being right. "Take her. Take all of them."

She was in the iron grip of two men as soon as the order was given, and they dragged her away from Marsha. A small woman, her face a roadmap of bruises and small cuts, stood outside the door, and Vivien wondered if that was going to be her fate. The woman stared at her with an almost sympathetic apologetic expression, and Vivien wanted to know who she was. Had the bruising come from someone trying to extract the information that led them here?

"What do you want?" They were outside, and she could see the campus police running toward them. She tried to call out to them to stop, but a pulse from the trident cut a beach ball–sized hole right through the center of the two lead cops' chests. The gruesome sight made the others pull up and take cover.

"Stop it," she yelled. "They can't hurt you."

"Your days of giving commands are over, Princess." She, Marsha, and Etta were shoved into the back of a van, and it started moving almost immediately. From what she could see, the battered woman was in the driver's seat, and the one in charge was in the middle seat looking back at them.

"Who are you?" She studied the woman's face, amazed how much she resembled Pontos. If she was related, the implications weren't good.

"Queen Daria Oberon. You're the woman my idiot brother chased for so long. I thought he was pathetic until now. You look like someone he'd lose his head over."

Vivien felt the warmth of Marsha's hand when she reached for hers, and she threaded their fingers together. "What do you want? Kai's already beaten your family once. Why take the chance of it happening again?"

"I'm not my brother, Princess, and stop thinking I'm taking you somewhere she'll never be able to find you. I want her to show herself. Once I kill her, Galen will have no choice but to surrender her throne to me, and we'll finally take our rightful place here." Daria's laugh was grating, so the family resemblance went further than looks. Steve always had the same effect on her.

"Your rightful place? You have no place here."

"Say anything like that again, and I'll make sure Kai's last glimpse of you will sicken her." Daria came over to the seat and grabbed her face in a tight grip.

She closed her eyes and sent her thoughts out to Kai. She wanted Kai to remember, above anything else, *I'll always love you. I'm sorry if I fail you and our child.* The possibility of losing her baby brought tears to her eyes. She loved the little girl as much as she did Kai. How could she be so close to happiness, only to lose everything?

CHAPTER EIGHTEEN

W hat the fuck?" Kai yelled as she drove her trident into the ground. "What's going on?" she asked Edil. The call from Vivien was short, and she sounded terrified.

"One of the guards called before we lost communications and said a force overtook them, and they were headed to Etta's office." Edil was running to keep up with Kai and Frankie. "She didn't know who they were, but she thought she recognized Bella Riverstone, who appeared beaten and bruised."

"Whoever Bella's working for is lucky if that's all I do to her if something happens to Vivien and the others. The only way she knew about Etta and got Vivien there was if Bella told them." Her heart felt as if it was trying to make its way out of her chest. She'd feared very few things in her life, but losing Vivien was about to send her into a black hole of rage.

"This isn't the time to lose your head, sister," Frankie said as they piled into his SUV. "She's going to need you to keep calm to get her back."

"She's going to need me to help her keep her head, don't you mean? I'm sure whoever has her is going to kill her, if only to make me suffer." Yelling at Frankie wasn't going to help anything, and she took a deep breath. "Sorry, it was my plan all along to draw Bella and whoever is with her out, but putting Viv in the middle of it damn well didn't figure in. It was a stupid oversight, and I can't believe I didn't consider it. Don't worry, I remember what needs to be done to win."

"No one knows better than me how much you love my sister, so both those things are true. I watched you almost sacrifice yourself to keep us safe when you faced Pontos. This time you'd better show no mercy and finish this. Vivien's expecting no less." Frankie placed his hand around her bicep, and she nodded before parking close to Etta's office.

Agents and officers from a multitude of different law enforcement agencies assembled in front of the building, and her people got out and closed their eyes, working as one. What needed doing didn't require a lot of input from her. It took her team a few minutes, but all the humans who'd been running around trying to figure out what had killed the two men on the ground stopped and took a deep breath. Confusing them was the only way for her to get in and find who the hell had done this. She kept trying to reach Viv through their connection, but she couldn't sense or hear her. More than anything else, that made her panic.

She ran up to Etta's office and noticed Vivien's broken phone on the floor. The office was messy, but that was Etta's state of being. The only thing out of the ordinary was the small medallion close to the only available visitor chair. She stared at it, her stomach turning, and Frankie pressed against her shoulder to get a glimpse of it.

"What is that?" Frankie pointed to the design on one side.

"The Oberon royal crest. This is from planet Atlantis." She came close to sitting down when her legs got weak. Bella and her mother weren't the only ones who'd followed Francesca Yelter, but their forces on Earth weren't large enough to overthrow her mother. The coin meant forces had again arrived from planet Atlantis without their knowledge. Now that they had Vivien and figured out she was carrying the heir to their throne, this problem would have no easy solution. All her planning might be for nothing if she couldn't fight the battle she wanted because it would endanger Vivien. "Who the hell left this?" In her gut she knew they hadn't dropped it by accident. The clue was too deliberate to be a mistake.

Kai's phone rang, and she almost ripped her pocket to get to it. "Mom," she said to her mother Galen. They were on their way and were probably close by now. She should've called and warned them off, but her only thought had been getting to Vivien.

"What's happening? We talked to your guards, but they didn't have a lot of information yet."

"Someone took Vivien and left a mess behind. If you want to see what a trident will do to the average human, I'll send you pictures. They also left an Atlantean coin behind." She handed the coin to Frankie and motioned for everyone to move out. The mind warp they had in place downstairs wouldn't last forever, and the coin was the only thing meant to be left behind. She was sure of that.

"Okay, we're an hour from our landing spot," her mom Hadley said. "Send a helicopter, and we'll make arrangements to muster the rest of the troops we have in the area. I'm not deploying anyone until I have a place to aim them."

"Isla can take care of that. I'll call as soon as we get back to the house. We'll talk then because the plan we had in place won't work now." They went out, and the bodies had been loaded into their vehicles. Their ashes would be sent to their families, but any trace of what had happened to them had been erased with one small pulse that had wiped every cell phone and camera within a two-mile radius. "Be careful."

The crowd was still around, so she took the moment to get a better look to see if anyone stood out. Two women with military postures dressed identically at the back of the thickest group of spectators caught her eye. "Frankie, Edil," she said softly. "There."

She started running right after speaking and was glad that they kept up. The taller of the two women was shaking her head as if trying to clear it, and her eyes went wide when she noticed Kai almost on her. It was easy to see she was trying to regain control of her body and run, but it was too late when Kai clubbed her over the head with her closed trident, before reversing course and hitting the other one, knocking them both out.

"Load them and bring them back to the house we have set up for the guards. I don't want them in Viv's place."

They were headed back to Vivien's vehicle when she stopped and closed her eyes again and held tightly to her shell. Vivien's voice in her head made her want to stop the world to hear it. She pressed the heel of her hand to her forehead and wanted to scream when she heard what sounded like a faint good-bye. Frankie held both her hands and shook his head. She would celebrate the fact that Vivien was still alive and use Frankie as a megaphone for what she had to say to both Vivien and Marsha.

"Ready?" she asked Frankie after she'd sent her message. She didn't get a response.

"They'll be okay, won't they?" Frankie's face was wet with tears, but he wasn't hysterical.

"Whoever this is will be sorry they ever came here."

The house was a hive of activity, and she needed the quiet to think. Earth might as well have been as huge as the universe if you had a short period of time to find three individuals hidden there. If these people were vindictive, she'd never get to Vivien in time.

"Should I call my parents?" Frankie asked. He was breathing hard, his knuckles white on the door. "I don't want them surprised if we don't find them right away. I'm surprised they're not over here already since they have their shells."

"Get them over here. My parents should be here in a few hours, so they can talk them through this." They headed inside, and the guards had brought some of their equipment over to monitor their radar. "I give you my word—I'll find them, and I'm sorry I haven't asked about Marsha. Have you felt anything or gotten any communication through your shell?"

"I can feel she's in trouble, but she's not totally freaking out just yet. I hope whoever has them has a tolerance for sarcasm," he said and laughed weakly. "I want to have a chance to tell her how I feel. I've been an idiot up to now, thinking she'd think I was some sort of stalker."

She put her arms around him and held him once they were inside. "You'll have that chance, but try to keep your head clear. Think of the priestess we questioned. If they have someone else talented at reading minds, we don't want to give anything away."

"What about the two women you captured?"

"Want to come with me?" She headed next door through the yard. The two were shackled to chairs and were looking around the room like they were trying to find an escape. "You're never getting away from me, so stop wasting your time."

"We don't take orders from you, scum," the taller one said. Edil slapped her so hard blood sprayed out and hit Edil's shirt.

So they definitely knew who she was. "Usually, we'd go through this dance of me beating the shit out of you, and you trying to hang on to your sanity, but we don't have time for that today." She expanded her trident and motioned for Frankie to do the same. "Today I'm going to surgically remove everything I can without killing you until you tell me what I want to know."

"I thought your mother didn't like that kind of thing," the smaller woman said. "That's what Bella told our leader."

"Look around," she said, swiping her trident across the hair at the side of the woman's head and slicing it off. "Do you see my mother anywhere?"

"What do you want to know?" the taller woman said, giving in quickly and showing how deeply her devotion went. "All we know is that we were ordered to accompany the team to that place and take your woman. Where they're going or what's planned isn't something we were told."

"Who are you taking orders from? Tell me, and make this whole process something you'll survive."

"Our queen, Daria Oberon." The name made her blood run cold. Just like Pontos, this woman would aim for the heart without thought or remorse.

"Edil, get what information you can." Kai left her to it. She knew who she was up against now.

They walked next door, and she went up to their bedroom in an effort to think of what her next step should be. The only things she had to go on were the two visions they'd had, and she tried to decipher anything she hadn't been able to glean before, but the result was the same—Viv being pulled away into darkness. She'd thought putting enough guards around them would keep them safe and control the scenario, but that illusion had shattered today. She needed her moms to get there so they could figure out their next move.

"Don't blame yourself, and I have faith that everything will be fine," Cornelia said, coming in without knocking. Viv's mother was a nice woman, and she'd been able to break Pontos's mental game without any help from her. "You know, when Vivien was a little girl, I found her awake late one night staring at the sky as she sat on that window seat."

"She still does that some nights. We might live in the depths, but we can still see the night sky." She smiled when Cornelia reached over and wiped her face of the tears she didn't realize she was shedding.

"I used to tell them old stories about seashells to make them feel better about whatever was bothering them or making them sad." Cornelia's smile was full of melancholy. "That night she was still suffering because we hadn't believed her story about the girl she and Frankie saw who might've been eaten by sharks. For the longest time I thought she had imagination enough for all of us."

"I'm sorry I ever did that." Her childhood whims had brought her Vivien, albeit years later, but had caused a rift in her family.

"I'm not. The story I told her that night was about a girl who thought there wasn't a place for her in the world. The girl had no voice and thought no one truly believed in her. Because she felt that way, the girl believed her life would be one of despair. One night, though, a loving sprite visited her, and she knew in time she'd find all the answers she sought in the stars." Cornelia joined her in her tears.

"That's a beautiful story." She held her mother-in-law's hand and tried her best to comfort her.

"I told her that one day there'd be a place for her in the heavens, and once she found it, she'd be the point by which her love would navigate their way home. That's what you are to her, Kai. You'll be her home." Cornelia hugged her and kissed her cheek. "Now stop feeling sorry for yourself and bring our girl home. You're the only one who can find her and do that."

"She sent me a message, but whoever has her has been able to prevent her from sending another one."

"With the shell, you mean?" Cornelia stared at her and reached for her own.

"Yes, like this," Kai said, showing her. "It was her. I know it was."

"You'll have to forgive me. All this is so new to me, and I'm still trying to learn the ins and outs of your gift. I could sense Viv's distress, but I'm way out of my depth when it comes to getting a detailed message."

"There's nothing to forgive," Galen said, coming in to join them and placing her hand on Kai's shoulder, "and my kid is a capable teacher when she sets her mind to it. Believe me when I tell you we'll exhaust everything at our disposal to bring Vivien back."

"Cornelia, I'd like to introduce you to my mother, Galen Merlin. Mom, this is Vivien's mom, Cornelia." She put her arms around her mom for a tight hug. That had always made her feel better from the time she was a child.

Cornelia didn't seem fazed, which was good. "Your Majesty, it's a pleasure to meet you, but I wish it had been under better circumstances. I'm trying my best to keep my cool, but you have to find her. If this was a simple kidnapping and demand for ransom, Winston and I would've paid it by now."

"Neither of us have enough to pay what these people want. Our only option is to find her and eliminate whoever took her." Her mom sounded like she was at the end of patience and was ready to burn whoever stood in their way.

They joined her mother Hadley who was comforting Winston. She sat and Frankie joined her. He stared at the water in the pool and took her hand. The memory of Nessa and Jyri came to her, and she thought of what they'd said. It couldn't be that easy.

"Laud," she said. "Have you gotten any updates from the guards working on Tanice? Pontos had to have known if anyone else was coming. Or have you gotten anything new from your search?"

"I think we've gotten all the information we're going to get out of Tanice." Laud sat with them and had a hard time meeting her eyes. "You'll be immediately informed if we have anything new."

"This isn't your fault, my friend. We put security on Vivien and Marsha, and they were outnumbered. The ones to blame are Bella, her mother, and everyone who followed them against my mother. When I find them, there will be justice." She'd never been one for revenge or an all-consuming rage, but Bella's stupidity had gone too far. If it cost her Vivien, she wouldn't need a trident to deliver the killing blow.

"We'll do better next time, but I'm sorry the guards failed."

"Let's not get into circular conversations about blame, and let's get back to Tanice. I think she's the one who holds the key to all this. She was Pontos's lover and fiancée. That means she has a vast knowledge of planet Atlantis's court and ruling family." When Nessa and Jyri talked about the past, maybe it wasn't just *her* past they were talking about. "Is there something we can do that'll open her mind to us?"

"Like the priestess we're transporting there?" Laud sat back, seeming lost in thought.

"You made progress making her think she was sitting with her lover Pontos, but we need information on more than what he had planned. Pontos is dead and his plan died with him. Whoever Sol has sent now is continuing what Pontos started, only this is someone new and much better organized. According to the guards we captured, the one who captured Vivien and the others is Queen Daria Oberon. Have you had any indication someone landed recently? Is Daria Sol's wife or daughter? Either way, they have revenge as well as conquest on their mind."

"I've been putting into place everything we talked about as well as tracking down anyone who might've helped Bella and Pontos, but I'm afraid I don't know what relation she is to Sol."

"Bella and her mother escaped, so there have to be some people in our realm who are still feeding Bella information if they grabbed Vivien so easily. Right now, we need to concentrate on Vivien, Marsha, and Etta. Any traitors within the capital will be dealt with eventually." She stood and paced as an idea started to take root. "To find the answers, we have to ask Pontos's girlfriend some different questions. I want to walk into this fight with *all* the answers."

"What do you want to ask her?" Laud said, already on her way to the monitors. Frankie and their parents followed.

The cell that held Tanice came on the screen, and she appeared content as the guard sat with her, stroking her hair. Her mother Galen explained, for the benefit of the others in the room, "There's a new technique we've perfected, where, with a little help, the prisoner sees someone other than the guard. In this case Tanice thinks she's talking to her lover—the man who tried to kill Kai outside your house."

"Steve, you mean?" Winston asked.

"Exactly," her mother Hadley said.

"Call the guard out and give her some instructions," Kai said to the control room at the facility.

"Yes, Highness," the woman said a few minutes later.

"It's a lot to ask, but I need you to make a bond with her and ask the following questions." Kai explained what she wanted, and the woman nodded. "Try to make it as fast as possible."

They all watched as the woman went in and lay down next to Tanice and started talking to her. She held her and kissed her like only a lover would, and Kai wondered if this romanticized version of Pontos ever existed. Tanice seemed to respond, and she started to whisper in the guard's ear. A mental bond of this kind was hard when there were no feelings for the other person, but she'd had no choice.

"Do you remember how annoying my sibling and parents were?"

the guard asked, and Tanice laughed as if sharing an inside joke. "I've been here so long I can't remember everything. Do you?"

Tanice hesitated and Kai held her breath. The more time that went by, the farther away Vivien slipped. This had to work. This idiot had to talk.

"Daria was annoying," Tanice said as she laid her head on the guard's shoulder. The name made Kai pay closer attention. "At least we got away from all that. Once we take over, do you promise to bring my family with the first wave?"

"Of course," the guard said, placing her hand on the back of Tanice's neck. "Now show me how much you love me."

There was no more talking, and Vivien's family glanced around the room, appearing confused as to what was going on. It took another ten minutes for the guard to excuse herself and walk out. The staff hooked a device to the guard's head that resembled the setup for a brain scan. This device was able to pluck the thoughts Tanice had shared while they were in an intimate embrace and render any images. When they saw what had been retrieved, it didn't surprise her to see an almost twin to Pontos. So Daria was Pontos's sister, not his mother. Sol Oberon had only one heir left, it was a daughter, and he'd sent her to finish the job.

"Does this help, Highness?" the guard asked.

"It does, but I need you to continue to ask questions about the Oberon family. Anything that can help us will only better prepare us. Thank you." She mentally sifted through the information she already had and made a decision. She stood and motioned for her guards. "Get ready to move, and make sure you're loaded for anything."

"Where are we going?" her mother Hadley said.

"I'm going to where Vivien and I first spent time together. Frankie was right—the answer lies in our past, but the complete picture lies in *both* our pasts. Pontos is dead, and his sister is here not only to avenge him but to finish what he started. This has as much to do with Sol as it does with the vipers he raised."

"Laud, start monitoring Earth for the same frequency Pontos used, and report any trace of it," her mother Hadley said. "We need a team who's willing to travel and destroy the ships left on the moon. We've been monitoring them to see if anyone returns, but no one has. Once we have Vivien and the others back, we'll start working on what to do about the pathway here so no one else can follow the Oberons."

"It can't be destroyed without some flashback to our world, but I'm sure we'll think of something," her mother Galen said. "Don't forget to call, and take care of Frankie." There was no question that Hadley was going with her.

"I promise both things." She kissed Galen before turning to Vivien's parents. "We won't come home without her. I have a wedding to attend this weekend, and I'm planning on being there."

"Don't forget to bring yourself home too, and good luck," Cornelia said.

Kai went upstairs and put on her uniform. After the battle with Pontos, it had been upgraded, and this uniform was now standard issue for everyone. She'd had some commissioned for Frankie and Vivien too. She wanted them to swim wherever they wanted but also wanted to keep them safe.

Frankie met her outside the master bedroom in the navy-blue suit, carrying his trident. He looked ready, and she said a small prayer that his fighting would be as good as the fit of the uniform.

"Are you sure about me coming? I don't want to screw up."

"I wouldn't recommend it," she said and winked. "You don't want the entire nation thinking that breeding men out of our realm was a good thing. All you need to do is stick close to my mother and follow her lead. The other thing to remember is aim well, and shoot to kill anyone not with us."

He laughed and shook his head. "Thanks, that adds no pressure."

"You're welcome, and remind me to tell Viv I thought of a baby name."

"I'll tell her that right after teasing her about what Mom bought her to wear to the wedding. After everything Marsha did to avoid Mom's idea of cute, I'd think she'll vote for Marsha Jr. as a good baby name."

"Keep dreaming, and let's get going. I'm sure the two of them are good and pissed by now."

As they got underway, Kai thought about the fight on her doorstep. She'd been born with a prophecy guiding her to a future with Vivien. Taking a wife from the human world wasn't something she'd overthought, but her decision to pursue Vivien had put her and their child in harm's way. The guilt of something happening to her was something she'd never get over, but she tried to put that out of her mind. Her mom Hadley had taught her the importance of going into a fight with the right mindset.

Instead, she thought of the life she'd have with Vivien and how different that would be from how her parents lived. She'd spend more time in the human world than any other queen, and that would hopefully make their child even more empathetic to the link between their race and the humans. Some might not care for that, but the majority of Atlantis would benefit from a better relationship with humans. And as for spending more time topside, if Queen Elizabeth could spend her summers at Balmoral, they could spend their summers in Louisiana and the Gulf of Mexico.

All she had to do was get this done, and the only things to worry about after that would be diapers and early morning feedings.

CHAPTER NINETEEN

The delta at the end of the Mississippi River was a place Vivien thought of as art that was constantly changing and perfecting itself. This canvas was left to run wild, to cut the veins that made up the acres that were used for farming. The river was tamed by levees years before, but here it was left to leave its mark however it wanted. The result was a picturesque design she'd never ignored on her trips offshore. Only nature could create such a stunning embodiment of change and flow. Focusing on it out the window gave her a sense of calm that allowed her to breathe past the panic of not being able to reach Kai through their link, which she'd thought was indestructible.

Marsha was next to her, and Etta was on Marsha's other side. Both of them had stayed quiet from the time they'd been pushed on board and locked inside the main cabin of a medium-sized boat. It was her job now to make sure whatever came next didn't involve swimming underwater for any length of time. She and Etta would survive, but Marsha would die quickly and painfully.

"Where are we going?" she asked Bella.

It hadn't made much sense that the woman who'd orchestrated this whole thing was locked up with them and looked like she'd been mauled. She wasn't falling for Bella's submissiveness. Bella hadn't made eye contact once in the time they'd been traveling. Whoever had put all those bruises on her face had to have been on Daria's side, because Bella had escaped before Galen caught and tried the traitors. Any bruising from that would've faded long before now.

"Do you think they'd mind if I punched her?" Marsha asked. "If she's the one responsible for all this, she deserves it."

Vivien smiled at Marsha before turning her attention back to Bella. "You can cut the act, and I hope you're happy with your choices." She didn't raise her voice, and Bella's head moved slightly from its bowed position, showing she was listening. "You've betrayed your entire nation and queen for this? I mean, look at yourself. Was it worth it?"

"I'm sure you'd never understand. Our nature is to conquer and lead. That's the Oberon heritage, and it's in my blood." Bella was soft-spoken and meek sounding, but she was still caught in the fantasy she'd woven for herself. "Someone like you was never meant to rule."

"You started this before Kai ever met me, so don't start lying now. Is it that Kai didn't choose from within the realm, or is it that she didn't choose *you* from within the realm?" It made sense now. "Your family put you in a position where you'd be in Kai's path, and she was supposed to fall for you and continue the Oberon line here. Is that right?"

"Stop before your mouth gets you into more trouble than you're already in. Daria is here to show true power and strength. It's something Galen has never done." Bella finally lifted her head, and her expression was one of true hatred.

"I think your first guess was right on the nose," Marsha said and laughed. That only deepened Bella's sneer. "Kai must've seen you on a daily basis and found you lacking if she never tried to sleep with you. It didn't take my friend here that long to get her naked and wild."

Etta laughed softly at Marsha's cutting wit.

"Shut up, human." Bella's voice finally rose from her fake whisper, and she touched her split lip when it began to bleed. "Daria will wipe the planet of your plague."

"So biblical, huh, Viv?" Marsha smiled and shook her head. "Where's your mother? Did the great Daria find her more appealing? That would make it two women in a row to reject you, if that's what she did to you," Marsha said, pointing to her face.

She squeezed Marsha's hand, knowing her well enough to realize where the teasing would go if given free rein. "You do remember what happened to Pontos, right?"

"Pontos was only the first wave. Daria has come with greater numbers, and when added to the voices of my sisters who think like me, Kai will be forgotten before her body is cold." Bella laughed, sounding deranged.

"You speak for Daria, do you?" She smiled and waited. "Marsha's right. Your face tells me otherwise, and the fact that your mother isn't here makes my friend even more right. Daria used you like she's going to use a lot of people—to get what she wants. It's you who's going to be forgotten, but not by everyone."

"You're damned right." Bella leaned forward, and Vivien expected her to try to hit her. "I'll be a hero to my people."

"I doubt that. You talk about Daria like she's a goddess, but in reality all she's done for you is kill your mother and beat you like an animal. That you'd think she's going to treat our sisters any differently is laughable. Every slave Daria makes of your sisters will guarantee they'll never forget you and what you've done. They'll curse you to the goddess for the rest of the miserable lives your new leader has in store for them." She finished as Daria came in and sat next to Bella and took her hand. The way Bella flinched made her think Bella wasn't long for this world, and that her verbal pledge of loyalty wasn't totally heartfelt.

"What's gotten into you?" Daria grabbed Bella's hand, and Bella grimaced as if Daria was squeezing too hard. "You've finally found your voice and think you can speak for me?"

"I was telling them about how you're here to win the entire planet. Kai will die, as will Galen's reign." Bella tried to keep up her loud voice, but it had died away before she was done.

"Where's Wilma, her mother?" Vivien pointed at Bella and made sure that her voice wasn't hard to hear. "I'd like to tell her to fuck off too."

"Wilma's dead," Daria said with an evil smile. "Lying is always repaid by death."

"Even after she got you here? And I thought your brother was an asshole." She was in no way someone who loved confrontation, but this was the exception to the rule. "He died begging for his life. Is being a coward part of your family line?"

"Do you honestly think you can goad me into a fight and survive?" Daria let Bella go and gave Vivien her full attention. "I can name every king in my family line, and why they came into power. It had to start somewhere. The answer lies with Nessa, and I understand she's worshipped here."

"We all interpret history differently, but only one side can be right."

"The truth is the little bitch left her father to die at the hands of our people. Poseidon's name died out just as soon as she gave it away to some commoner, and the people followed her anyway." The way Daria lunged forward and grabbed her by the chin made her blink, but she'd be damned if she was going to flinch like Bella had. "Now that weak bloodline has come full circle and chosen a human. Galen doesn't deserve this planet."

"Then throw me and Marsha over the side and use our loss to tear down Kai when you face her." She jerked out of Daria's grasp and straightened her back. "You probably won't go with that choice, though."

"Why do you think so?" Daria went to grab her again.

Vivien grabbed her hand in a death grip, keeping her from touching her. "Pontos bragged about what a great warrior he was before he faced Kai. Once they started, he had to be backed up by all the people he'd brought with him. Sounds like you brought enough to prop you up when the time comes, just like he did." She shoved Daria's hand away but kept hold of Marsha's hand to keep her face neutral. She wasn't going to show fear. "I think it's easy to see through your plan. You're going to hide behind me, hoping Kai loves me enough to surrender before you have to fight her."

"It's funny that you're keeping this up. You're crazy if you think you'll get inside my head." Daria sat back down and slapped Bella when she stared at her.

"Maybe all I am is a human, but I can see right through you." She had to hope that Daria had no way to know she'd been made an Atlantean in their joining. "Wilma's dead, and I'm sure the battle it took to end her life must've been something the historians will write about when it comes to your glory." She laughed, and Daria's face twisted into something ugly. "If she resembled Bella, she must've been a worthy opponent. It's clear now that the Oberons know how to rule by beating great enemies." She laughed again and didn't look away from Daria even if her brain was screaming this was suicide. Sometimes you had to fight through your fear, though, and show strength in order to gain even a miniscule edge that might provide a gap to escape.

"Do you think dying at my hand now will make you a martyr the people will rally around?" Daria was starting to get angry, but instead of moving she hung on to Bella by her hair.

She could tell Bella wanted to pull away to stop the pain, but trying what Vivien had and grabbing Daria's hand wouldn't end as well for her. "I think the idea of coming here, taking over a whole planet, and killing Kai and her family sounded like what we call a cakewalk. You thought that because of the information you'd been given, but you're about to find that neither Kai nor her mother is going to let go of the crown that easily. And even if you can make it through them, you don't have enough people to defeat every military force on this planet."

"The humans have no forces," Daria said, screaming now. "Stop trying to talk me into killing you. Believe me, it won't be that hard."

Vivien laughed incredulously. "Who told you that? The human race isn't as backward and helpless as you think. There are huge military forces all over the planet. If Bella didn't tell you that after you put all those bruises on her, then she's tougher than she looks." She laughed and pointed at Daria. "You've touched me, and doing that in front of Kai will be the only permission she'll need to rip your head off."

"Which is it then? Will she kill me for touching you or for killing you?"

She waited to answer as she tried to connect with Kai, needing the strength to finish this without ending up with a trident in her chest. "You figure it out. You'll never be the warrior Kai is, and Pontos said as much. He told me he had a sister, and he was glad I didn't remind him of her. You were a joke to him and your father."

"Shut up."

"Why? I'm not Bella, and I have every right to tell you the truth. You're stuck here, and you're going to have to fight, but you're never going to win. At least you'll die like your brother. That would be swiftly and easily." She felt her shell warm, and she glanced at Marsha and Etta and got a slight nod from each of them. Hopefully, that meant they'd felt the same thing.

"You want to drown? Is that it?" Daria stood and grabbed her with both hands, and she moved Marsha's hand to the waistband of her shorts.

No matter what, she didn't want Marsha to let go. The river's current was brutal and a known killer. She'd be able to swim through it, most likely, but Marsha would have no chance. "On the contrary, I want to live to see Kai kill you and everyone with you, starting with her." She pointed to Bella and was surprised that she totally meant it.

They were out of the delta and into the very beginning of the Gulf. From here it would be an easier swim when it came to keeping Marsha's head above water, if it came to that. She was about to keep up her taunting when something hit the boat, throwing Daria and her people to one side. Daria swore and shoved away from them, heading to the front of the boat to see what was going on. Bella was bleeding from a cut on her head and looked dazed.

The ship had been hit in such a way that it pitched to one side but wasn't punctured. Once it was on its side, though, they started taking on water. Whatever it was hit them again, which meant this was deliberate, and by bracing themselves they stayed in their seats. She took one last look out the window and saw that the boats around them were piles of smoking wreckage. The water was starting to rise and Marsha's panic with it.

"Don't let go of me, no matter what," Vivien said. The windows cracked under the pressure, and Etta stood at their back as she and Marsha finished pushing the panes out so they could swim away. She grabbed Marsha and stepped into cold brown water. She let go of the ship and the current slammed into them, propelling them forward. She held tightly to Marsha to make sure she didn't slip away into the deadly flow. Even in the murky water, she could see Marsha's eyes were open wide, and she was struggling to get away from her, in full panic mode.

She pressed her lips to Marsha's in a tight seal and blew into her mouth. She did it on every other breath so she could keep Marsha alive and swim at the same time. Marsha stopped moving and put her arms around her neck instead of her waist and was ready whenever she blew into her mouth. Etta was swimming in front of her and pointed to the line of grass on the bottom, below the swift-moving current. One of the Sea-Doo type vehicles the guards used around the palace was sitting close by, churning up the silt at the bottom.

Frankie motioned frantically from where he sat on it, clearly watching for them, and she let Marsha go when he reached for her and placed a breathing device over her mouth. It was a tight fit, but they all got on, and he gunned the machine and took off. Two other similar vehicles came into view behind them with Hadley and another woman giving them cover. The small pieces of cement sticking out of the bottom gave away their location, and Vivien broke the surface, knowing who would be waiting.

The sun was in her eyes, and she was having trouble seeing, but she recognized the arms that lifted her up until she was out of the water. "You found me," she said before she kissed Kai with a desperation born of the fear she'd never be able to do it again.

"Your mother told me a story about a girl who found her place among the stars. To me you're my star, and I'll always find you." Kai put her down and ran her hands down her arms until she reached her abdomen. "Are you okay?"

"We're both okay, and it's not my birthday, but if you're thinking of getting me something, beating the crap out of Daria Oberon is at the top of my list." She smiled tiredly when she made Kai laugh. "She says she has enough people to put up a fight this time."

"She did have a larger force than her brother, but they should've done a better job of changing their communications frequency. It's still in our network memory. While my mother and Frankie mounted a rescue mission, I led the forces and took care of the warriors she'd brought with her. I knew they wouldn't let anything happen to any of you." Kai moved them to where they'd sat all those months ago on Raccoon Island. The barrier island off the Louisiana coast was one of Kai's restoration projects, and they'd spent an afternoon here when they were getting to know each other. Kai had taken her snorkeling and shown her the land expanders.

"She has Bella with her, and it sounds like Daria killed her mother Wilma." Vivien looked around, but they seemed to be alone out here without guards.

"Our focus was getting you, Marsha, and Etta, so Daria and the others were able to get away," Frankie said, sounding miserable.

"Stop worrying—you did a wonderful job. Now, Etta, take Marsha with you and find cover. The guards are around, but I wanted to finish the job of drawing Daria out. You did your job beautifully, by the way. Remind me never to make you mad."

"You were listening in?" Vivien asked.

"I couldn't reach you for the longest time, but suddenly you came in clear as day. It helped me figure out which of the boats you were on." Kai kissed her and let her go to accept her trident from Frankie but still held her hand.

"How did you know it was Daria? We didn't know until she actually introduced herself."

"Tanice just needed to be asked the right questions. We used the system Bella set up with the priestess of reading people's thoughts and got a picture of who was here." Kai put her hand up to her shell and nodded. "The last of the surviving invaders are being driven here by our people."

"If Daria is with them, it'll take her less than a minute to make you want to punch her. And I didn't think it was possible, but there's such a thing as too much self-confidence."

The people with Daria all came out of the water together like a synchronized swimming team, and Kai stepped in front of her. She loved Frankie and Etta, but they weren't any match for the trained soldiers standing with Daria, and she was glad to see Laud and Hadley as well as a troop of warriors standing behind them.

"Surrender now, and I'll just use you as an example until I lock you away," Daria said, standing in knee-deep water.

"See, I told you she'd be too afraid to face you," she said loudly, and Kai turned and smiled at her. She shrugged and blew Kai a kiss.

"Once I'm through with you, I'm going to enjoy ripping her tongue out." Daria lunged and swung her trident like a bat and brought it down, aiming for Kai's head.

Kai used her trident as a shield, and Daria laughed as she hit it repeatedly in rapid succession trying to weaken her hold. Vivien saw someone running from behind them and screamed before Bella shot a pulse at Kai that hit her in the back. She dropped to her knees. She couldn't watch her love die, not again.

Kai wanted to laugh at Daria's style of combat. If there was a hammer and nail way of going about things, her distant cousin had perfected it. The idiot had been hammering away at her from the moment she came out of the water like she was intent on driving her into the sand. She thought the easiest way to end this was to push her over and literally blow her head off, but she'd promised her mother Galen a different outcome.

She brought her arms up and blocked another blow, then kicked Daria in the side. Before she could follow up, she heard Vivien scream, making her lose concentration. It didn't happen often anymore, but she had nightmares sometimes about the pulse Pontos had gotten off. The damn thing had come close to pulverizing her chest and lungs, and she had a feeling the same thing was happening again.

The anticipation this time made her keep her eyes open as she waited to get hit, thinking she didn't want Vivien to have to live through this again. She wasn't sure which of them was more surprised when Frankie got off his own shot and hit the pulse before it hit her. He quickly returned fire on Bella, and Daria screamed like a wounded animal when she went down, which didn't make sense, but Daria seemed to need her to navigate this world.

"You need someone like Bella to fight your battles for you?" The taunt sent Daria into a froth, and she continued her attack with the renewed force of her anger. As she drew back for another blow, Kai pushed her back with her foot, and Daria dropped her trident. Kai rushed forward before Daria could turn the weapon back on her and shoot. The trident swung around, but before Daria could aim it, she kicked it out of her hand toward Vivien.

"You bitch," Daria screamed, rolling to avoid another hit. She was on her feet and running toward her with her arms open wide as if she was ready to hug her.

Kai went with the momentum and allowed herself to be tackled to the ground. She flipped Daria over her and was back on her feet as Daria let out a breath of air that sounded like she was in pain. Daria wasn't about to give up, though, and she began a second running attack in the same fashion, making Kai think she was a slow learner. This was the type of fight strategy that would get you latrine duty in her mother's forces. She moved with Daria again, but this time she wasn't going down. The raging bull came close enough for her to sidestep and deliver a punch to the side of Daria's face.

It was satisfying to watch Daria's head whip back. She tried shaking it off as she swung back. The soldiers with Daria stepped closer when Kai hit her two more times, followed by a kick to her ribs. A few of them raised their weapons to stop her from hitting Daria again.

The Atlantean guards fired first, and the water surrounding the island turned red, bringing Ram and Ivan into the fight as they took a couple into the deep with them. Daria stopped for a moment to watch what had happened before rushing her again. Their fight lasted another few minutes, until Kai had Daria on her knees with her fist ready to deliver the killing blow.

"Go ahead and kill me. That's what your people have done to us for eons. You've left us to die." Daria glared up at her with the defiance of someone who knew death was whispering in her ear.

"Your people never change. You blame everyone except those who deserve it. It's time to step up and take credit." She gave Daria what she wanted and brought her fist down. The fight went out of her, and she slumped back on the beach.

The few remaining soldiers from Daria's group had already laid down their weapons and were kneeling on the beach. Seeing Daria motionless took the rest of their courage, and their shoulders slumped as they looked at the sand. Laud took the opportunity to place everyone in restraints and had them loaded on the large transport docked nearby. The last person put aboard was Bella, who was regaining consciousness from the stun pulse she'd taken from Frankie. When they lifted the stretcher, Bella came to and tried to get up.

"You're very lucky that nothing happened to my mate," Kai said, placing her hand on Bella's chest to keep her in place. "I don't believe in killing for revenge, so you're in no danger of that."

"You're letting me go?" Bella sounded skeptical and glanced around as if to see who else was still alive. "Even you're not that forgiving."

"What you did is simple to prove, Bella. It's treason, and you know the punishment for that." She stepped back and allowed the guards to take over.

"You're going to kill me later? Why not let your pet do it now?" Bella was as angry as Daria and it made no sense. If anyone in her mother's employ had enjoyed the privileges of that position, it had been Bella.

"Death is the easiest solution, don't you think?" Kai smiled down at her, and Bella glanced away. "I can promise you a long life where you'll get everything you want. I'll ask my mother to spare you myself. My prayer is that your life lasts a thousand years so you can think about what you've done—and lost because of it."

"What are you talking about?" Bella rubbed a spot on her chest and grimaced. "Why couldn't you just be more aggressive? None of this would've happened if you'd only taken what we deserved."

"Killing humans to take the land makes no sense when very few of our people want to live on land. We are happy, prosperous, and content. Our realm is vast and expanding every day with careful outreach to the human world. That will only help both our peoples, but for you it wasn't enough." Kai held her hand up when they started to move Bella away. "Power should never be pursued by placing a foot on someone's throat. It's earned with respect and service—at least that's the only way to keep it."

"Where are you taking me?" Bella's voice rose when they picked up the stretcher.

"You're going home, Bella." Vivien answered her question for her. "You should be happy. Like Kai said, you're getting everything you've ever wanted. You'll spend the rest of your life in the company of the Oberon princess you served so well. If it was Kai you wanted all along, then you're getting squat."

Kai walked them over to Etta and Marsha, who was being held by Frankie. "Thank you both for keeping Vivien safe."

"I think you got that wrong," Marsha said. "If anyone kept us safe, it was Viv, and we'll discuss later why everyone in the family can breathe underwater except me. It's not fair."

"Trust me, it's a good thing," Vivien said. She leaned over and whispered in Marsha's ear, and whatever she was saying was making Marsha nod. The way she looked at Kai and then Frankie made her wonder what Vivien was saying.

"Really?" Marsha said.

"Really. I'll talk to the head priestess and see about getting you some."

"Do you guys want to sail home? You're welcome to come with us, Etta." She started for the beach where some of her people had dinghies waiting to take them to the *Salacia*. Laud already had people taking care of the cleanup of boats and bodies before anyone reported anything.

Once they were aboard, they went over what had happened, and Kai told them about the body the guards had found. Wilma had been floating not far from where they'd first spent time together. Fortunately, their people located the body and were able to dispose of it. Had the sheriff's office gotten involved and tried to identify her by DNA, that would've been a problem.

"Why?" Marsha asked.

"Our genetic makeup is much different than yours. We share a little strand of DNA since it's what helped man evolve to where you are, but that's it. If Wilma had been found, it would've been hard to shut down the investigation that would've come of it." She raised the sails and left Edil to navigate.

They were at the mouth of the river a few hours later, and the sails came down as they passed the cluster of Coast Guard cutters surrounding the half-sunken ship they'd rammed to release Vivien. It was the only bit of evidence her people hadn't tidied up yet, but human investigators wouldn't find anything that would lead back to them.

"Did you know they were here?" Etta asked. "How did you find us?"

"Daria left a coin in your office, and I kept trying to reconnect with Vivien through our shells. Once I saw the coin, we scanned for the pattern of frequency used by Pontos's boxes. Once we had that, we were able to catch up to you. I was able to feel Vivien, so your ship was the only one we laid carefully on its side," Kai said.

"I don't know what blocked me, but we need to figure out what it was, so it won't happen again," Vivien said.

"We have plenty of time to study that, and to question Bella and Daria. All we have left is to find anyone else in the realm who was working with those two and bring them to justice."

"Thank you for getting here so quickly, Highness," Etta said.

"I had every faith in you, baby," Vivien said, kissing Kai's cheek. "But I'm with Etta. Thank you for finding us before that lunatic figured out I'm pregnant."

"From here forward, it's all naps and lazy afternoons wherever you'd like to be."

"So you really are having the next head guppy," Marsha teased Vivien and almost got pushed overboard.

"Let me call my parents," Vivien said, taking her phone from her.

Her parents said they'd be waiting for them at the dock close to the French Quarter. It wasn't meant for luxury cruisers, but Winston's connection would save them an hour's drive when they tied up.

"What happens now?" Marsha asked. "Those idiots were really going to hurt us."

"All the people from our realm will be tried for treason, and all the invaders with Daria will be kept like we have the people we've rounded up from Pontos's attempt. Once we complete all that, my mother will pass judgment." She sat with her arm around Viv and was in the mood for a nap. She'd never been so emotionally exhausted. "Being found guilty of treason is a death sentence like it is in the US, but my mother is no killer. At times it's unavoidable, but our queen has a merciful heart."

"Being stuck under the frozen tundra doesn't sound like a picnic either," Viv said.

"This time it might be a different outcome."

They stopped talking after that and enjoyed the scenery as they motored up the river. The Palmers were waiting when they reached the city, and her mom was with them. Kai felt the heat of her blush when Cornelia held her and cried as she thanked her over and over again. She could feel the relief coming off Viv's parents in waves. Vivien's call and their shells let them know everyone was okay, but seeing them after what had happened drove their emotions.

Their dinner was filled with laugher and stories of Kai's childhood thanks to her aunt Clarice later that night, and she was glad the families didn't need much help in getting comfortable around each other. They told everyone good night so they could lock the door on the master bedroom and enjoy the rest of the night. Kai was happy to hold Vivien against her and think about a lifetime of spending time like this and not having to worry about strategy for whatever came next.

"When they called and told me they'd taken you, I thought my heart would stop." She decided to take her mom Hadley's advice and admit her fears as well as her love. "The reality that I wasn't there to protect you was brutal."

"It wasn't easy for me either, and when I couldn't feel you I almost panicked. I had faith that you were still okay and tried to keep my head. All I needed was a chance to get off that boat and back to you." Vivien pressed closer to her and kissed her. The press of her stomach between them reminded Kai of all they could've lost. "I know it was scary for both of us, but it turned out okay. That's what we need to concentrate on."

"Now that this is done, are you ready to marry me? It'll help with all the looks you get when people think I'm not paying attention. A ring on your finger will be a great way to tell them you're taken, but I can't blame them. You're the most beautiful woman I've ever met."

"If you don't shut up and touch me, I'm sending you next door for another lecture from your mother on romance." Vivien had put Kai's parents in the guest room next to theirs, and Kai wasn't interested in making a lot of noise. Her family already had enough stories about her to last a lifetime.

"My mother Hadley would love that, but I think I know what I'm doing." She rolled them over and kept her complete weight off Viv. "Do you think I know what I'm doing?"

"I don't know." Viv moved her hand down and ran her fingers through her own sex so she could run them over Kai's lips. "You might have to prove that to me again."

She moved down and put her mouth on Viv while Viv threaded their fingers together. "You taste so good."

"Baby, not the time for descriptive conversation." Viv lifted her hips and finally let her go, so she could grab her hair and push her head more firmly against her. "Right there, don't stop. God," Vivien said and moaned so loudly she figured her parents would have a few comments later on.

She felt Vivien let go, and she immediately started crying. It had happened a few times before, but now it was like a dam had given way. "Hey…hey," she said, coming up and taking Vivien in her arms. "Did I hurt you?"

"I wasn't crying because I was in pain, honey. Sorry, it's all this crap, and the baby is starting to drive my emotions. The thought of having to raise our baby alone was making me just a tad crazy." Vivien used the sheet to wipe her face. "The whole time you were fighting her, my heart had stopped, and even though it was obvious you were a better fighter, one mistake…" She shuddered. "I want all this to be over."

"It will be. My mother made me promise not to kill any of them unless it was necessary, but especially Daria and Bella. She has plans for them, and if she gets her way, this won't be a problem again." She kissed Vivien and ran her hand up and down her back. "I'm not saying life is going to be perfect, but we'll make it what'll make us happy."

"I love you, and you're right. The only thing that might ruin my happiness in the near future is you realizing my mother got you something to wear for the ceremony. Hopefully you'll still love me when you realize you can't turn her down." They laughed at that, and if that was all she had to worry about, life would be easy from here.

"If the word *lace* is in any way included in the description, you'd better start running."

"Don't worry. I have ways of making it up to you." Vivien kissed her before moving down the bed.

CHAPTER TWENTY

The white dress Vivien and her mother had found was a simple silky sheath, clingy enough to accentuate the curve of her stomach. It had a slight train in the back, and her mom had ordered a small ring of blue fairy flowers for her hair that held the small veil in place. She looked pregnant, and she was glad. They would've gotten married anyway, baby or no, but she wanted to remember the fact that she was expecting. She turned to the side in the full-length mirror in her old bedroom at her parents' place and stared at herself.

"Vivien Palmer, you've never cared about what you were wearing your entire life, so don't tell me you're about to start now." Her mother was sitting on the bed, watching her with a smile.

"I love the dress," she said, running her hands down her side. "It's okay, right? You know Kai's family. This doesn't look very royal. I mean, it's not that fancy."

"All Kai will care about is if you meet her at the altar, and her mother might be a queen, but she owns a pair of jeans with a hole in the pocket." Cornelia stood and kissed her cheek. "You're already married, so I thought this time around it could be more relaxed. I'll force the formal affair on Frankie and Marsha."

"I promise I'll help you with that, and all I care about is what Kai thinks anyway."

There was a knock at the door. Her mother had picked the perfect place for a wedding, and it was time to go. "Hey, Dad." She put her arms around her father and closed her eyes as he hugged her. Ever since their talk with Kai, when he'd asked for the truth of who Kai was, something in her parents had shifted, especially in her father. He was more demonstrative with his feelings, and it healed something in her that had been broken from the day he'd told her not to tell foolish tales. It was nice to have him back.

"You look beautiful." He held her hands and looked into her eyes. "I know you're not my little girl any longer, but your mom and I are here for you and Frankie, no matter what. Remember that—and also not to take shit from anyone."

"I'll remember."

"The thing that popped into my head this morning is you telling me, right after you delivered your last project, that you wished you ruled the seas or could meet the person who did."

"I did say that, and you doubted me when I told you I believed that job was held by a woman. I was right."

"You were, and it's time to go and meet her at the end of an aisle."

She and her mother had visited the Longue Vue Gardens often when she was a child, and tonight it was open only to their guests. The lawn at the back of the house was spectacular and perfect for a wedding. She waited with her father until Kai's parents were seated with her mother. Marsha and Frankie were their only attendants and had agreed to her mother's plan—dress was casual, but everyone was color-coordinated in different shades of blue like the sea that had brought them together. Her mother was only willing to relax to a point.

"Thanks for doing this. I'm sure you'd have chosen something on the beach with just the two of you and a justice of the peace, but I think every father dreams of walking his daughter down the aisle." Her father kissed her cheek and squeezed her hand. "She's a lucky woman."

"Thanks, Daddy, and I think bringing Kai here was the first step in making all of us okay." She stood on her toes and kissed him back. "You did that by dragging her away from that job in the North Sea, so in a way, we've all been lucky."

She placed her hand in the bend of her father's elbow and started their walk to the canopy of flowers, where Kai and the priest were waiting. Kai's smile was all she could see, but she did notice the relaxed white linen shirt and loose pants Kai had on that matched the simplicity of her dress. Her mom had kept her promise to keep it simple while still capturing who she and Kai were as a couple. Kai might've been royalty, but she wasn't pretentious.

The rest of the ceremony wasn't long, and their vows were

repeated much like they were at their first wedding, and then it was time to kiss, and she relished it. She'd loved both ceremonies they'd had, but this one was more about friends and family gathering because two people met, fell in love, and decided to spend the rest of their lives together. There wasn't a lot of pomp and circumstance, but there was laughter and a fun atmosphere that Kai seemed to be enjoying as well.

"Ladies and gentleman, I present to you Kai and Vivien Merlin," the priest said.

The party started after the applause, and the guests hit the bar while she got Kai alone for a minute. "Do you think all these people will notice if I drag you behind a tree?"

"Not yet, Mrs. Merlin. I want to dance with you, and I promised your mom we'd be good about taking pictures." Kai kissed her again until she jumped a little when Vivien pinched her ass.

"Come on, the sooner we start, the sooner we get to sail away."

She knew some of the guests were business partners of her father's, but she was too happy to care when she and Kai shared the first dance before her father got a turn. An hour later, they were sweating and laughing with their friends. More than one of her old college friends appeared interested in getting to know some of the guards better as things slowed down.

"Call us and tell us you arrived," her mother said to Kai when it finally came time for them to leave.

"Yes, ma'am," Kai said.

"Tell me, Your Majesty," Marsha said as she and Frankie walked with them to the waiting car.

"No, we're no longer allowed to keep serfs," Kai said. "You can visit anytime without having to feed me."

"Not what I wanted to know, wise guy. I had a question about these gills." Marsha touched behind Kai's ear and pulled her down so she could whisper in her ear. Whatever she said made Kai blush as she answered in kind. "Even in the bathtub?" Marsha said so that everyone could hear.

"It could be a puddle, but yes." Kai looked at Frankie's blush and shook her head when she joined Marsha in laughing. "Have fun experimenting, just don't forget to feed him. It's not as intense if you're dehydrated and starving."

They waved one more time from the boat as they set off downriver toward the spot they'd explored together when they first met. "Think we'll find treasure?" she asked Kai as she stood in front of her with her hands on the wheel.

"I already did. The next two weeks are more about getting you naked and doing things to you that you can't share with Marsha."

"I love the way you talk to me." She watched as Kai set the autopilot and sat her down. It didn't take long for the sky to light up with stars and for the temperature to drop enough to make it comfortable. "I'm looking forward to our time off."

"I am too, love. Are you ready?" Kai stood and lifted the sails once they were in open water. The boat jerked forward, and it cut a wake that seemed to leave civilization behind. For the time being, it was just the two of them.

"For this, and everything that comes." Vivien stood in front of Kai and placed her hand on her abdomen. Their lives would never be completely their own because of who Kai was, but she was looking forward to this child as well as any others that they'd be blessed with. She hoped their reign would last a thousand years and always be remembered as a time of peace and innovation that melded their worlds to make their homes better.

Her dreams now centered on Kai and what they'd found together. With the goddess's blessing they'd have years to share, love, and build on the world they'd create together. She was ready for whatever came next.

EPILOGUE

Five months later

"Push, Highness," Dr. Jac Dalton said for what seemed like the five millionth time that night. Vivien glared at the woman, and if she had the strength she'd have punched her.

She'd been miserable for the last couple of months and was convinced she was having a forty-pound baby. That morning when her water broke, she wanted to celebrate—it was finally over. Now she wasn't so sure, since the kid acted like she was content to stay where she was.

"One more, love," Kai said, holding her hand.

"The next person who tells me to push is getting exiled to the desert." They'd come back to the queen's retreat with both sets of parents along with Frankie and Marsha as her due date neared. Galen had been nice enough to offer when she realized how important it was to have the family together when the baby was born.

They needed to share this, after the public trials of Bella Riverstone and the small number of accomplices who'd helped her gather information on Kai's family. If they'd wished for death, Galen wasn't in a giving mood. Daria, Bella, and the rest of the troop of fools were loaded back on the remaining ship on the moon. They programmed the navigation system to return to Atlantis, while also making it impossible to change course. Once it arrived, it would self-destruct, wiping away the path to Earth with it.

Their people had worked on erasing all traces of the coordinates of Nessa's path as well as wiping all mention of Nessa's voyage from the

Atlantean ship archives, since the ship was connected to the systems on the planet Atlantis. Even if the planet Atlantis continued to sustain life, no records would remain. The likelihood, though, was that the original civilization of Atlantis was already gone, and the ship returning to it would find nothing but a planet void of life. And then the ship would self-destruct, leaving no further enemies to deal with from among the stars.

Some of the people who'd come with Daria appeared relieved when Galen passed judgment, and surprisingly the only one who'd begged to stay and be given another chance was Bella. Galen had denied the request. Once they confirmed the ship had arrived on planet Atlantis, Galen had ordered communications stopped between the two rulers and those frequencies purged from their system. It was time to let go of the past.

"Breathe," Kai said softly. "You're doing great, so listen to me."

She'd been in labor for hours and was exhausted. "What?" She kept her eyes closed and took some deep breaths.

"My mother loves this place. Did you ask her why it was so special to her?"

"No, I meant to, but it slipped my mind."

"When she got close to giving birth, she came here and waited. She wanted to give birth in the deepest part of our ocean, so I'd know the depths of her and Mama's love for me." Kai kissed the side of her head and placed her hands on her abdomen. "The story I've been told all my life is that I was born in this room under a sky full of stars and calm seas. When I finally came out, she said she cried and made one wish."

"What was it?"

"We'll have to be holding our little girl before I can say the words."

"Sneaky, honey." She sat up a little and bore down with the little strength she had left. It took four more pushes before she heard the cry of a baby, and the sound did make her cry. She hadn't seen her yet, but she was already in love.

"Your daughter, Highnesses," Jac said as she handed Kai the baby.

Kai gazed at her face for a moment before laying the baby across her chest. "She's beautiful."

"Oh," she said, touching the baby's face. "She looks just like you." The dark hair and long body didn't come from her. "Welcome to the world, Callan."

"Your mother and I wish you love, adventure, and calm seas," Kai said. "Go and seek them all until you find your happiness on the compass of your life. We will love you until the end of times."

The beautiful words made her heart swell with love for the most wonderful woman in the world. "I'm glad you and Callan will have this place in common." The baby started crying, and Kai helped Vivien sit up so she could feed her. "Are we ready for this?"

"Like you said, love. For this and everything to come."

About the Author

Ali Vali is the author of the long-running Cain Casey "Devil" series, the newest being *The Devil Incarnate*, and the Genesis Clan "Forces" series, as well as numerous standalone romances, including three Lambda Literary Award finalists: *Calling the Dead*, *Love Match*, and *One More Chance*.

Originally from Cuba, Ali has retained much of her family's traditions and language and uses them frequently in her stories. Having her father read her stories and poetry before bed every night as a child infused her with a love of reading, which she carries till today. Ali currently lives outside of New Orleans, where she enjoys cheering LSU and trying new restaurants.

Books Available From Bold Strokes Books

Can't Leave Love by Kimberly Cooper Griffin. Sophia and Pru have no intention of falling in love, but sometimes love happens when and where you least expect it. (978-1-636790041-1)

Free Fall at Angel Creek by Julie Tizard. Detective Dee Rawlings and aircraft accident investigator Dr. River Dawson use conflicting methods to find answers when a plane goes missing, while overcoming surprising threats and discovering an unlikely chance at love. (978-1-63555-884-5)

Love's Compromise by Cass Sellars. For Piper Holthaus and Brook Myers, will professional dreams and past baggage stop two hearts from realizing they are meant for each other? (978-1-63555-942-2)

Not All a Dream by Sophia Kell Hagin. Hester has lost the woman she loved, and the world has descended into relentless dark and cold. But giving up will have to wait when she stumbles upon people who help her survive. (978-1-63679-067-1)

Protecting the Lady by Amanda Radley. If Eve Webb had known she'd be protecting royalty, she'd never have taken the job as bodyguard, but as the threat to Lady Katherine's life draws closer, she'll do whatever it takes to save her, and may just lose her heart in the process. (978-1-63679-003-9)

The Secrets of Willowra by Kadyan. A family saga of three women, their homestead called Willowra in the Australian outback, and the secrets that link them all. (978-1-63679-064-0)

Trial by Fire by Carsen Taite. When prosecutor Lennox Roy and public defender Wren Bishop become fierce adversaries in a headline-grabbing arson case, their attraction ignites a passion that leads them both to question their assumptions about the law, the truth, and each other. (978-1-63555-860-9)

Turbulent Waves by Ali Vali. Kai Merlin and Vivien Palmer plan their future together as hostile forces make their own plans to destroy what they have, as well as all those they love. (978-1-63679-011-4)

Unbreakable by Cari Hunter. When Dr. Grace Kendal is forced at gunpoint to help an injured woman, she is dragged into a nightmare where nothing is quite as it seems, and their lives aren't the only ones on the line. (978-1-63555-961-3)

Veterinary Surgeon by Nancy Wheelton. When dangerous drugs are stolen from the veterinary clinic, Mitch investigates and Kay becomes a suspect. As pride and professions clash, love seems impossible. (978-1-63679-043-5)

All That Remains by Sheri Lewis Wohl. Johnnie and Shantel might have to risk their lives—and their love—to stop a werewolf intent on killing. (978-1-63555-949-1)

Beginner's Bet by Fiona Riley. Phenom luxury Realtor Ellison Gamble has everything, except a family to share it with, so when a mix-up brings youthful Katie Crawford into her life, she bets the house on love. (978-1-63555-733-6)

Dangerous Without You by Lexus Grey. Throughout their senior year in high school, Aspen, Remington, Denna, and Raleigh face challenges in life and romance that they never expect. (978-1-63555-947-7)

Desiring More by Raven Sky. In this collection of steamy stories, a rich variety of lovers find themselves desiring more: more from a lover, more from themselves, and more from life. (978-1-63679-037-4)

Jordan's Kiss by Nanisi Barrett D'Arnuck. After losing everything in a fire, Jordan Phelps joins a small lounge band and meets pianist Morgan Sparks, who lights another blaze—this time in Jordan's heart. (978-1-63555-980-4)

Late City Summer by Jeanette Bears. Forced together for her wedding, Emily Stanton and Kate Alessi navigate their lingering passion for one another against the backdrop of New York City and World War II, and a summer romance they left behind. (978-1-63555-968-2)

Love and Lotus Blossoms by Anne Shade. On her path to self-acceptance and true passion, Janesse will risk everything—and possibly everyone—she loves. (978-1-63555-985-9)